Every Witch Way but Wolf

Magical Misfits Mysteries - book 4

K.E. O'Connor

K.E. O'Connor Books

EVERY WITCH WAY BUT WOLF

ISBN: 978-1-915378-45-3

Written by: K.E. O'Connor

Chapter 1

Glitter guns

"You go around the back of the barn. I'll go in the opposite direction, so we can finally catch this troublemaker." My whiskers twitched, and my booping snooter wrinkled as I avoided a thin trail of sparkling glitter. If I got that on my toe beans, it would be lights out.

Sammy, my ever-faithful feline companion, nodded. His tabby fur was fluffed all over his stout body, and magic glimmered around him. "When I first met Ajax, I thought she was nice, but these enchanted pygmy hippos are twice as mean as their larger relatives."

I jumped over Zandra and Finn, giving my wonderful witch a sniff to ensure she was still breathing. They were the victims of encountering Ajax's glitter and not getting out of the way in time. This enchanted pygmy hippo could shoot magnificent blasts of glitter from her rear end. One whiff of it, or if you got any of it on your skin, and you sank into a speedy unconsciousness.

Adrienne and Joel, two recent ghoulish additions to Finn's volunteer team, ambled around the corner. They held hands as they shuffled toward us, oblivious to the chaos they'd wandered into.

"Hey! Keep out of the way. Ajax is on the rampage again," I yelled.

Adrienne frowned and shook her fist in the air. "She's nothing but trouble."

Joel grunted his agreement. He still wasn't much of a talker, even after being around me and Zandra for a month. But in that time, I'd grown to trust these ghouls. And Adrienne had turned into a remarkably caring ghoul. The opposite of how she was when she was a scatterbrained magic user parenting Zandra through her early years.

"They could help us bring down Ajax," Sammy said. "Maybe the glitter parps don't affect ghouls."

"Better to keep them out of it. Adrienne, watch over Zandra and Finn. They'll be confused when they come around. Let them know everything's under control."

"Sure thing, Juno." She shuffled over, still clasping Joel's hand. They made such a sweet couple.

Once I was certain my witch was being looked after, I dashed around the side of the barn. Sammy went the opposite way.

There was never a dull moment at Finn's animal sanctuary. The critters he took in were lost or lacked direction. Some had been mistreated or had trust issues, while others simply needed gentle re-education before it was safe for them to go back into the world.

But this enchanted pygmy hippo was a whole other level of messed up. Ajax trusted no-one, stole food, and knocked out anyone who stopped her from doing what she wanted. I didn't like to think that some critters were born bad, but this one had me wondering.

"Need a hand?" Binky, my new cougar friend, bounded into sight.

"Always. I didn't expect you until later. Watch out for the glitter."

Binky bounded over a line of glitter with ease and landed on a fine set of paws. "Tia is busy at the bakery with a rush order, so I was kicking my paws and had nothing to do. I figured I'd come and see what you were up to. Getting in trouble again, by the looks of it."

"Trouble found me. Ajax got out. Watch out for her rear end or anything sparkly."

"Her again! When will she figure out this is a great place to stay?" Tia trotted along beside me as I hunted for Ajax.

"It takes some longer than others. This way. I'm sensing strong magic." I slid an appreciative glance over Binky. She was transformed from the sorry-looking creature forced to kill for an unstable dark magic user. Her fangs were long and sharp, her fur gleamed, and the scars that had once littered her fragile body were gone.

She caught me looking and winked. "My fur has never been so glossy. Tia has been feeding me up ever since I got back to her."

"It's no less than you deserve. Follow me." I slid around the barn and almost collided with Sammy.

He dodged me at the last second. "Hey, Binky! No Ajax?"

"Not this way. She can't have given us the slip."

"Over here." Binky was racing away from the barn toward the back fences. "I see glitter. Only a few specks, but it must be Ajax."

"She's making a run for it. We can't let her get out of the sanctuary." I charged after Binky.

"We'll stop her." Binky flashed me a full toothed smile before bounding away.

"I see her!" Sammy said.

"We can use a pincer maneuver to stop her. I'll go up the middle. You two flank me left and right."

Binky diverted left, and Sammy went right, while I rocketed straight ahead, getting closer to Ajax's wobbling rear end.

She glanced over her shoulder and squealed, her stubby legs speeding up as she raced toward the fence.

"No, you don't. You haven't finished your rehabilitation. It's unsafe for you to be in the wild. Not until your glittery flatulence is under control."

"Leave me alone. I don't need anyone. I'm better off on my own." Ajax's voice was high with panic as she thundered closer to the fence and what she thought was freedom.

"You're not. No familiar is. I know you've had a rough time, but we'll find you someone better. A perfect companion who appreciates your uniqueness."

"I want nobody." She blasted glitter at me, and I narrowly avoided getting a face full and passing out.

Ajax had been discovered chained in the basement of a magic user gone rogue. He'd dabbled in power he couldn't control, and it sent him mad. He'd become convinced Ajax was tainted with evil, so he kept her a prisoner for months. It was thanks to a visit from me and my wonderful witch, Zandra Crypt, as part of our animal control job, that Ajax had been saved.

But because of that mistreatment, Ajax had a deep hatred for everybody. It was no surprise.

She darted left, heading toward Binky.

"I've got her," Binky yelled.

Ajax launched into the air and flipped over Binky's back.

Binky was moving so fast, she had to skid, almost flipped over herself, and wheeled around. "Did you see that? She's fast for a stubby gal."

"It was impossible to miss." I joined Binky, and we chased Ajax. This little hippo had impressive skills.

She was heading back to the barns, which was perfect. She'd be easier to corner and herd to safety.

But Ajax didn't make it easy on us. We completed three more circuits of the barns, and even I was winded before she finally slowed.

I nodded at Sammy to divert around the back of the barn so we could cut her off. Sammy sprinted away.

I stayed with Binky, darting past Zandra and Finn, happy to see them waking. Randal Nix had joined them. He was another new volunteer at the sanctuary, although his volunteer efforts were more to do with Zandra spending time here than because of his love for mucking out pens. Those two had a serious crush on each other, but neither was brave enough to make the first move.

When I got a moment, I'd rectify that. My witch had been on her own for a long time, and she deserved some sweet in her life. And Randal Nix was definitely that. A sweet, obliging, loveable tech mage geek. Just what she needed.

I rounded the corner with Binky beside me, and we slowed. Ajax was powering down to a trot, her beautiful gray mottled skin gleaming with sweat.

"You don't have to fight us. You've got everything you need here," I said. "No one will hurt you. This is a haven for familiars."

"I've been promised that before." Ajax wheezed out a breath. "Always lies. I had a bond I thought was unbreakable, but then it was ruined, splintered beyond repair by that idiot's greed."

"It was horrible what happened to you." Binky chuffed out consoling grunts through her nostrils. "I was mistreated by someone, too. They filled me with unnatural magic and used me as a weapon. I hurt a lot of people because of it."

Ajax was now walking, her head down. "I've heard your story. It's tragic. But mine is worse. Why don't you understand that I want to be alone? It's not much to ask for."

"Then you'd be lonely. And why have that when you can be here? Maybe even find someone new to bond with when the time is right." I approached slowly, not wanting to startle Ajax in case she took off again.

Not that she'd get far. Ajax was cornered. She had nowhere to go.

A wheezing sound from the entrance of the sanctuary caught my attention. I glowered as a huge coach limped in through the open gates, the engine spluttering and complaining.

"More non-magicals?" Sammy peered at the vehicle.

"If it is, it'll be the third group this month."

The coach door opened, and a tall, thin man with lanky shoulder-length, mousy brown hair climbed out. He looked around then patted the side of the coach and shook his head.

I breathed in deep and frowned. "It's definitely more non-magicals invading the sanctuary."

"How do they keep getting through the wards?" Binky stepped forward, her huge head raised as she inhaled the pungent aroma of sweaty feet and armpits drifting from the coach.

I glanced at Ajax, concerned she might make a run for it. But she knew when she'd been defeated and was settled on her haunches, a grumpy look on her face. "No idea. I've spoken to the Magic Council about defective wards, but they've been checked and there was no problem. This can't keep happening to Crimson Cove. It's too much of a risk to have non-magicals blundering around. They could wander into a spell and get their brains fried."

"Hey! Excuse me. I could do with some help over here." The guy who'd climbed out of the coach raised a hand and walked toward the barns. He wore a red jacket with a yellow logo on the right shoulder.

"You watch Ajax. I'll go see what he needs." I trotted away from Sammy and Binky and joined Finn and Randal, who were approaching the guy.

"Sorry to crash your party, but the coach has been playing up ever since we got into Crimson Cove," Coach Guy said.

"How odd." Finn was all dazzling smile and relaxed, while Randal stepped from foot to foot, looking like he needed a bathroom break. "You get it serviced regularly?"

"Always. Can't bring the customers out on a dodgy coach. And I've got a golden oldies special today, and they complain like crazy if the ride breaks down." Coach Guy chuckled. "At least this'll give them something to talk about with the grandkids."

"You planned a day trip to Crimson Cove? It's rarely on anyone's list of fun places to visit." Finn had his angel wings pinned neatly behind him, even though non-magicals shouldn't be able to see magic. Occasionally, it happened, though. Someone with latent abilities saw something they shouldn't, and that raised tricky questions and required a mind wipe. Never a safe move to perform on those with no power.

"Well, it wasn't the plan, but I guess we're stopping for now. Can't go anywhere until the coach is fixed." Coach Guy looked around. "What is this place, anyway? A petting zoo? Please say yes. I can pretend I added a free stop to the trip. My golden girls love a bargain."

"I can't help you there. This is my animal sanctuary," Finn said.

"Oh! Perfect. It's open to the public? We've been driving for two hours straight, so everyone needs to stretch their arthritic bits. Do you have a public washroom? Cafe?"

Finn glanced at Randal. "I'm not set up for crowds."

"It's just my old girls, and they're no bother. And we've got toilets onboard they can use. They'd love to see some of your animals. Might make up for the coach breaking. Would you mind? Of course, I'll make a donation to your project. I've got a budget for activities."

Finn tilted his head from side to side. "Most of the barns are off-limits. We've got animals in rehabilitation, and they can't be disturbed."

"Heard and understood. We'll only go where you tell us. Or give us a guided tour. That way, you can make sure none of my ladies misbehave." Coach Guy looked down at me. "You're adorable. My old ladies would eat you up."

I gave him a cool look. No one was eating me, old or young.

He chuckled as I narrowed my eyes. "I guess not that adorable."

"Don't mind Juno. She's protective of her territory. Isn't that right, cutie?" Finn leaned down and scratched between my ears.

I meowed my displeasure, since talking in front of a non-magical was never wise. They often fainted or screamed.

"How about I look at your engine?" Randal said. "I'm good with mechanical things. It's a hobby of mine. If I can get you going quickly, you can be on your way."

"That'll be great. I was wondering if it overheated. It had an oil change recently and new filters, and there's gas in the tank, so I can't think what else it could be. I'm no good with engines, and the driver is even worse. I just ride along to keep the old dears happy and make sure no one gets lost during the walking tours."

"Happy to help if I can," Randal said.

"I'd appreciate that." Coach Guy tipped an imaginary hat at Randal and nodded at Finn before they walked back to the vehicle.

I stepped on Finn's foot once they were out of earshot. "I don't like this."

"Neither do I." Zandra joined us a few seconds later, her eyes still bleary from getting a glitter shot. "It's doing us no good to repress our powers when the non-magicals wander in."

I nodded. If we repressed our natural urges, things exploded. I knew all about that. My magic had been strange ever since I was turned into an enchanted cat. Slowly, I'd been regaining my abilities, but my power was twitchy, so I held off from using it too often, despite the temptation. And right now, my magic wanted to blast out. It acted up at the strangest of times. Usually, when there was trouble around.

"Randal will get the coach fixed," Zandra said. "Then we can get them out of here. How's Ajax?" she said to me.

"Sammy and Binky are looking after her. She's miserable, though. And I'm unsure how we can make things right for her. Nothing I've said has gotten through."

"We'll keep trying," Finn said. "What do you always say, Juno? We never give up on an animal."

"I couldn't agree more." Finn was far from a perfect angel, but he had a solid gold heart when keeping animals safe.

"We should check on the rest of our residents to make sure there are no surprises waiting if the non-magicals look around," Zandra said.

"I'll do the far end barns where the baby dragons are housed," Finn said. "Can you handle the rest?"

"No problem. We're on it." I trotted away with Zandra, and we spent twenty minutes making sure the animals were content. They had plenty of food to keep them occupied, which made it less likely they'd blast out inappropriate jets of magic if non-magicals got too near or too nosy.

Zandra was shutting the barn door on the rogue cat familiars' pen when there was a scream. Another swiftly followed it. Then another. Within seconds, piercing wails clogged the air.

"What now? Ajax had better not have blundered over and shot them with butt glitter." Zandra raced around the side of the barn with me on her shoulder.

My eyes widened as I took in the scene. "Uh-oh! It's not Ajax causing the hysteria."

"Oh, my broomsticks! What are they doing?" Zandra's mouth dropped open as Adrienne and Joel shambled hand-in-hand toward the coach.

Chapter 2

Greetings from the ghouls

"We have to stop them." My gaze was on the non-magicals who'd emerged from the coach. Instead of wisely getting back onboard when they spotted two ghouls heading toward them, they were running for the barns.

Well, some of the old ladies were running. The rest hobbled, one speed-slid using her walker, and another limp-ran using crutches.

"You don't think they want to eat them, do you?" Finn hurried over.

"Of course not," Zandra snapped. "They're just curious. I've been around them long enough to know they don't give into their urge to take a bite out of anyone."

"Even when the potential food source is running, screaming, and smells of Parma violet dressing?" Finn pointed to the flailing non-magicals. Most of the old girls had gotten a steam up and motored along at a decent pace, heading into even worse danger.

"Zandra, you deal with Adrienne and Joel. I'll work with Finn and Sammy to stop the non-magicals from getting into the barns," I said. "If they do, they'll be magicked to death before they've adjusted their support stockings."

"And if they see the baby dragons or Binky..." Finn shook his head. "Let's move, everyone."

I yelled for Sammy, hoping that in the chaos, the non-magicals wouldn't notice a talking cat, and he bounded out of a barn a second later.

"We need to go on a charm offensive. Non-magicals are easy to distract, and they always stop to take pictures of something as cute as us," I said.

"You won't make them forget they've just seen two flesh eating ghouls." Finn jogged along beside us as we drew near the first group.

"You underestimate our cuteness. We're adorable. We just need to get them to notice us."

"It's too risky. Let's see if angel charm will do the trick. Hey, ladies. There's no need to be scared. Those ghouls aren't real," Finn called out. "There's a cosplay event going on around here. Nothing to worry about."

Several of the ladies slowed and turned. All their gazes were appreciative as they ran over Finn's toned form. I resisted the desire to roll my eyes.

"What's cosplay?" one lady said.

"Fancy dress," another said. "I've seen nothing like that before." She jabbed a finger at Adrienne and Joel, who'd stopped and were staring at the groups of flailing pensioners. They'd better not be thinking about which group to eat first.

"The wonders of special effects. I'm impressed by how fast you all moved. You ladies must work out. You're so limber." Finn had caught up with the group and was dazzling them with smiles.

While Finn charmed them, we dashed after the next group that was dangerously close to a barn full of unstable critters.

"You head to the right and cut off that smaller group. I'll deal with this bunch," I said to Sammy.

We split up, and I dashed in front of six pensioners. I hid behind a rock, and as they got close, I darted out, my tail up as I used my sweetest meow to get their attention.

One old girl stopped and grabbed her friend's arm. "Will you look at that? He looks like Muffin Moo Baby Face. Hello, angel."

I wrinkled my booping snooter. I was not a he. I meowed again and lifted one paw off the ground.

"Are you lost, sweetie?" She ducked and made kissy sounds as she held out her fingers, rubbing them together to encourage me nearer.

I flopped onto my side and exposed my stomach. I couldn't guarantee I wouldn't scratch if she touched it, but everyone liked the challenge of touching a cat's stomach. Death or glory.

"Gladys, come take a picture," the woman I'd so easily beguiled said. "I want to show my grandchildren what an adorable, fluffy darlin' we found on the tour."

"Oh, what a cutie pie." Gladys returned with the rest of her friends, and they cooed around me while

I allowed my photograph to be taken, while keeping a watchful eye on Zandra as she shuffled Adrienne and Joel out of sight.

Bony fingers settled on my stomach and tickled. It took all my willpower not to bite and claw. Instead, I closed my eyes and thought happy thoughts. This tummy intrusion was for the good of Crimson Cove. These non-magicals could never discover what we had in these barns. It would flip their minds upside down, and they'd never be the same.

Finn walked over with his new group of admirers. "Welcome to Creature Comforts animal sanctuary. May I invite anyone for a coffee? It's my way of making it up to you for having a fright. I assure you, we don't have people dressed up as ghouls wandering around every day."

"A coffee would be lovely," Gladys said. "Are your animals up for adoption? This kitty is cute. Are they all cute?" She kissy-faced at me.

"Sadly not. This is a special needs sanctuary. And Juno is dear to me. I couldn't bear to part with her." Finn winked at me. "This cat has unique talents."

"Those zombies were too realistic to be let out unsupervised," another lady said. "I've got a pacemaker. I can't get shocks like that. I was looking forward to a sedate amble around a stately home, not the walking dead greeting me."

"Let me get you a coffee and a muffin. My little way of saying sorry." Finn caught hold of the woman's hand and kissed the back of it. "I'd hate for such a beauty to feel unwell because of me."

The woman preened and blushed under his praise. "Perhaps a nice sit down and a hot drink is what I need. Come along, ladies. Drinks and muffins are on this stud."

After receiving several more tickles and pets, I was left alone. I resisted the desire to give myself a tongue bath. Perhaps I'd allow Zandra to give me a proper bath later with suds and a loofah. The taste of non-magicals was never pleasant on the tongue.

A Sammy sounding squeak had me tensing. I dashed around the barn and discovered him being squeezed by a plump child in long beige shorts with chocolate stains around his mouth.

Sammy was squirming in the child's grip, unable to get away. His eyes were wide, and his paws scrabbled in the air.

"Let him go." I growled and narrowed my eyes at the grubby brat.

The child's eyes grew as large as saucers. "Did... did you just talk?"

Sammy squeaked again. "He's horrible. He jumped on my tail."

The child stared down at Sammy. "You, too? So cool. What else do you do?"

"Obliterate individuals who injure us." Magic sparkled out of me as my anger grew. No one hurt my Sammy and got away with it. "Where did you come from? You're not a pensioner."

The child wrinkled his pudgy nose. "Whoa! You really talk."

"Focus, small being. Why are you here? Don't make me ask again."

He scowled at me, his surprise at our talking ability quickly gone. "My gran dragged me on this dumb trip. I didn't want to come, but I'm glad I did now I found you. You're both coming home with me." He squeezed Sammy tighter.

I coiled, preparing to blast this miscreant child with everything I had so I could get Sammy back unharmed.

A blur of movement rocketed out of the barn. Binky slammed her enormous front paws against the child's shoulders, sending him reeling as he hit the dirt. She stood on him and growled in his face, exposing her fine fangs. "Let the cat go if you want to live."

My magic still sparkled and wavered, tugging against my control and encouraging me to destroy this unwelcome intruder.

The child didn't protest against Binky's order and released Sammy. He raced over to me, his tail dragging on the ground. It looked dislocated.

"What... what..." the child stammered.

"I am your nightmare," Binky said in a voice that would terrify all but the hardiest of beings. "Never hold an animal like that again. They hate it. From now on, your motto is to be kind to all. And I'll be watching you to ensure you live by that. If you step out of line, you'll regret it. Do we have an understanding, small, smelly person?"

Binky was magnificent as she growled and hissed over the child, who'd developed a dark stain on the front of his shorts.

"I don't hear you agreeing with me," Binky said.

"Yes! Yes! I will. I'll be good."

"Do you promise never to harm an animal again?"

"Never. Sorry, I didn't know."

Sammy placed a reassuring paw on my head. "It's okay, Juno. He just scared me. One second, he was petting me, then he pulled my tail and grabbed me."

Magic bubbled around me. I was losing control of my power. "Your magnificent tail is damaged."

"It'll heal with a spell."

I hissed out my annoyance and, with no small effort, got my magic under control.

It took several deep breaths and more words of reassurance from Sammy, but I recovered.

I needed to watch myself. I was still getting used to having increased abilities since discovering part of my stolen power and reabsorbing it, and I needed to re-learn how to be an all-powerful demigoddess, or this could go horribly wrong, fast.

"I was worried about you." I nuzzled Sammy's face, while nuzzling his tail and pulsing out healing magic.

"I always worry about you, too."

We indulged in a few seconds of bonding, and after checking to ensure his tail was pain free, I trotted over to where Binky had the child restrained.

"He's learned his lesson. Let him go." I fixed a glare on the small person. "Remember my friend's words."

The child crawled back like a crab. "I'm gonna tell everyone I heard animals talking."

I growled at him. "Foolish brat. No one will believe you. If you say anything about this, your friends will abandon you, and you'll find yourself at the doctor as your family figures out why you believe animals talk. They may even poke about inside your brain and take out a few bits. You wouldn't want that, would you?"

He gulped. "I... I didn't think about that. I won't say nothing."

"Anything. You won't say anything. Good boy. Go find your grandparent. I hope she has a change of clothes for you."

The child backpedaled then turned and raced away, his arms pin-wheeling.

Binky blew out a breath and slid me a glance. "I hope you don't mind me getting involved. I thought you were about to go nuclear on that kid."

"For a minute, so did I. Thanks for stepping in and saving the day."

She grinned at me. "That's what friends are for."

There was an enormous sneeze from inside a barn, and a faint plume of glitter appeared in the air.

"Uh-oh. Some of the non-magicals must have found where I stashed Ajax," Binky said.

We raced to the barn to discover the door open and four non-magicals staring with their mouths open as Ajax gave another enormous sneeze and showered them with glitter.

"I didn't know glitter came out of your nose and your rear end," Sammy said.

Her gaze skittered our way. "What do you know, I'm magical. The magic comes out of all orifices. Why are these pointless beings in here?"

"An unhappy accident," I said. "Stop covering them in glitter. You have no idea what your magic will do to them."

Ajax smirked. "I know exactly what it'll do. They're under my control. It's how I convinced them to open the pen door. Now, I plan to use them to escape."

I hissed at her. A glitter sneezing hippo controlling non-magicals would be a nightmare. "You could kill them. You know we shouldn't use magic on them."

"They wandered in uninvited and poked around. What else was I supposed to do?"

"Show restraint." Binky inspected one large paw and pulled a twig out from between her pads.

"Says the enormous cougar who just made a child wet his pants. I saw. You can't tell me what to do after that display of aggression."

"I didn't use magic on him." Binky growled. "I was saving a friend. You're doing this so you can manipulate the non-magicals and get your own way. Be grateful for what you have here."

"It's all the same thing. What's that saying? Tomatoes, tomatoes."

I stepped forward. "I can't let you do this."

Ajax sneered at me. "What you gonna do to stop me? Show me your belly like you did those old codgers? I'm not falling for your tricks."

I scraped a paw on the ground and tested my magic. It faltered but then stabilized. What I was about to do was a huge risk, but this situation would get out of hand if I didn't try. I drew in a deep breath, centered myself, and pulsed out a spell that covered the non-magicals. They wavered on their feet then slumped to the ground.

"Hey! Why did you do that? They're my way out of here." Ajax stamped over to the unconscious non-magicals and snuffled around them. "Wake up! Help me!"

"That's exactly why I did it. Now, get back in your pen and behave," I said.

"And if I don't?"

I narrowed my eyes at the misbehaving hippo. "I'm always on the side of the animals, but you try my patience. This place is here to help you. I understand you've had a hard time and your past was rough, but that's what it is. It's the past. Now, you have two choices. You dwell on your past and make the rest of your life miserable, stay unhappy and hurt everyone around you, or you focus on the positive and the good."

"Oh yeah, Freud. How am I supposed to do that?"

"You control your thoughts and your feelings about the past. Use that for good. Use that to realize you can have a happy life, you can trust again, and you will find someone who loves you and treats you right." I coiled my white tail around my paws. "While you immerse yourself in dark thoughts and let your brain chatter away and tell you the world is terrible and everyone will hurt you, that's what will happen. You're in control of that chatter, and only you can drown it out. Become a better pygmy hippo."

Ajax lowered her head and huffed out a few breaths. "It's too hard. I got hurt."

"Life isn't easy, but it's how we respond to that difficulty that makes the difference. Focus on the good, think about the positive, and be hopeful."

After scuffing her feet in the dirt for a few seconds, Ajax turned and ambled into her pen.

Binky trotted over and secured the door. "Right choice. It isn't always easy, but when you work at it, things get better. I know that from my own experience."

"I'm taking a nap," she mumbled.

Binky re-joined me and Sammy.

"What should we do with these unconscious non-magicals?" Sammy said.

"We'll fake a gas leak story," I said. "We've done it before when non-magicals have gotten too close for comfort. Let's get them in the fresh air, and the magic will wear off. I only used a tiny amount."

"It did the job." Binky sniffed at one of them. "How should we move them?"

I sighed. "The old-fashioned way. Any more magic, and their hair will fall out."

It took us a few minutes to drag the non-magicals outside.

Once they were slowly rousing, Binky turned to me. "I'd better get out of here. If they see me, I'll cause more panic."

"Of course. Not everyone is comfortable being around such a magnificently large cat. Thanks for your help."

"Anytime." Binky nodded a goodbye at Sammy and me then bounded away.

"Hey, what's going on? Are they okay?" Coach Guy trotted over, concern on his long face.

I stepped back and lifted my tail. I couldn't tell him what happened, so I tried to look happy.

Sammy sparked a small spell in the air while Coach Guy checked his passengers. Immediately, a strong smell of gas drifted around us.

Coach Guy lifted his head and sniffed. He looked around and waved frantically at Finn, who was handing around mugs of coffee to his new fan club. "You've got a problem. It smells like a gas leak. I think it's affected my ladies."

Finn jogged over. "Huh, you could be right. This place is old, and things always go wrong. They're okay, aren't they?" He was looking at me as he asked the question.

I discreetly nodded as I settled next to Sammy.

"Ugh. What happened?" a lady in the dirt mumbled.

"Stay where you are, Betty. You got exposed to a gas leak, but you'll be fine. Take plenty of deep breaths." Coach Guy caught hold of her hand and patted it. "Best we say nothing to head office about this, though. You don't want them to stop you coming on these trips because you're too big of an insurance risk, do you?"

"Oh, no. Of course not. I love these trips." Betty rubbed her forehead. "I dreamed I saw a small hippo sneezing glitter."

Finn chuckled. "That's quite an imagination you've got there."

Coach Guy's eyebrows were raised as he nodded. "What kind of gas have you got running this place?"

"Nothing unusual." Finn rocked back on his heels. "When everyone is awake, come join the others. We're having coffee and cake. That'll make you feel better."

"That sounds nice, doesn't it, Betty? You rest, and I'll check on everyone else." Coach Guy scratched my head. "You're so pretty."

I pretended to preen under his praise, even though his fingers smelled of cheesy chips.

Randal jogged over a few minutes later and gave a thumbs-up. "Good news. The coach is fixed."

"You hear that, everyone?" Coach Guy called out. "We'll soon be on our way. Although we've already had an adventure. What with zombies, gas leaks, and a broken engine."

"Maybe the universe is telling you something." Finn was all smiles.

"Oh, we've faced worse. We once drove through a storm where it rained frogs."

"I was on that trip." Betty was struggling to her feet, aided by Finn. "We thought Armageddon had struck."

Coach Guy laughed. "It was just freak weather. A localized tornado dipped into a stream and picked up most of the wildlife and dumped them on the coach. Gave us all a fright, though. We made the front page of the local paper, didn't we, Betty?"

"I got a quote in print." Betty nodded eagerly.

"Tell me all about it over coffee." Finn held out his arm for Betty to take.

"I'll bring the others over as soon as they're ready." Coach Guy leaned in close to Finn. "And let's keep this quiet. We haven't got much insurance, and I don't want anyone making a claim against either of us. You get my meaning?"

Finn stepped back and patted him on the shoulder. "Loud and clear. No one wants too much attention, do they? When questions get asked, problems arise."

"Exactly! We're on the same page." Coach Guy high-fived Finn.

Half an hour later, and after the unwelcome visitors had finished their refreshments and been hustled onto the coach, the vehicle chugged out of the driveway.

I stood with Zandra, Finn, Randal, and Sammy. Adrienne and Joel were safely inside, chewing on boiled brains. We breathed sighs of relief as the coach turned the corner.

"Why do these non-magicals keep showing up?" Zandra said. "Every time they're here, they cause trouble."

"I've asked the Magic Council about the wards, but they assure me there's no problem," I said.

She arched an eyebrow. "And do we believe them?"

"I'll keep trying."

"Maybe the non-magicals are evolving," Randal said. "They could be becoming more sensitive to magic. Smarter."

We looked at each other and laughed.

An approaching vehicle caught my attention. I lifted my booping snooter and sniffed as a sleek black SUV rolled into the animal sanctuary.

"More non-magicals?" Sammy said.

I let out a sigh. "No. This has dominant werewolf stink all over it. When will these guys pack up and leave Crimson Cove?"

Chapter 3

A walk on the werewolf side

Emron Laker appeared from the SUV. Our paths had crossed several times since the werewolves arrived to conduct negotiations and end a dispute between the White Ridge and Amber Cross packs.

He was a prime werewolf, filling every inch of his dark fitted jeans and crisp, white shirt. He reminded me of a pirate, with his slicked back, shoulder-length dark hair and beard. The fancy sword slung low on his hip only added to the air of pirate chic. Throw in an eye patch and a talking parrot, and he'd be signed up for the next *Pirates of the Caribbean* movie.

Emron strutted over, his hand raised in greeting. "What's with the coach?"

"Unwanted visitors." Finn stepped forward and shook Emron's hand. "How are the negotiations going?"

He rolled his shoulders after he'd released Finn's hand. "They're going. We're taking a break. It's been a tense few days, and everyone needed time out to blow off steam before the wrong words got snarled out."

"So, no progress?" Although Finn looked relaxed, his wings fluttered behind him. Angel Force was dealing with the nightly fights among the rival werewolf packs. And those fights were intense, bloody, and leaned toward fatalities more often than not. So far, there'd been no deaths, but the longer these negotiations went on, the likelihood of that increased.

"I've got things under control. This isn't my first negotiation." Emron rested a hand on the hilt of his sword. It was lodged in a black leather scabbard, so I couldn't see the blade, but the handle was a deep polished silver with a gold band wrapping around the hilt.

"Of course. Just hoping for positive news so the residents don't get any jumpier. I think it's all the howling. We're not used to it." Finn was smiling, but it was a strained smile.

"Can't do anything about that." Emron looked around. "It's a fine piece of land you've got here. And I've heard people say you run a sanctuary on this plot."

"Sure do. Are you looking to adopt?"

Emron chuckled. "Not as such, but I am looking to acquire land and have animals free roaming."

Finn tensed. "To hunt?"

Emron's grin grew feral. "Well, it is what werewolves do when we need a meal. I've yet to decide if it'll be a wildlife refuge or something with purpose."

"Refuges have purpose," I said.

Emron crouched until he was almost eye level with me, adjusting his sword so it didn't bash against his broad thigh. "My apologies. I didn't mean to offend. Of course, I'll look after any animal in my care. I appreciate you pointing out my error." He reached out a hand, and after a second of hesitation, I touched it with a paw.

Zandra nudged me with her toe. We knew to be careful around werewolves. Their tempers were hotter than the center of a volcano. And werewolf negotiators came with a special sauce, so they could control tense situations with a primal power that wasn't to be messed with. If you crossed a negotiator, and they unleashed that power, you'd be in for a world of torment.

Emron stood. "Would you mind showing me around the sanctuary, Finn? I need an idea of how much land I need and what quality to invest in. I want to grow crops to feed the animals."

"Fatten them up, he means," Sammy muttered.

I gave a half-shrug. I wasn't keen on werewolves, but we were predators, too, so I understood the hunt instinct. But I didn't appreciate the cool way Emron described his desire to have a ready meal on his doorstep.

"You're welcome to look around. It's quiet now we've gotten rid of the coachload of non-magicals," Finn said.

Emron canted his head. "They were non-magicals? In Crimson Cove? Is that safe?"

"Not for them," Zandra said. "That's why we discourage them. We like this town quiet."

Emron raised a hand. "I get your meaning. Since we've been here, the town has gotten livelier. And I apologize for any inconvenience the werewolves have caused. After a tough day of negotiation, they blow off their frustration. Let me know if there's been damage or trouble caused, and I'll ensure things are made right. I don't want Crimson Cove turning away the werewolves the next time we need a safe haven to negotiate."

"You don't think these negotiations will work?" I said. "I know the last three have ended in a stalemate."

"Do you now? Why the interest in wolf business, little cat?"

I hissed softly. "To ensure those I care about are never at risk of werewolves' steam rolling over anyone who gets in their way."

Emron nodded. "Perfect answer. And the negotiations will work now I'm here. But we're walking a fine line, and that can be snapped with the wrong word." He lifted his head and drew in a deep breath. "If you want to hear from the werewolves' mouths how things are going, the alphas are running close by."

I wrinkled my booping snooter. This could get tricky. Too many dominant werewolves in one place made things tense.

I'd spotted Leon Margot and Decker Duke strutting around Crimson Cove like they owned the place, and I didn't want that much alpha testosterone near my wonderful witch.

Finn clapped Emron on the shoulder. "Let me show you around. I expect you could do with a break from the alphas, too."

Emron inclined his head. "Much appreciated. I get satisfaction from my work, but only when I have enough downtime to recharge the wolf. Otherwise, he gets snappy."

Finn flashed his eyebrows at me as he led Emron away.

No one was keen on the werewolves being here, but it was only right they had a safe place to conduct negotiations. Crimson Cove may appear to be a sleepy little town on the outside, but it was a draw for those in trouble and in need of a refuge. A place to heal wounds and rebuild. Requests for help were never turned away, no matter how inconvenient it was to the residents.

Just as Finn was showing Emron around a barn, two huge werewolves appeared at the far end of the field. One was an enormous black creature with a white tail tip. The other was a tawny brown with a huge ginger ruff around his solid neck. Two smaller werewolves, one pale brown and the other an ash gray, accompanied them.

The two alphas raced each other and shoulder barged hard enough to make the ground shake. It was rough play, but that's exactly what it was. Play. That was how the werewolves operated.

The smaller werewolves trotted behind, keeping a respectful distance from the alphas, knowing that getting involved in that level of roughhousing would kill them.

"First non-magicals, now rampaging werewolves," Zandra said. "I'm unsure which is worse."

Randal had been quiet during the conversation and scuffed his foot through the dirt, looking like he wanted to be anywhere else but here.

"You're not a fan?" I said to him.

"I don't find werewolves easy to be around. I don't get the posturing, and they don't understand my tech. I've butted heads with a few werewolves."

"And lived to tell the tale?"

"As you can see, I'm still breathing." His smile was lopsided. "If I were a werewolf, I'd be the bottom of the pack."

Zandra nudged him with an elbow. "Maybe you wouldn't be alpha, but who wants that? All that fighting, negotiating, and standing up against others who want your spot. It would be exhausting. Better to be lower in the pack. You'd make a great negotiator."

A flush crossed his cheeks. "You think so?"

"Sure! You'd be amazing at that. You help people to see all sides of an argument. And you always make me calm when we're together."

I smiled as Randal continued to blush under Zandra's praise.

An animal alarm cry shot out of a barn, quickly followed by another.

Zandra stepped forward. "They're sensing the werewolves." She waved her arms at the wolves. "Hey, you can't be here. This is an animal sanctuary." She strode off, and I jogged after her, Randal and Sammy following.

"Be careful. Don't annoy the werewolves," I cautioned.

"Why not? They've annoyed me." She kept waving her arms. "Slow down."

The werewolves kept bounding around, body slamming each other, nipping and snarling.

"They need something stronger to pay attention to me." Zandra zapped out a spell and slammed it into the ground in front of the werewolves.

All four of them whipped around and snarled at her.

She kept the magic shimmering on her fingers. "I told you to quit. This is a refuge for animals who need help. You barging around and causing noise is alarming them. You must hear their distress."

The alphas snarled, cocked their heads, exchanged a glance, then paced toward us. They were flanked by the other two werewolves, who looked no less aggressive, their heads down, eyes blazing amber, and hackles raised.

"You want me to deal with them?" I stepped in front of Zandra.

"Nope. I don't want you going up against four mean looking werewolves," Zandra said. "Besides, they don't scare me."

My wonderful witch was fearless, but I wished she had less bravado. It would make it easier to keep her alive.

She held out her hands, magic blazing on her palms. "Last chance to leave. You shouldn't be here."

The two alphas exchanged another glance. They kept walking, but as they did so, they shifted from four paws to two feet. Once they'd shed their magnificent werewolf fur, they were naked. The other two werewolves remained in their furry forms.

Zandra looked away from the well-muscled, handsome, naked as the day they were born, guys in front of her.

I was more than happy to get an eyeful of their delicious nakedness. "Greetings. I'm Juno, and the magnificent witch who requested you cease and desist your rambunctious activities is Zandra Crypt. The stunning tabby beside me is Sammy. And that's Randal."

"Hey, Juno. Zandra. Sammy. Randal. Nice place you got here." The tall, dark, delicious werewolf reached out a hand. "I'm Decker Duke. This is Leon Margot."

Zandra kept her eyes averted. "Any chance you brought clothes with you?"

He lowered his hand, a wicked smile on his face. "Of course. Hugh, if you'd do the honors."

The smaller brown wolf trotted over. He wore two neat packs attached to a collar around his neck. Decker took one and turned his back, taking his time to slide into a black T-shirt and khaki shorts.

Leon remained naked, his hands on his hips.

"As delicious as those abs are, you can also put them away," I said to him.

He laughed. "Too much for you?"

"I'm enjoying the view. But..." I glanced at Zandra, whose face was crimson. "There's a way of doing these things."

He shrugged and clicked his fingers. The other werewolf trotted over and deposited a single pack of clothing on the ground.

"Nico, change," Leon ordered.

Nico shuddered and transformed into a toned, slender male with dark eyes that flickered everywhere. He had no clothing, so remained naked, his hands covering his modesty.

Decker nodded at the ash gray wolf, who stood silently beside him. "You can change too if you want."

The wolf, Hugh, nodded. A few seconds later, a slender guy with shaggy light brown hair grinned at us. Fortunately, he'd brought clothing, which he quickly put on.

I surveyed the werewolves. All handsome and sure of themselves, although the alphas radiated their power like lighthouse beacons. "This is a refuge. Best you find somewhere else to play tag."

Decker rubbed the back of his neck. "We meant no harm. We were out for a run and got carried away."

I nodded. "If you must run in this area, stick to the fence line. That way, the animals will be less likely to sense you and panic."

"You should have signs up if you don't want us running around." Leon tossed his blond hair off his face. "We can't be the first werewolves to show up in Crimson Cove."

"We have werewolves. Most of them have manners, though," Zandra said.

"Is that so?" Leon's gaze tracked over Zandra. "I like a spicy female. Let me take you out while I'm here. Show you I'm a harmless pup."

"I'm not free."

"I haven't said when I want to take you out."

"I still won't be free."

He bared his teeth. "And I love a challenge."

"I'm not the challenge you want to deal with," Zandra said. "Focus on your negotiations."

"I can do both. And I always get what I want, eventually." He reached forward as if to cup Zandra's face.

I stepped in front of her and issued a warning hiss. To my surprise, Randal also stepped forward.

"Zandra's made it clear she's not interested," he said.

Leon's gaze flashed to Randal, his eyes flickering amber. "And I suppose you think she's interested in you?"

A bright flash of color traced across his cheeks, but Randal's shoulders were back and his head high. "Whether she is or isn't, it's none of your concern. Focus on the fact she turned you down."

"Or she's playing hard to get."

"She's also right here and capable of speaking for herself," Zandra said.

Leon chuckled.

"Sorry, I was trying to help." Randal's shoulders lowered. "This guy is bothering you."

"Never apologize to a potential mate," Leon said. "They hate to see weakness."

I stamped on Leon's foot. "Good manners are never considered weak. Back off."

Leon's top lip curled. "You'd better have serious magic inside those cute little paws before you challenge me."

"My murder mittens know how to deal with an annoying werewolf who won't take no for an answer." I extended my claws and bared my fangs.

He chuckled again. "Adorable. That's something I'd love to see."

"You will, if you keep pushing your luck."

Decker, Hugh, and Nico stayed out of the situation, although Nico was tense, as if waiting for an order. He must belong to Leon's pack. They'd all probably seen Leon operate like this and knew it never turned out well if they interfered.

I despised a bully, though. Sure, werewolves were strong and knew their place in the supernatural world, but that didn't allow them to be entitled jerks.

"I'll take you somewhere nice. Fancy dinner, dancing, whatever you like. You just say the word," Leon said to Zandra, not appreciating how foolish it was to ignore me.

"I'll say one word. No," Zandra said.

"That's not nice. Here's me, being friendly, and you're making life difficult."

"You're the only one making things unpleasant," Randal said. "It's time to go."

Leon's hand shot out, and he shoved Randal. "I'm going nowhere. Decker, don't you think this puppy is putting his neck on the line? He must be into his female if he's willing to go up against us."

"Only you. You started this." Decker's tone revealed boredom and a dash of exasperation. "I've got no issue here."

"He challenged me. You heard him." The air crackled with tension. This werewolf was spoiling for a fight, and he didn't mind who he started it with.

"No challenges were issued," I said. "Let's walk away from this while we all still can."

"I'm going nowhere," Leon snarled through his teeth. "This pup stood up against me. Don't you know who I am?"

How tempting it was to roll my eyes at such an egotistical comment.

Randal stood firm, and I admired him, even though he stared a violent death in the face by going up against an alpha werewolf.

"We should get back to the negotiations." Nico kept his head lowered, so he didn't meet anyone's gaze. "They're starting again in half an hour."

Leon raised a finger. "They'll start when I'm ready."

Decker growled. "You don't run these negotiations. Stop wasting time."

"I'm not done here."

"You need to be," I said. "There's nothing for you here."

"Not until I get my retribution." Leon shoved Randal so hard he staggered back.

"That's enough." Zandra sparked magic on her fingers.

"I'm only getting started, sweetheart. Let's see what it takes to get a reaction out of this guy." He swung a left-right punch combination at Randal.

Randal ducked both punches. His eyes were wide, but he was in a crouched position, ready to fight.

"Huh! You've got moves, pipsqueak. Now, I'm interested." Leon lunged at Randal and tackled him to the ground. They rolled around, everyone dodging out of their way to avoid being knocked off their feet.

Randal put up a brave fight, but he was no match for an enormous alpha werewolf. Within seconds, Leon had him in a headlock and was choking him.

Zandra lifted a hand to cast a spell, but Randal caught her eye and shook his head.

"I've got this," he wheezed out.

"All you've got is a mouthful of dirt and an apology that needs to be made," Leon said. "Until I hear that, you're going nowhere."

"Here's your apology." Randal yanked something out of his jeans pocket and slammed it against Leon's arm. Leon went rigid, his hair stood on end, and he flew back, sparks flickering across his body.

Randal rolled onto his hands and knees and sucked in lungfuls of air. Leon remained flat on his back, twitching as magic rolled over him.

I dashed over to Randal with Zandra and Sammy. "What was that?"

He glanced up at me, his face red and eyes watering. "A gadget I've been working on."

"Leon is out cold," Zandra said. "That was incredible."

A smile crossed Randal's face. "You think? It was nothing."

"It was more than nothing." Decker walked over and helped Randal to his feet. "It's not often I get to see Leon fall flat on his back. Nice work. Would you lend me that device?"

Randal opened his palm to reveal a small, flat gold disc. "It's still in the testing phase. I've been figuring out how to channel my tech mage magic into objects. It means I'll always have a supply of magic."

"Was that your strongest spell?" Decker examined the gold disc.

"No, I'm just messing around with this. I forgot I had it in my pocket. When Leon was choking the life out of me, I figured it could be useful."

Leon groaned and tried to get up but staggered and fell on his face.

"Hey, what's going on?" Emron strode over, Finn behind him.

"Werewolves being feisty," I said. "One of them bit off more than he could chew."

"What happened to Leon?" Emron held out a hand to assist Leon up.

He batted it away and clambered to his feet, resting his hands on his knees and shaking his head. "That happened." He jabbed a shaking finger at Randal.

"It's no less than you deserve," I said. "You were disrespectful to my wonderful witch and then issued a challenge against Randal for no reason."

"There's been a misunderstanding." Emron stood in between Leon and Randal so they couldn't eyeball each other. "These negotiations are making everyone hot under the collar. My apologies if things got out of hand. It won't happen again."

"He owes me," Leon said.

"Randal bested you in the challenge," I said. "You lost. Accept that. Or aren't you alpha enough to know when you've been beaten?"

Leon growled at me. "I demand a rematch. This time, no trickery or gadgets. We fight with fists."

Emron placed a hand on Leon's shoulder. "You don't need a small skirmish to distract you from achieving your goal."

Leon bared his teeth again. "I'll get what I want. From everyone."

Emron squeezed Leon's shoulder then stepped back. "I suggest we arrange a feast for tonight. Something everyone can enjoy. Take our minds off things."

"Best if the packs choose different venues this time," Decker said. "Last night got out of hand. Some of my guys were stalked on the way home. Anything you want to say about that, Leon?"

"It wasn't stalking. My pack was being cautious. They heard a few things they didn't like."

Decker ran his tongue across his teeth but didn't respond.

"I'm having the pizza parlor," Leon said.

Decker raised a hand. "We'll take the café, so long as it's not another vampire night."

"And, of course, anyone in Crimson Cove is welcome to join either party," Emron said. "We don't want residents thinking they can't use the stores and restaurants while we're here."

"We have other plans," Zandra said, "but thanks for the invitation."

Emron rested a hand against his chest. "It's our loss you'll not be joining us. Perhaps another time."

"Sure. Perhaps."

After a few muttered words to Leon, Emron looked at us and nodded. "Forgive any high spirits. No harm done. We'll leave you to it. Enjoy the rest of your day."

Decker nodded a goodbye, as did Nico and Hugh, and the group headed off. As they reached the boundary, they turned back into werewolves and sprinted away.

I wrinkled my booping snooter as Emron disappeared. He was full of smooth lines and platitudes. Could anyone be that perfect, or was it an act?

Zandra lifted me onto her shoulder and scratched under my chin. "You okay, Randal? You didn't have to stick up for me."

He stuffed his hands into his jeans pockets. "I'll always look out for you. And I know you can take care of yourself, but sometimes it's nice not to have to, isn't it?"

"It's more than I'd have done. Those werewolves have been a nightmare since taking over the town," Finn said.

"Ever the gentleman." I batted the air close to his nose.

He reared back and grinned. "Zandra has enough people looking out for her without me getting involved."

"And as I keep telling everyone, not that you seem to listen, I can look after myself." She grinned at Randal and then looked away. "But now and again, it's good to know who's got my back."

"If we could just get rid of the werewolves and the non-magicals, we'd get things back to normal in Crimson Cove," Finn said, a rueful smile on his face as he watched Zandra and Randal blushing.

"I've never considered this place normal, but I agree. It would be nice if non-magicals stopped blundering into wards and frying themselves, or werewolves stopped snapping at each other," I said.

"They'll be gone soon," Randal said. "Should we see how the animals are doing? Make sure none of them got too spooked."

We all agreed that was a great idea.

I hopped off Zandra's shoulder and let her walk ahead with Finn and Sammy so I could speak to Randal uninterrupted. "Good work with Leon. I hate it when anyone is disrespectful to my witch."

Randal nodded, his expression intense. "I know she has incredible power, but I saw red when Leon wouldn't take no for an answer. Who does that?"

"Someone with a lot less sense than you. Keep up the good work. I approve."

He grinned at me. "Thanks, Juno. That means a lot. Do you... Do you think I have a chance? I like Zandra, but she could have anyone she wants."

"And she will. Zandra will make the right choice, but it's always wise to make it clear you're interested."

"I am. I mean, I don't want to be a disappointment to her. She's way out of my league."

"She's not. Keep doing what you're doing." I bumped into him with my side as we walked. "And if you keep knocking down werewolves like that, you'll have plenty of interest from the opposite sex."

He hunched his shoulders. "There's only one person I'm interested in. I just hope she likes me, too."

"Time will tell." I had every hope this budding romance would turn into a blossoming relationship in no time, with a gentle shove from me.

Chapter 4

A heeled horror

I sat in the passenger seat of the van as Zandra unloaded the last of the feral kittens and placed them inside the office, ready to be moved to a pen in the quiet space at the back.

My eyes narrowed as four werewolves dashed past in fur form. It looked like tonight would be the same as the previous night. The werewolves would press pause on their negotiations, take over Crimson Cove, and make everyone's life less pleasant.

Zandra shut the back of the van and joined me, leaning against the side as even more werewolves raced past. "Same old, same old. I was thinking we could eat out tonight, but I'm not going for pizza if the place is filled with greedy wolves again."

"Let's keep out of their way until the negotiations are finished." The less my wonderful witch had to do with the werewolves, the better.

"How's it going?" Barney Hoffman, our gruff, supportive boss, emerged from the building. "I just moved the ferals into their pens." He held up a hand to show several deep slashes.

"Thanks, Barney. I was about to do that. We were just watching our furry visitors," Zandra said.

He pursed his lips. "It's not ideal, but ever since I've been here, Crimson Cove has been a safe space for those looking for a resolution to trouble. This has been a haven for hundreds of years for those who struggle. Some of the old talks and agreements were even sealed in blood."

"Sounds gruesome," Zandra said.

"It happens more regularly than you think," I said.

Back in the day, they wrote treaties in the feuding parties' blood to show they were committed to reconciliation. And, of course, blood magic was one of the most powerful forces a magic user could unleash.

"They used blood as ink?" Zandra shuddered.

I nodded, but added no more commentary. I'd seen my fair share of negotiations as a demigoddess prior to my unwanted transformation into a cat. Some of the baser supernaturals still found it reassuring to use blood magic power to ensure agreements would be almost unbreakable.

"It won't be for much longer," Barney said. "I met their negotiator, Emron, this morning. He said they'd had a breakthrough. Another few days, and they can put the details in writing."

"Do you think they'll get that far?" Zandra said. "I heard the talks have failed before."

"This negotiator knows what he's doing," Barney said. "He'll make it right, and we'll get Crimson Cove back to the happy little haven it always is."

After we said our goodbyes, Barney locked the office and ambled away, heading home for a quiet evening.

I still had to work on finding him a familiar to bond with, since the attempt with Sammy had failed, but I was in no rush. It took time to find the perfect match for a magic user. I should know. I'd had many failed bondings in the past, and it wasn't until I'd discovered Zandra that I realized how marvelous a genuine bond was.

"Let's grab food before the werewolves take over," Zandra said. "What would you like?"

I hopped out of the van. "Something fishy."

She tipped her head back. "It's always fish with you. I was thinking pizza."

"You can put fish on pizza, can't you? Perhaps a seafood medley. But no octopus. It's chewy."

She grimaced. "I'm with you there. Nothing with tentacles."

"Where is he?" A shrill female voice had me lowering my ears.

I glanced over my shoulder and spotted a stunning Amazonian woman with silky black hair down to her waist and flawless bronze skin striding along. Hugh and Nico scurried on either side of her, their positions submissive.

"I'm sorry, but Emron said he shouldn't be disturbed," Hugh said.

"Idiot! He didn't mean me. He always wants to see me. Why are you making this so difficult?"

"She's fun," Zandra muttered. "What's up with her?"

"Werewolf drama. They should get their own reality TV show."

We lagged behind the bickering group, since we were headed in the same direction. As we drew closer to town, I was unhappy to see two groups of non-magicals milling around. They were taking photographs and staring into the store windows. How had they snuck in? I blamed the werewolves for distracting everyone.

"I can tell him you're here. When he has a moment, I'm sure he'll find you," Hugh said.

The stunning brunette stopped, turned on one heel, and slapped Hugh across the cheek. "How dare you. I'm no one's afterthought, and I demand to see Emron immediately. He hasn't returned my messages."

Hugh clamped a hand across his flaming cheek. "I'm sure he wants to. He's busy with the negotiations." He glanced at Nico, desperation in his eyes.

Nico nodded. "It's true. Emron specifically requested downtime. Today was a tricky stage in the negotiations, and—"

"I care nothing about that. My needs are more important. Why won't you tell me where he is?"

Zandra stopped walking and watched the argument. "No wonder Emron is avoiding her if she's this high-strung."

I nodded. "She must have werewolf in her to make Hugh and Nico cower so much." I lifted my booping snooter to get a whiff of her power. There were musky werewolf undertones mingled with another type of shifter and something I couldn't identify. Rare magic always intrigued me.

"Werewolf and a bad attitude, by the looks of it. She shouldn't have slapped Hugh. The poor guy was only passing on information."

"If you don't tell me where he is right this second, you'll regret it." The brunette loomed over Hugh. "And he'd better not be with another woman. If you're covering for him—"

"No! No! He wouldn't do that to you."

She grabbed Hugh by the shoulders and slammed magic into him.

He staggered back and yelped, his body sparking with whatever spell she'd thumped him with.

Several of the non-magicals who'd been perusing the stores turned to watch, confusion on their faces as their brains attempted to decode what they'd witnessed.

"We have to stop her," I said. "She could hit a non-magical with her spell and kill them."

Zandra was already on the move, headed toward the argument. I dashed along with her, glaring at the angry female, who was reaching for Hugh again as he cowered. Nico raised a hand, looking like he wanted to stop her, but hesitated.

Whoever she was, she had superiority over them. I didn't get the stink of a full werewolf, but this female had enough power to intimidate these guys.

Full female werewolves were rare and considered a prize for any pack. Even a female with partial werewolf powers was a rarity. Wielding such power meant they got away with bad manners and crass behavior simply because they could.

"Is there a problem here?" Zandra stopped beside the group.

The stunning female glanced at her. "What's it to you?"

Zandra leaned in close, her stern expression making it clear what she thought of the intimidation tactics. "We have non-magicals close by. You shouldn't use your powers. It's unsafe."

She gave a delicate snort. "It's their fault if they get in my way. They shouldn't be here." She curled her fingers into Hugh's shirt. "Tell me where he is."

Hugh's gaze shot to Zandra, and he shook his head when he spotted magic sparking on her fingers. "It's okay. This is Katrine Nominski. She's been seeing Emron."

"Been seeing! That suggests I'm no longer involved with him, and I am. You know that." Katrine narrowed her almond-shaped eyes. "Promise me he's not with another woman."

"I'm... I'm sure he isn't," Nico spluttered out. "Emron's focus is the pack negotiations. He wouldn't get distracted when working."

"Including by me? I'm no distraction." Katrine arched a perfectly groomed dark eyebrow. "He'd welcome me being here. There's more to life than dealing with difficult wolves who don't know how to behave."

"You're right. Of course." Hugh hung limp in her grip.

Katrine's hard smirk distorted her face. "I wouldn't be here unless this was important. I must talk to him."

"Emron will be happy to talk once the negotiations are over," Nico said.

"Not good enough." Katrine spoke through gritted teeth. "I've been holding back my power because I don't want to hurt either of you. You're usually such good little wolves, but this is outrageous. You have the nerve to tell me if I can see my boyfriend. I should rip those scraggly pelts off your backs while you're still alive. Or demand you be cast out of the packs. You won't survive alone as runts."

"Enough!" Zandra said. "You're drawing too much attention."

Katrine didn't bother looking around, simply shook Hugh again.

This werewolf babe needed taking down a few pegs. As tempting as it was to zap her so she landed on her peachy butt, I took the mature route and pulsed calming magic to take the edge off her temper.

Katrine inhaled deeply, and her head twisted so her stony gaze fixed on me. "Nice try, kitty, but my gift means few spells work on me. When they hit, the magic filters into me. It gives me new powers."

"You're a spell taker?" Zandra took a step back.

My stomach knotted. Spell takers, also known as magic rippers, power grabbers, and spell stealers. No one liked them, and everybody feared them. They were the parasites of the magic world.

Katrine chuckled. "Have no fears, witch. I'm not interested in what you've got. Your magic has a chaotic flare that would be too much trouble to tame. But your fluffy companion interests me. That spell was tainted with curious flavors of the old days. We should talk."

I grimaced. I had zero intention of sharing anything with this harpy.

She smirked again when neither of us responded then turned back to Hugh. "One last time. Where is Emron?"

The werewolves glanced at each other and nodded.

"Leon's pack is in the pizza parlor again. It's their favorite place. It's at the end of this street. You can't miss it," Nico said. "Emron planned on spending an hour with them and then an hour with Decker's pack. Then he was heading to his base to review progress."

"But he doesn't want to be disturbed," Hugh said. "He's still working, even while the others enjoy downtime before tomorrow's meeting."

"Of course he is. Always doing some deal." Katrine made a noise of disgust in the back of her throat as she shoved Hugh away. "You're both as pathetic as ever. No wonder you've never had mates. Never going to get them, either." She turned and stomped off on ridiculously high-heeled black knee-high boots.

As mature as I considered myself to be, I zapped her with a spell that made her stumble. She righted herself, smoothed her crimson dress, and carried on. Huh! She really could absorb most magic.

"We're keeping away from that one," Zandra muttered to me. "We don't want a spell stealer in Crimson Cove. Everyone will be too afraid to use their magic."

I nodded. Katrine was someone to watch if she stayed around. I'd have to recruit my magical misfits to keep track of everyone who was a threat to Zandra.

"Thanks for coming to our rescue. And sorry about Katrine." Hugh straightened his crumpled shirt.

"You're welcome. I was worried her magic could hurt a bystander." Zandra side-eyed the non-magicals who'd gone back to staring at the stores now the show was over.

"Of course. You've got a lot visiting. Also sorry for everything the werewolves have done since we came to Crimson Cove. We're a bit much for most people."

"Sure. It's been an experience having you here," Zandra said. "You shouldn't put up with what Katrine does to you. That was mean."

"I kind of have to. She ranks above me."

"She's not a full werewolf, though," I said. "I smelled a mix of magic."

"Werewolf, coyote, and somewhere in her ancestry, there was a magic user with the ability to take powers." Hugh shivered and touched his slapped cheek. "Katrine creeps me out. She knows the hold she has over anyone who wrongs her. And she's quick to take offence, so you always have to be on your guard."

"So we noticed," I said. "Katrine's really in a relationship with Emron?"

"They've been dating on and off for years," Nico said. "She always shows up and makes a mess when he's not paying her enough attention. Emron is high profile, so he often crosses paths with our alphas. Katrine is never far behind, causing a scene and making sure she gets noticed."

Hugh shook his head. "They're as bad as each other for sneaking around with other people, though. Although, if you think Katrine is bad, you should meet Emron's wife. She's got ice queen running through her veins."

"Emron is married, and he has a girlfriend?" I said.

"Several girlfriends. Although he doesn't call them that. He calls them companions. And he charms them all into thinking they're his perfect female." Nico grimaced.

"And you two cover for him?" Zandra said.

"Not normally, but Emron is important to these negotiations, so our alphas ordered us to ensure he doesn't get distracted." Hugh blew out a breath. "It's not easy. Katrine is a handful."

Zandra folded her arms over her chest. "Doesn't Emron's wife mind about these other women?"

Nico lifted his shoulders. "Their marriage was formed because of alliance needs rather than passion."

"That must still be tough to accept," I said. "Werewolves are proud, and they should be devoted to their mates, no matter the circumstances of their joining."

"Sure. But sometimes personalities don't fit, even if the alliance prevents battles," Nico said. "Emron doesn't talk about Grace much. That's his wife. But it's frosty between them. I don't think they see much of each other."

The werewolves had my sympathy with match-making. With such a limited supply of female werewolves to steady the primal power encouraged by the moon, males were often twitchy and prone to bouts of destruction. They made matches to stop war, not provide blissful happily ever afters.

"We should check in on the packs," Nico said to Hugh.

"We'll walk with you." I fell into step with the werewolves alongside Zandra. "Any idea when the talks will end?"

"We're hoping for the end of the week," Hugh said.

"Which suggests things are going well?"

"It's hard to say. Concessions were made today, but as you've noticed, we're a tricky bunch. One wrong word, and it's back to square one."

"We'll be out of here soon," Nico said. "And we really are sorry for messing up your town. I like Crimson Cove. You've got great wild runs."

"So long as you don't aggravate the sanctuary animals, you're welcome to make use of them," I said.

Nico tensed and breathed in deeply. "Leon needs me. I have to go." He patted Hugh on the shoulder. "See you later?"

"Sure. I need to get going, too. Decker will wonder where I am." Hugh nodded at us then loped away.

I walked with Zandra, conscious of the raucous laughter coming out of several stores being monopolized by the werewolves. "It sure sucks to be in bottom of the pack in werewolf land. You get the worst jobs."

Zandra nodded, frowning as we passed the rowdy pizza parlor brimming with Leon's pack. Sorcha's café was also full to bursting with werewolves. "How about we forget the takeout? I can't face muscling through the crowd of testosterone to eat."

"You want me to tackle them?"

She grinned. "I'd love to see you beat down these fuzz balls. Another time, though." She scooped me up, and I settled on her shoulder.

"I'd do it. Especially for a seafood medley pizza with a side order of fried cod in butter."

Zandra chuckled as we hurried past the pizza parlor. "There's not much you won't do for fish."

"You know me so well." I stared at the werewolves as they tore into triple meat feast deep crust pizzas. "What shall we do for dinner, though? I was looking forward to something fishy and doughy."

"Vorana will have leftovers. I'm in need of a quiet night and a movie. How about you?"

"That's an acceptable compromise. Will your mother and Joel be joining us?"

"With Sage's agreement. Maybe they could watch the movie through the window. Sage is still tense whenever they're in the basement."

"It's no surprise. She has the memory of Vorana's life being at risk when Adrienne broke in."

"I get it. We'll figure things out. Come on. Let's have a night off. No work, no werewolves, and no worries."

I nuzzled her ear. That sounded purrfect to me.

Chapter 5

Moon fall

"Psst! Juno, wake up."

An insistent prodding on my hindquarters disturbed me from my delicious slumber. I rolled over and came face-to-face with a wide-eyed Sage.

I wriggled to the edge of the bed so as not to disturb Zandra. "What is it?"

"Come with me."

"It's early." I glanced out the basement window. It wasn't even dawn. "If you're worried about Adrienne and Joel coming back, they're staying at Cannibal Bill's tonight. They won't bother Vorana."

"I'm not worried about the ghouls. There's something going on outside. Can't you hear?"

I tilted my head, but the basement was well-insulated. "You sure you didn't have a nightmare? Imagined some evil creature creeping toward you."

Sage sniffed. "I imagined nothing. There's something going on, and I don't like it."

After checking Zandra hadn't been disturbed, I rolled off the bed, did a full body stretch, ensured my fur wasn't too fluffy for polite company, and followed Sage up the basement steps. She was in her harness, so used magic to propel up the stairs.

"What do you think is going on outside?" I whispered.

"This way. I've been watching out the front window for ten minutes. It's bad."

As I drew close to the window, I slowed. A long, eerie howl echoed through the night. "Are the werewolves playing up? If they keep doing this, they won't be welcome back in Crimson Cove, no matter what they need to negotiate."

"They're not messing around. That howl suggests distress. And it's not just the werewolves out tonight."

I joined Sage at the window and looked onto the quiet street. There was a half-moon overhead that partially lit the road. I was about to ask Sage what I was supposed to be looking at when a blur of white flashed through the sky.

"Was that an angel?"

"They're everywhere. Cythera must have called out the entire troop."

"Because of something the werewolves have done?"

Another unnerving howl flooded the night, and two large, black shapes darted along the road.

"I don't know what's going on, but it can't be good. Werewolves don't howl like that unless there's serious trouble in their pack."

"What kind of trouble?"

"Trouble we don't want in our town."

We remained by the window for fifteen minutes. More angels flashed past on the wing, and several more werewolves sped past.

"We should investigate," I said. "We don't want this trouble reaching our witches."

Sage arched her neck, her gaze going to the ceiling. "Too late for that. Vorana is shuffling into her slippers. She'll be down here any minute."

"Those howls will disturb Zandra, too. She's not a deep sleeper."

We watched for another minute until Vorana's shuffling footsteps drew nearer.

"Hey, what are you two doing up at this time?" She stumbled into the living room, rubbing her eyes.

"Go back to bed." Sage kept her gaze on the window, her tail pointed straight behind her and her ears pricked.

"I heard a howl. I thought for a second it might be you." Vorana shuffled closer.

"I don't sound like a tortured werewolf," Sage said.

Vorana half-smiled. She opened her mouth to say something, but another howl pierced the night.

"That was it! That's the sound that woke me. What's going on out there?" All signs of sleepiness were gone as she hurried to the window in her book print pajamas.

"We were just going to find out," I said.

"The angels are about, too?" Vorana pointed to the sky.

"What are you all doing up?" Zandra appeared in the doorway.

I ran over and hopped onto her shoulder. "There's a small problem with the werewolves. We'll deal with it."

"Uh-uh. You're not going out there if there's a pack of marauding werewolves causing trouble." Zandra hurried over and peered out the window. "I'll try Finn. See if he knows what's going on."

I jumped off her shoulder, and she went back to the basement and returned a moment later with her mobile snow globe. "I'm not getting any reply."

"Finn must be busy taming the werewolves," Vorana said. "I've seen six angels whizz past since I've been here."

"Where are they headed?"

"No clue, but they're moving with purpose. And those howls cut you right to the bone. Something has ruffled the werewolves' fur."

"I'll grab a jacket, and we can go see what's happening," Zandra said.

"Bad idea. You and Vorana stay here. We'll take a look." I nudged Sage. I didn't want my witch dealing with werewolves when they were stressed. Stressed wolves bit first and asked questions later.

Zandra arched a bed messy eyebrow. "You think we can't handle the werewolves?"

"I know you can handle anything you set your mind to, but it's best this way. Besides, if I go with Sage, we'll blend in. We're smaller, so we won't be noticed while we're figuring out what's going on."

"We'll all go together," Vorana said. "This is our town, and we're not letting the werewolves take over and make a mess of things."

I exchanged a worried glance with Sage.

"Don't look concerned. Zandra's right. We know how to take care of ourselves." Vorana leaned down and kissed the top of Sage's head.

Despite my concerns, there was no point in arguing. And once Zandra dug her heels in, there was no chance of getting them to budge.

Five minutes later, we stepped out onto the porch. The second I was outside, I tensed. The air was alive with werewolf power, and mingling with that power was unbridled rage.

I looked up at Zandra. "You sure you want to do this?"

She flipped up the collar on her jacket. "Positive."

I stuck close to her as she headed out to the road.

Sage was glued to Vorana's side, both of us in ultra-protective mode to ensure no harm came to our witches.

Three werewolves sped past but didn't slow or pay us attention.

"They're headed in the same direction," Vorana said. "If they keep going straight, they'll end up in the woods. Maybe there's been a werewolf fight at their camp, and it got out of hand."

A small, ash gray werewolf I recognized hurried past. I chirruped at him.

He slowed, lifted his muzzle and inhaled, his gaze landing on me.

I raised a paw. "Greetings, Hugh. What brings you and the other werewolves out? It sounds like trouble."

Hugh hesitated, took a step back as if being drawn away by something, but then turned to us. As he trotted over, he transformed from four paws to two feet, but he was naked for only seconds. He had a small backpack attached to him, and he smoothly turned and pulled on shorts and a T-shirt before jogging over.

"Sorry for the disturbance. We've had an incident," he said.

"What's going on?" Zandra said.

"Emron's dead."

Zandra and Vorana gasped.

"What happened to him?" I said.

Hugh gulped in a breath. "Someone hit him with an axe and then chopped off his head."

We all stared at him in disbelief.

"He was decapitated?" Zandra said. "With an axe?"

"I'm not sure of the details. It's a mess. I've been doing what I can to calm the packs down, but everyone's angry and looking for a fight."

There was fresh bruising on Hugh's forearms. "You've been fighting, too."

"No option. The other wolves won't listen to sense. Leon's got them riled up and is demanding justice for Emron. He ordered his pack to find the killer. I encountered two of his wolves, and they lunged at me when I told them not to hunt. I'm having more luck with my pack, but they don't have to listen to the bottom werewolf if they don't want to. And none of them want to do anything rational at the moment."

"Where did it happen?" Vorana said.

"In the woods. Emron set up his quarters between the two pack camps. He was found in his tent about half an hour ago."

"Who found him?" I said.

Hugh glanced around as a howl ricocheted through the night. "Katrine. She finally tracked down Emron, and they had a huge argument. He was angry and humiliated and told her to go. She left but must have changed her mind and come back to reconcile."

"Or kill him," Zandra said.

Hugh's eyes widened, and a low growl slid from his lips. "I didn't think about that. I mean, she's strong, but she's not a full werewolf."

Having seen Katrine in action, I easily believed she was nasty enough to decapitate her lover if he didn't give her what she demanded.

"Could she have used her spell stealing magic on Emron?" Zandra said. "She weakened him and then attacked him with the axe."

Hugh moved his mouth from side to side as he considered the possibility. "They were always arguing, but that's how their relationship was. I never got a hint things were really bad. Not chopping someone's head off bad, anyway."

"Katrine was raging when we saw her with you," Zandra said. "Maybe she no longer wanted to be a part of that team, but Emron wouldn't let her go."

"There are safer and easier places to kill Emron than when he's surrounded by werewolves," I said. "Katrine took a huge risk if she did this."

"She has a temper," Zandra said. "We witnessed that when she whacked Hugh."

Hugh's cheeks flushed, but he nodded. "This'll ruin our negotiations. Emron was making progress. We were close to success." There was another ear damaging howl close by. "I've got to go. Leon is demanding justice. Decker's angry, too. It took three werewolves to calm him enough, so he didn't order us to hunt the killer."

I nodded thoughtfully. Two packs of rampaging, blood lusting werewolves seeking to tear someone to pieces was the last thing this town needed.

"You go," Vorana said. "I hope the werewolves settle soon. For all our sakes."

Hugh dashed off, removing his clothing and changing behind a tree to save his modesty before he loped off in werewolf form.

Vorana blew out a breath. "A werewolf murder in Crimson Cove will get us unwanted attention if this isn't cleared up fast. You really think it was Emron's girlfriend who did this?"

"Katrine is on my suspect list," I said. "That woman is scary, and it takes a lot to terrify me."

Zandra arched an eyebrow as she looked at me. "You have a suspect list?"

"Of course. So do you."

She shrugged. "Maybe. I'm thinking."

"If the werewolves go on an all-out hunt for Emron's killer, it'll be carnage. More people will die." Vorana lifted Sage and settled her in her arms, giving her head several kisses.

"Angel Force is already on it," I said, as another angel swooped past, leaving a trail of warmth and a few white feathers.

Zandra's nose snitched into a cute button. "We all know the angels can be less than effective, especially in times of crisis. Cythera's probably scheduling meetings for the rest of the day to figure things out."

"True. And by the time they've decided what to do, half of Crimson Cove will have been destroyed," I said.

There was a whoosh of warm air overhead, and Finn landed angel style, one hand fisted on the ground. He stood and shook out his feathers. "Hey. Have you heard the news?"

"From Hugh," Zandra said. "Any idea who killed Emron?"

"Not a clue, but we have to contain the werewolves. There are rumors of a house-to-house search being led by the packs. Magic sparks will fly if this gets out of control." Finn rubbed the back of his neck. "And the situation at Angel Force feels the opposite of controlled."

"We were just pondering the same thing," I said.

Finn's forehead wrinkled as he nodded. "It gets worse. I found out yesterday the coach that broke down at my animal sanctuary wasn't an isolated visit. Four more coachloads of non-magicals are arriving in the morning."

Vorana puffed out her cheeks. "And if they collide with the werewolves, it'll be a bloodbath. The non-magicals will blunder around and aggravate the werewolves."

"And they'll only need something small to push them over the edge and bite." Worry crossed Zandra's face as she tugged on her hair.

I flicked my tail. "What can we do to make sure that doesn't happen?"

I stood with Vorana, Sage, and Sammy near the entrance of Finn's animal sanctuary later that same day.

None of us had gotten any more sleep as we'd worked on a plan to prevent the non-magicals from getting close to the marauding werewolves.

We'd decided on diversionary tactics and would act as an official welcome party to the coaches, who would conveniently break down thanks to our magic outside the sanctuary.

We'd gotten food from Sorcha's café, entertainment, and safe, guided walks so the non-magicals wouldn't lose limbs or be beguiled by any glitter parping hippos while looking around. And by keeping them here for as long as possible, it gave Angel Force time to calm the werewolves. Something they had yet to achieve.

"Heads up," Zandra said around a yawn as she hurried over to join us. "The first two coaches are here. They just triggered the magic on the road, so their engines should be malfunctioning. They'll be rolling in any time."

Vorana passed her a mug of coffee. "We've got this. We'll keep them so entertained, they won't even think about going into town." She tweaked the glittery bow tie she'd put around Sage's neck to achieve maximum cuteness factor.

Sage had gritted her teeth through every humiliating second, since she knew it was for the good of Crimson Cove and its residents. I also sported a bow tie and an adorable top hat covered in red glitter. It was tacky, but it would enthrall the non-magicals, without casting a single spell.

Vorana patted a pile of second-hand paperbacks on a table next to her.

Zandra looked at the books and grimaced. "You sure your books will be enough to entice them to stay? Most of them will take one look at that mangy pile of paper and walk away."

She swatted Zandra's arm. "Of course! And you're the weird one for not enjoying reading."

"Zandra likes books well enough," I said. "Although mainly the spell books her mother gave her."

"At least they're useful." Zandra flipped through a paperback.

"Books are always useful," Vorana said. "Whenever you've had a tough day, all you do is open a book and escape into another world. You can experience anything you like and be whoever you want when you read."

"Maybe I already like who I am," Zandra said.

"There's always time for escapism." Vorana pointed at the table. "And I've set up a competition, so anyone who buys a book gets entered into the grand prize to win Sorcha's amazing dessert hamper."

"I might be convinced to buy a book to win that," Zandra said.

"That's against the rules." Vorana waggled a finger at her.

"Aren't we making up the rules, since we're running this show?"

She grinned. "If you promise to read at least one paperback next week, you can enter."

Zandra groaned. "I'll think about it. Maybe I'll just buy a cake from Sorcha. All the pleasure and none of the torture."

Barney hurried over from the main gate. "I've seen a coach. Everyone, action stations."

We all had a part to play in this illusion. Vorana was selling books and encouraging people to enter the prize draw, Barney was doing guided tours, Zandra was dealing with the refreshments, and Sammy and I had our charm turned to maximum, so we could distract the non-magicals. Hopefully, there'd be little petting involved, but I was resigned to being mauled by strangers. I just had to remember this was for the good of Crimson Cove and to ensure no non-magical lost his head to a werewolf.

We turned as the first coach rumbled through the gates. Its engine sounded like it was about to explode as it wheezed. It was followed by a second unhappy coach, the passengers looking out of the windows anxiously, unhappy their day trip had been cut short.

"Here we go, people," Zandra said. "Everyone ready with their best fake smiles."

I hopped onto Zandra's shoulder. "It would be easier if we zapped them. We could send them to sleep then turn the coach around and get them out of Crimson Cove. We could even implant nice memories of all the fun they had without them ever coming near a werewolf."

"Nice idea, but all that magic would make their heads explode. We wouldn't be able to explain that to Angel Force."

"We could use tiny amounts of magic. They'd barely feel it."

She leaned her head against my side. "I reckon they would. We'll just have to smile and wave and convince them this is the best place to spend their time and not bother with Crimson Cove."

The first coach ground to a halt with a hearty wheeze of defeat, and the same smiling, tall, thin guy with lanky hair climbed out. He looked around then lifted a hand as Barney strode over to greet him.

Zandra walked over too, but we stayed back a few feet.

"Hey, there! If I didn't know better, I'd say that road was jinxed," the tour guide said. "This is the second time I've broken down on this road."

"I'm sorry to hear that." Barney stuck out his hand. "I'm Barney Hoffman. I run animal control in the area."

"Gus Bainbridge. Head tour guide for Delectable Travels. Nice to meet you. You weren't here when the coach broke down the last time."

"No, I just help out now and again. And it's your lucky day." Barney's smile was a touch over-stretched, but he put on a solid show of being an affable host.

Gus scratched the back of his head. "How so? The coach breaking down doesn't feel lucky."

"Oh, no. Of course not. But we're having an open day. Perhaps your passengers would like to spend the day here rather than go into Crimson Cove? And there's a problem with the main road into town, so I doubt your coach would squeeze along the narrow diversion route."

"Huh! First I've heard about it. I should check with HQ."

"No need. We're all complaining about it. Stay here. We have games and prizes for people, refreshments, and tours of the sanctuary. No charge. And there's plenty of green space if people want to walk around or have a picnic."

Gus looked back at the coaches. "You know what, you've saved the day. I've got two parties of golden oldies to look after, and my assistant called in sick this morning, so it's just me. They were already complaining about how long it was taking to get here. Then the engines went wrong, and it was the last straw. Several of them were asking for refunds."

"Then we can make it up to them. They'll have a wonderful time. What do you say?"

Gus nodded. "I say, yes. This is perfect. Give me ten minutes to calm the passengers and let them know the slight change of plans, and we'll get things rolling."

"This is going to work," I whispered in Zandra's ear.

"Just so long as Angel Force keeps the werewolves out of this area, we'll be fine," she muttered.

Finn was acting as liaison between the packs, and he'd made an agreement with Decker and Leon to keep their werewolves away. But with tempers raised and passions high, I wasn't certain the furry beasts would stick to it. I'd keep an eye out for any who broke the rules and would chase them away.

But no werewolves appeared, and the following three hours were a blur of activity. The coach passengers, all mature ladies and a few gents, decided the animal sanctuary was the perfect place to spend the day.

Some had even brought picnics with them and were settled in the field, munching sandwiches and sipping from plastic mugs. The rest were checking out the games and activities, and Vorana did brisk business at her second-hand bookstore. The golden oldies loved a bargain.

And Barney was rushed off his feet, ferrying pensioners around the barns, and making sure none of them petted the animals.

Even the animals behaved as if they sensed something serious was going on. They most likely did. Tension flickered through Crimson Cove because the werewolves were so unsettled, and they'd remain so until Emron's murder was resolved.

Finn wandered over, his white shirt crumpled and his hair looking like he'd repeatedly raked his fingers through it. "Just checking in to let you know our big dogs are behaving."

"So are our small wrinklies," I said. "Mostly."

He looked around. "They are something else. I've been here ten minutes and lost count of the number of times I've had to say no to someone adopting a magical creature. Can you imagine what would happen if they took anything with magic into their world?"

"Carnage and chaos." I hopped onto Zandra's shoulder.

Finn leaned back against the barn Zandra had propped herself against and sighed. "They'll be gone soon."

"And then you'll focus on the murder?" Zandra said.

"It's all I've been doing, when I'm not werewolf spotting. Although I keep getting called away by Cythera for progress reports. She's almost as freaked out at having non-magicals in town as she is marauding werewolves."

"I've been wondering about the spiteful girlfriend, Katrine," I said. "She's not afraid to use magic to get what she wants."

"What's her motive?" Finn said.

"She found out about Emron's wife. Or issued him an ultimatum to leave his wife, and he refused."

Finn pinched his chin between his finger and thumb. "All possibilities."

"Or the wife found out about Katrine," Zandra said. "From what Hugh and Nico said about Emron's behavior, he's not been faithful throughout their union. Perhaps Katrine was a step too far, so his wife snapped."

"And snuck into Crimson Cove to behead Emron?" Finn shook his head. "That's a risky move."

"Maybe it was a risk she was prepared to take," I said. "Emron's been disrespecting her for years. And I've already said how prideful werewolves can be. I'm assuming Emron was paired with another werewolf?"

"Yes. Grace Laker. She's been informed about Emron's murder."

"How did she respond?"

"She howled, but there were no tears shed."

"Because she killed him?" Zandra said.

"Maybe. The scene is still being processed, so we'll know more soon," Finn said. "What about Leon? My encounters with him left a bad taste in my mouth. He takes alpha to a whole new level of jerk."

"Why would he kill Emron? He was mending fences with Decker, and Emron was helping make that happen," Zandra said.

"Perhaps Leon wanted to resolve the negotiations differently. A way that would guarantee victory for his pack. The negotiations weren't going his way, so he responded."

I curled my tail around Zandra's neck. "We saw how Leon operated when he blundered onto sanctuary land. He doesn't strike me as a nice guy."

We were silent as we considered motives and watched the non-magicals at play.

"They're both decent motives," Finn said. "The rest of the angels are working on a strategy to solve this."

I sat up straight. "You'll be involved, though?"

"That's the plan, now I'm back working for Angel Force."

"No regrets about returning to your old job?" Finn had recently had a crisis of confidence, and I'd needed to give him a stern talking to, to help him see he was on the right path.

He shrugged. "It's a work in progress."

Barney hurried over with a tray of empty plates. "I spotted werewolves on the boundary."

I tensed. "They're not coming in, are they?"

"No, but they're interested in what's going on." Barney's face was red, and sweat danced on his top lip.

Zandra took the tray from him. "Have a break. You've been running around ever since the non-magicals got here."

"We need to keep them happy and unaware of what we do." Barney didn't resist Zandra's urging to sit on a nearby hay bale. "It's nice to do something different. But I'll admit, I'll be glad when I'm behind my desk. Paperwork and meetings are less tiresome. And I'm worried the werewolves might cause trouble. Any progress on the investigation?" Barney looked up at Finn.

"We're working on it. The crime scene is being combed over."

Barney's gaze remained on the border. "I know the two alphas involved. Decker and Leon have been vying for the same territory for decades. They even battled over the same female at one point."

"Katrine?" I asked.

"No, Emron's wife, Grace. When she came of age, her family set her up as a prize for the highest bidder with the right credentials."

I wrinkled my booping snooter. Werewolves were odd creatures, always following the old ways, even to the detriment of their valuable females.

"Grace must have hated that," Zandra said.

"It's the werewolf way. She'd have understood her obligation to forge alliances." Barney dabbed the sweat off his top lip.

"Decker and Leon wanted her, but they lost out to Emron?" That was an interesting motive for both of them. Pining after the female they couldn't have because they weren't alpha enough to best Emron.

"They did. And there were several bloody battles, but eventually, Emron won."

"We met Emron before he died," Zandra said. "He was in great shape, but how did he beat two alphas?"

"Although Emron wasn't a pack alpha, his connections ran deep across the werewolf community. He had alliances that almost made him better than an alpha of a single pack."

"I expect he loved that," I said. "He wore his cockiness well."

Barney pressed his lips together. "Both alphas were unhappy, but they had to accept their overlord alpha's ruling. What he says goes. Emron secured Grace, and Decker and Leon had no cause to argue."

"Leaving a lingering grudge," I said. "It's a good motive for murder. For either alpha."

"Unless either of them is having a secret liaison with Grace, they gain nothing from this murder," Finn said. "If anything, the opposite."

"They'd slake their anger over losing her," I said.

"It would be an old anger. Grace was married to Emron for a long time."

"Maybe Emron goaded whoever killed him. Pressed a few buttons, and Decker or Leon saw red," Zandra said.

"An alpha always thinks of his pack first," Barney said. "Even when he's in a rage, he'll feel the connection to his werewolves. If either alpha did this, their days as leader are over, and their pack will be pulled apart. It would be the last thing either of them would want."

"Let's return to Katrine," I said. "She got in a lucky hit. When we saw her in town, she was bitterly angry. She was demanding to see Emron."

"And Emron would have been relaxed around her," Zandra said. "That could have given her a chance to injure him and then steal his power to make the killing blow."

"Using an axe suggests premeditation," Finn said. "Whoever killed Emron brought it with them. No one has stepped forward to say it belongs to them."

"Excuse me, the restroom toilet is overflowing. And Iris is feeling faint." A spry, silver-haired woman peered at us.

We'd been so engrossed in discussing murder, no one had noticed her approach.

"Here we go again," Finn muttered. He dragged out his best smile and headed over to the woman.

"Action stations, everyone," I whispered as more non-magicals wandered toward us.

The murder would have to wait. It was time to charm and misdirect some more.

Chapter 6

No one died!

What felt like the longest day of my life was drawing to an end. We'd spent all day at the sanctuary, dealing with the non-magicals as they streamed out of their coaches and demanded tours, refreshments, and bathroom breaks with alarming frequency.

It had taken every ounce of my willpower not to blast them with magic. Only Zandra's cautious words prevented any mishaps as my murder mittens wriggled with the desire to mind-wipe the visitors.

It was a useful learning experience but one I had no intention of repeating.

Zandra was flopped on her bed in our basement apartment, her eyes half-closed. "Let's hope that's the last we see of the non-magicals. Too many days like that, and I'll need a long vacation."

I hopped up and settled on her stomach. "That makes both of us. We need to keep applying pressure on the Magic Council to do something about the wards. Even though they've said there are no problems, there must be a fault they've missed.

These non-magicals shouldn't get in so easily. And they seem barely affected by our magic."

"Maybe Randal is right, and they're evolving. The next thing we'll see is some gray-haired old dear shooting spells while she clutches her pearls."

I shuddered. "What a terrible thought."

There was a knock on the basement door at the top of the staircase.

"Come on down." Zandra remained sprawled on the bed, so she wouldn't disturb me when I'd just gotten comfortable.

"But only enter if you're bringing food. And lots of it," I said.

Finn appeared on the staircase and headed down to join us. "Hey! I wanted to say thanks for everything you did today. I've come to take you to dinner. My treat."

"If you're buying, then we're in," I said.

"We'll split the bill," Zandra said. "Dinner would be great. Although I'm too exhausted to move."

"I was thinking Sorcha's café. I checked, and the werewolves aren't using it this evening, so it'll be quiet. I invited Vorana and Sage, too, but they're planning an early night."

"We can muster the energy to enjoy a free meal." I rolled off the bed and did a full body stretch.

"We're going halves." Zandra finally did her own less elegant roll, pulled on her boots, and grabbed her purse.

"I owe you. If we'd had to deal with all those non-magicals in Crimson Cove, it would have been a mess. As it is, the angels are struggling to handle those who snuck through after visiting my sanctuary."

"They're still getting into Crimson Cove?" I hopped up the steps ahead of the others, eager to fill my stomach with delicious treats.

"They're everywhere. They keep coming out of the woodwork like unwanted worms. It's strange, but it's as if something is drawing them here," Finn said.

"I was just saying to Zandra, it's a problem with the wards. The Magic Council could have added a welcoming ward rather than a repulsion ward the last time the magic was refreshed. It could be what's bringing them here."

"Cythera's spoken to them, and they insist everything is working."

"We need to keep pressing. We've all had dealings with the Magic Council, so we know they're less than perfect."

"I'm concerned something bigger is going on. More than a mess up with the wards." Finn opened the front door for us, and we headed into the pleasant evening air, only the faint tang of werewolf spoiling the aroma.

"Like what?" Zandra said.

Finn's mouth twisted to the side. "A few of the non-magicals noticed my angel wings. Just for half a second, but several angels have reported non-magicals coming up to them and asking why they're in fancy dress. Then they get a confused look on their face and stare into space. They're seeing through our glamor, and it's giving them a brain spasm."

I almost stumbled over my paws. "That's impossible. They can't see magic, and they can't see our supernatural enhancements." I was safe, and so was Zandra, but supernatural creatures, such as angels, changed werewolves, pixies, elves, to name a few, would be worried about this new development.

Finn shrugged as he strolled along the road. "I wouldn't have believed it if someone told me, either. But we're being extra cautious around the non-magicals, so we don't freak them out. Cythera has banned all flying."

"I'm sure you're thrilled about that," Zandra said.

He grinned. "Every cloud has a silver lining."

I ambled along the road while Zandra and Finn discussed the reasons the non-magicals could suddenly see us.

There was a time, a few hundred years ago, when I'd experienced a similar thing. We used to keep tabs on the non-magicals to make sure they weren't stumbling into places they shouldn't, but for several months, they'd been aware of our magic. It caused tension, and there'd been suggestions the non-magicals were relocated.

That had sounded a little too concentration camp for my liking, so I'd investigated, and uncovered dark magic users disrupting the natural order. Once they'd been obliterated by my fair paws, the problem went away.

But who'd want to disrupt the harmony in Crimson Cove? And surely, if anyone was using dark magic, I'd notice. My booping snooter was attuned to darkness, so I could ensure it didn't taint my wonderful witch.

We arrived at Sorcha's café, and I was thrilled to see no werewolves inside.

Sorcha waved us to an empty table at the back of the café and brought over menus. "How's it going?"

"We've been busy." Zandra gave her a brief low-down on our eventful day at Finn's sanctuary.

She winced. "You have my every sympathy. I was glad I could help by providing all the food. The non-magicals liked it?"

"There wasn't a crumb left. You were a lifesaver," Finn said. "Hungry non-magicals get grumpy, but your cakes hit the spot."

"Always happy to help." Sorcha looked up as a large party came in. "Can't stop. I've got a birthday celebration in this evening. Don't worry, they won't bother you. Let me know when you're ready to order." She dashed away to greet and seat her new arrivals.

Finn looked out the window. "Having all these non-magicals around is making it trickier to deal with Emron's murder. We have to tread carefully, so no one gets alarmed."

"I'm still certain Katrine did it," I said.

Finn shook his head. "I've interviewed her. Katrine admitted to arguing with Emron late last night, but she stormed out of Crimson Cove while he was still alive."

"She could have come back and whacked him with an axe." Zandra studied the menu.

"Katrine had a late-night doctor's appointment. Emron was alive when she left and dead when she got back. She couldn't have done it."

"Why was the appointment so late?" I said. "Seems like she planned a solid alibi."

"Normally, I'd agree. But werewolf doctors work mostly at night. It's when the wolves are more active. I checked with the doctor, and he confirmed Katrine attended the appointment. She wasn't here when the murder took place."

Zandra huffed out a breath. "She's mean enough to kill."

Finn nodded as he waved Sorcha over. "Agreed. She wasn't fun to interview. She kept snarling and snapping. At one point, I thought she'd stamp her feet. And she kept saying we'd regret questioning her."

"She's a charmer," I said.

Sorcha hurried over, an order pad and a pen in hand. "What will it be?"

I ordered the salmon soufflé with a side order of crispy bacon. Zandra and Finn ordered the pot roast and a basket of fries to share.

"Be back as soon as I can."

"What does the evidence suggest happened?" I said to Finn. "Have you finished processing the scene?"

"Yep. The attack with the axe was clumsy. It struck Emron's right shoulder, so it wasn't a mortal blow for a werewolf. Well, for anyone."

"Taking his head off was, though," Zandra said.

"No doubt about that. It seems Emron was forced to kneel and his own sword used. It was a clean slice from front to back, so the blow would have needed someone with super strength to drive the blade up and send his head clean off and rolling away like a bowling ball," Finn said. "His head landed by the entrance of the tent. And Emron wasn't slumming it in a two-person pop up, so it flew some distance."

We grimaced at the gruesome description.

"Cythera thinks it was a strong male, so she's focused on the werewolves," Finn said.

"She would be so narrow-minded. Females also have significant power," I said. "Especially female werewolves. They match their mates pound for pound for power."

"With Katrine's alibi checking out, we weren't sure where else to turn. There aren't any pack females at the negotiations."

"How about Grace?" I said.

"We're looking into her. But there was a development just before I left for the evening. It changes everything."

I yanked my gaze from the rack of glazed ribs that passed the table. "You found a clue to the killer's identity?"

"More than a clue. We found significant evidence that points to one werewolf."

"Who?" I leaned forward at the same time as Zandra.

"Werewolf hair and blood were found in Emron's tent. They don't belong to him." Finn seemed to enjoy stretching out the tension by not revealing who the killer was.

"Emron fought his killer before he was beheaded?" I said.

Finn tilted his head from side to side. "It's hard to tell. But Cythera is about to bring someone in under caution for questioning."

"Who's she cautioning?" Zandra said.

Finn drew in a breath. "Decker Duke."

Neither of us spoke as we digested this information.

Sorcha came over with our food and set down our plates. Her gaze went around the table. "Oh! Not fair! I'm missing a fun conversation. What are you talking about?"

"Emron's murder," Zandra said. "Angel Force is about to arrest someone."

Her eyes widened. "That was fast. I wish I didn't have to work. I want to know everything."

Before we shared, Sorcha was called away to the birthday party.

"Do you think Decker did it?" I said to Finn. "When we were talking earlier, we couldn't find a strong motive for him to commit murder."

"Cythera's focused on him. And if he doesn't have a solid alibi, she's planning on charging him."

"Is she certain he's guilty?" Angel Force was notorious for jumping to conclusions or thinking they had the right information, but getting everything around the wrong way.

Zandra toyed with her food. "Perhaps Decker was pushed too far. I know werewolves work for the good of the pack, but he could have had a second of uncontrolled rage. That would have been all he needed to decapitate Emron."

"What about the axe?" I said. "Someone bringing that into Emron's tent suggests premeditation."

"Whatever went on, we're clearing it up quietly," Finn said. "And you'll be happy to know animal control is involved, so I'm free to discuss the case with you."

"You would, anyway." I lapped up a chunk of warm soufflé.

He chuckled. "More than likely. Glenda Ridgeback is our main liaison through animal control, but I appreciate any backup you offer."

"Of course," Zandra said. "Whatever you need. Although I'm not experienced with werewolves."

"I am." My gaze was fixed on a scene outside the café. Several non-magicals had wandered past. "Perhaps we should take a step back from this investigation, though. We don't want to get on the werewolves' radar. Plus, we have Adrienne back in our lives. And you're getting to know your new stepdad."

"Stop calling him that! Joel is Adrienne's boyfriend. They're not married. I'm not sure ghouls can get married." Zandra looked at Finn for an answer, but he shrugged. "Besides, you're always the first to offer help when a supernatural needs help, especially when it's an animal."

"Yes, but these are werewolves. They sometimes bite first and ask questions later." And I didn't want my wonderful witch to start howling at the moon because she went toe-to-toe with a mean wolf.

"We're helping Finn," she said, a stubborn lilt to her voice.

I tugged my gaze from the non-magicals and gave her a stern look, but I was interested in figuring out who killed Emron. I'd deal with the werewolves if they troubled my witch. "Of course, we'll help. When do you want us on dog patrol?"

Finn gestured at the food. "Right after we finish this. The sooner we clear the werewolves out of here, the better."

Chapter 7

The killer unmasked?

After finishing our meal and Finn and Zandra debating over who paid, we walked to the Angel Force HQ.

Glenda Ridgeback was in the office when we entered. She was small for someone who turned furry regularly, with a fine set of cheekbones. She'd been posted to this branch of animal control temporarily, and although she had a prickly nature, she knew her stuff when it came to the animals. I enjoyed her company.

She lifted a hand when she saw me and Zandra. Glenda wore spray on denim jeans, flat black boots, and a T-shirt with a deep V-neck.

"Back in a minute," Finn said. "I'll make sure everything's ready for the interview."

"I see you got dragged into this mess, too." Glenda nodded at the chaos as angels darted around, not seeming to know what they were doing.

"Finn asked for backup," Zandra said. "How did you get involved?"

"Blame the job. Barney asked me to be the impartial liaison between the packs." She smirked. "He must be out of his mind. Or the stress has finally gotten to him. I'm not a natural negotiator, and I left my purse full of tact back in the nineteen-eighties."

"But they'll still respect you," I said.

Her eyes flashed amber for a second. "I wouldn't be so sure. I've had run-ins with both alphas."

Zandra grabbed a bottle of water from a table of refreshments and unscrewed the cap. "What kind of run-ins are we talking about?"

"Oh, you know alpha males. They always want what they can't have."

"They wanted you as a mate?" I jumped on an empty seat and curled myself into it, already feeling sleepy following my delicious soufflé.

"Why wouldn't they want this?" Glenda splayed her hands. "But I'm no alpha's mate, unless I choose to be. Although that didn't put Leon off. He went as far as proposing. Idiot." Her chuckle had a dark edge to it.

"You turned him down?" Zandra said.

"Of course. We'd have torn each other apart. Leon's a smug charmer, who thinks he's entitled to everything he likes the look of. Not happening in this case."

"You're not a fan?" I said.

"I have no issue with the guy, but I see why you asked the question. There's no bias here, though. I'll make sure werewolf protocol is followed and no wars get started because an angel drops a doozy." She rolled back on her heels. "I even admire Leon's spirit for having the nerve to ask. He didn't take it too badly when I told him to take a running jump onto a silver stake."

"What's the plan for questioning suspects?" Zandra said.

"I'll be sitting in on the major interviews. You've heard the angels think they've found evidence to convict?"

Zandra nodded. She glanced around. "Fur and blood from Decker Duke. Do you think it was him?"

Glenda raised a hand. "I'm not here to trawl the evidence and decide who's guilty. I just want to make sure no werewolf codes are broken. It's so easy to offend us, and some werewolves can hold a grudge."

"There you are. I've been waiting for you to arrive." Bertoli strode over with an unusually large smile on his face.

I lifted my booping snooter and inhaled deeply. "Are you in possession of fish?"

"A gift for you. I hoped I'd see you this evening. You like kippers, don't you?"

I stared at the large packet he placed on the desk. "I do. That's generous of you."

"Yeah, and strange." Zandra eyed the package. "What's Juno done to deserve gifts from you?"

Bertoli pressed a hand to his chest. "I was just thinking about how wonderfully soft her fur must be. May I pet you?"

"Only the head." I tensed for a second as Bertoli gingerly touched me. He must still be a little beguiled. It was only natural. I was, after all, magnificent and was still testing the boundaries of my recently reacquired powers. I must have used too much juice when I'd beguiled him into befriending Finn.

"You're even softer than I imagined." Wonderment shone on Bertoli's face as he grew more confident about petting me. He risked a swipe down my back, and I spun and glared at him.

"That's enough. Don't take liberties."

He rapidly blinked. "Sorry, I never would. I couldn't resist. Let me know if you enjoy the kippers, and I'll get you more. Whatever you like." He hurried off as he spotted Finn, waving enthusiastically and pointing at the kitchen.

Finn raised a hand, an amused look on his face as he walked over to us. "I can't decide if I preferred it when Bertoli was snarky. It feels wrong that he's so friendly."

"Why is he being friendly?" Zandra said.

I caught Finn's gaze and discreetly shook my head. Zandra most likely wouldn't approve if she learned of me beguiling Bertoli into being Mr. Nice Guy. I hadn't meant for him to become enchanted by me. I must work on creating clearer magic boundaries. Otherwise, the whole of Crimson Cove would fall under my spell.

That could be entertaining.

"Maybe he's reading self-improvement books," Finn said. "He's seeing the good in people instead of the bad."

Zandra didn't look convinced.

Finn cleared his throat. "Decker's interview is about to start. I can't let you sit in, but Glenda will be in there with me and Cythera. She'll keep us on the straight and narrow. You're welcome to watch from the room next door."

"It feels like it's our home from home," I said. "Bertoli, a coffee for Zandra and warm my kippers in the microwave and bring them in."

Zandra shook her head. "No warm kippers in any enclosed spaces. That'll be torture. Bertoli, put them in the fridge. We'll take them with us. Juno can eat them outside, where they can't stink out the place."

He ignored me. "I'm happy to warm them if you wish."

I sighed. I could never understand Zandra's distaste for the smell of fish. "It can wait. Make sure I don't forget them."

He dashed over, passed Finn a coffee, grabbed the kippers, and raced away to the kitchen.

"You have him well-trained," Zandra said. "What's the secret?"

"He must have realized how magnificent I am. Shall we?" I ignored Zandra's skeptical expression as we headed into a small room with a one-way glass mirror partition and settled in.

A few minutes later, Decker was brought into the interview room under angel guard. Although he looked angry, he wasn't resisting. But I understood the need for a heavy angel presence when confronting a werewolf murder suspect. I'd never met a chilled werewolf, and their tempers could go nuclear in a split second.

Cythera, Glenda, and Finn entered the room. The two angels who'd brought Decker in stepped back but remained against the wall, ever watchful, their fluttering wings revealing their nerves.

Finn ran through the formal introductions and got Decker to state his full name.

Although he was unhappy, he answered succinctly, didn't appear shifty, or as if he had anything to hide. It wasn't the behavior of someone who'd just committed a murder.

"How long have you been alpha of the White Ridge pack?" Cythera said.

"Forty years." Decker's voice had a slightly rough edge to it. "I succeeded the previous alpha when I turned one hundred."

"From all accounts, your pack is respected."

"Naturally. Unlike some, I'm not power hungry and always looking to expand."

"The negotiations between Leon suggest otherwise," Finn said.

Decker shook his head. "I only want to keep what I'm entitled to. What my pack is entitled to. We've had the same territory since I took over. We plan to keep it just as it is."

Glenda leaned forward in her seat. "Leon initiated a territory grab from Decker over ten years ago. He's been growing his pack, and the territories run adjacent to each other."

Decker nodded. "It's not ideal. I keep things as friendly as I can, but Leon keeps encroaching. Then my werewolves found markings from Leon's pack in our territory. It was a display of disrespect."

"You've been fighting ever since?" Cythera said.

"Not fighting, but there's been tension. Recently, it's gotten out of hand. We've tried to calm Leon's desire to expand, but nothing works. The guy is on a power trip." Decker's top lip curled, but it was his only sign of anger.

"That was how Emron became involved?" Finn said.

"Sure. The Wolf Council wants this sorted."

"What was your opinion of him?" Cythera said.

Decker let out a sigh. "He was smug and arrogant. I know that sounds ridiculous coming from an alpha werewolf, since arrogance runs through my blood, but he took things to another level."

"Which suggests you thought little him," Finn said.

Glenda smirked. "Everyone who knew Emron had that opinion. It was how he was. He always had to have the best, whether it was a car, a home, or a female. Then, when he got whatever he was chasing, he looked for the next best thing. It was never enough for him."

"True. But the guy got results," Decker said. "I'll admit I didn't consider him a friend, but he understood complex negotiations, and he was clear he'd hear both sides equally. If either of us over-stepped, he reminded us of that."

"Emron never favored one pack over the other during the negotiations?" Cythera said.

"That was never a problem. We had equal time to share our grievances and outline any potential compromises."

"And were you coming to a compromise?" Finn said.

Decker's bottom lip jutted out. "Both sides had made concessions. What does this have to do with Emron being killed?"

"We're looking into the motive for his murder," Finn said. "Perhaps you didn't think he was being fair."

"I had no problem with the guy. I wouldn't invite him to a party, but I knew he'd come through on these negotiations. I wanted him around."

"Or you wanted to get the negotiations to end and for a war to be declared," Cythera said.

Glenda sucked in a breath, and Decker growled low in his chest.

Cythera sat up straight, her wings fluttering. "We have to look at all motives."

Decker slid his hands behind his head and leaned back. "I don't want war. I'm tired of fighting. My pack needs to focus on what's important."

"Which is?" Cythera said.

"Family. We need more pups. And we need suitable candidates to turn into werewolves. It's a hard process to go through. Many of those who get bitten don't survive the transformation. I want to focus on that, not squabbling with some giant ego over land."

"Perhaps things would have resolved faster if there was a werewolf war," Cythera said. "You could defeat Leon and move on with your plan. You'd have more territory and Leon's werewolves."

Glenda glared at her. "Are you looking to start a fight? If you'd done your research on Decker, you'd know that's not how he operates."

"I appreciate that, Glenda," Decker said. "And I remember the Vulpin War from fifty years ago. I have no desire to return my werewolves to a situation like that."

"I mean no offence. And I'll be asking Leon the same questions to see his response," Cythera said.

Decker ran his tongue across his teeth. "Sure. Diplomacy is tedious, especially when dealing with Leon. He won't give an inch until you've given five, and he loves to exploit every opportunity for his own gain. But I was staying the course because there are better things to do than fight. All my werewolves are tired of the stress, and we can't be at peace while Leon is jabbing at us. With Emron dead, the process falls apart, and the fighting continues."

"Where were you at the time of Emron's murder?" Cythera said. "He died between two and three AM."

Decker hesitated. He adjusted his position and crossed his arms over his chest. "I was alone."

"He just lied," I said. "He was fine being prodded about the negotiations, but the second they asked where he was, his demeanor changed."

"What's he hiding?" Zandra said.

"The evidence the angels have suggests he's concealing a murder."

"You have no alibi?" Cythera said to Decker. "Surely, your pack would vouch for you."

"They would if I asked them to lie. And don't be surprised if Leon's entire pack stands up for him. But I encourage mine to tell the truth, even if that isn't an easy thing to do."

"Where were you?" Finn said.

Decker's gaze flashed to Finn. "In my tent, about to go to sleep, when I heard shouts and howls. That's when I knew something terrible had happened."

"Not a single one of your werewolves can vouch for you being in your tent at that time?" Cythera said.

"Maybe one of them saw me go in, but I can't guarantee it. And as I said, I don't get my werewolves to lie for me."

"Which means you have no alibi," Cythera said.

Decker growled again. "I don't need an alibi, because I did nothing wrong."

"You should focus on that alibi," Finn said. "It's important."

Decker's nostrils flared. "Why? What have you got on me?"

Finn and Cythera exchanged a glance.

"Don't keep me in suspense. You wouldn't be interviewing me first if you didn't think you had something to suggest I was guilty."

Cythera nodded. "We have evidence at the crime scene that shows you were there around the time of the murder."

Decker's eyes flared amber for several seconds. He drew in a long, slow breath. "What evidence?"

"Have you recently been in a fight with Emron?" Finn said.

"No. We occasionally butted heads during the negotiations but nothing physical. What evidence have you got on me?"

"You're sure about that?"

"Positive. Why?"

"Your blood and fur were found in Emron's tent," Cythera said.

Decker rested his hands flat on the table, and his shoulders heaved up and down. "This is a mistake."

"You know how he was killed?" Finn said.

Decker appeared stunned as he processed the information. "Emron was hit with an axe, and then his sword was used to take his head off."

"Only a powerful individual could have managed such a clean and swift beheading," Cythera said.

"Which means you think it was a male werewolf." Decker jerked a thumb over his shoulder. "Angels are strong. Maybe one of yours did it."

Cythera simply raised an eyebrow.

"Decker looks shocked about the evidence found," I said. "He's struggling to control his temper."

"How else did it get there if Emron didn't fight back when Decker attacked him? And Decker admitted they'd never had a confrontation," Zandra said. "Blood and fur don't blow in on the wind and settle at a crime scene."

"Technically, fur could. Mine gets everywhere."

"True. I'm always finding your fluff in my coffee. But Decker and Emron aren't camped near each other. It couldn't have gotten in there by mistake."

Decker inhaled slowly, his gaze directed at Cythera. "What about the axe? Or the sword? Weren't there prints on them?"

"The axe had been wiped clean. We found nothing useful on the sword. Whoever did this tampered with the evidence."

"It wasn't me."

"The evidence we have doesn't lie," Cythera said.

"It's lying now. Maybe..."

Cythera's wings fluttered. "Yes. Do you wish to confess?"

Decker snorted. "Never. But maybe I'm being set up."

"Who would want to do that?" Finn said.

Decker went quiet. He finally looked up, and there was a mixture of frustration and anguish in his eyes. "All I know is it wasn't me."

There was a thud, and several yells came from the main office.

Zandra pulled open the door to the room we sat in. "Werewolf alert! Decker's pack must have figured out what's going on."

I ducked out of the room and discovered Decker's fifteen werewolves crowded into the open-plan office. They were surrounded by anxious angels, their wings extended, all crouched in readiness to fight the wolves.

Cythera and Finn had emerged from the interview room and were taking in the scene.

"What's the meaning of this?" Cythera strode over to the pack. "You can't all be here."

Hugh slid around the side of the pack and stood up straight, his shoulders back, his face pale. "I'm here to confess. I murdered Emron."

Chapter 8

I killed Emron

No one spoke. The angels appeared frozen in indecision, all of them glancing at Cythera and waiting for an order. The werewolves behind Hugh were also stone still, their gazes flicking from him to the angels and back again.

Cythera broke the silence, her intense ice-blue stare on Hugh. "You're confessing to Emron's murder?"

He lifted his chin. "Decker is innocent. He had nothing to do with what happened to Emron. It was me. Let Decker go."

"No, it was me." Another werewolf stepped forward, quickly followed by another. Soon, the room was full of werewolves confessing to the murder.

I hopped onto Zandra's shoulder. "This is all we need. The werewolves are protecting their alpha by pretending they did it."

She pressed a hand against my side. "They must have sensed he was in trouble."

"Or he sent a signal for them to come to his rescue."

Hugh kept shouting he was guilty, but the other werewolves out-yelled him, and he was quickly shoved to the back of the pack.

Finn joined us, his expression wary as he kept a watchful eye on the werewolves. "This is just what we need. Although I'm not surprised it's happening. We all know how protective a werewolf pack is when any member is in trouble. And my research into Decker shows he's well-liked."

"What will you do with them?" Zandra said.

"We've got evidence to show Decker was in Emron's tent. If he'd admitted his involvement, the case would be open and shut. But this," he gestured to the shouting werewolves, "this messes everything up."

"And slows your investigation. I admire Hugh's spirit," I said. "Despite being bottom of the pack, he was the first to speak up and help his alpha."

"Maybe he had no choice," Zandra said. "Perhaps the other werewolves insisted he sacrifice himself. He's the most expendable. Losing him to get their alpha back wouldn't have been a debate that took long."

"Everyone be quiet!" Cythera extended her wings until they were an impressive eight feet in width. White flickers of angel magic sparked across them, giving her a golden aura of power. "I said, silence!"

The werewolves stopped yelling and paid her attention.

She speared each werewolf with a glare. "While I admire your loyalty to your alpha, your confessions aren't helping the situation."

"But I did it." Hugh's voice could be heard, but I couldn't see him, since he'd been stacked away behind the rest of the werewolves.

"No, I did it," another werewolf said.

"It was me."

"Ignore him. I did it."

Cythera raised both hands. "That's enough. Since you're all confessing, you'll have to be interviewed. We'll check your motives and your opportunities and discuss the method of killing. But if I discover any of you lying, I'll charge you with wasting angel time."

The wolves stood firm, unbothered by Cythera's threat. She waited a moment, but none of the werewolves changed their minds or left.

"Very well. Angels, divide up the werewolves and interview them individually." Her gaze flickered around the pack. "Where's the small one? The one who first confessed? I'll start with him."

Hugh dodged to the front of the group. "That's me. And I did it. You don't need to interview anyone else. And let Decker go."

"I'll decide who I interview, when I interview them, and who gets released. Follow me." Cythera turned and stalked away, shadowed by a scurrying Hugh.

The next five minutes were taken up in a flurry of activity as angels picked werewolves to interview. While they jostled each other and the tension grew, I made sure Zandra kept out of the action.

"We should help," she said, "but I don't want to get tangled in this mess."

Cythera reappeared, still with Hugh in tow. She opened the interview room containing Decker. "Angels, remove Decker and place him in a cell. I need this space to interview Hugh."

Decker stood from his seat. "What's going on? Why are all my werewolves here?"

"Most likely because you summoned them." Cythera's tone was crisp. "You're only making things worse by involving other people."

Decker's gaze slid to Hugh, who hovered behind Cythera. "What have you done?"

"You didn't kill Emron," Hugh said. "I had to make sure you were free."

Decker closed his eyes for a second and pinched the bridge of his nose. "I didn't ask you to do that. Any of you."

"We'll always protect you," Hugh said. "You're our alpha. We know you didn't kill Emron."

Decker focused on Cythera. "This is a ruse. None of my werewolves were involved. They're here to protect me, nothing more."

"I killed Emron," Hugh said. "I'll keep saying that until someone believes me."

"Angels, take Decker to the cell." Cythera was unmoved by Decker's words.

"Now's our chance to escape," Zandra whispered.

"Let's hear what Hugh has to say before we go," I said.

"You're sure you don't want to leave? You have kippers to consume, thanks to your new best friend, Bertoli."

I hesitated. I could go for a huge kipper meal. "Kippers later."

We headed back into the room and only had to wait a moment before Hugh was in the seat vacated by Decker, shifting around and chewing on a thumbnail.

Glenda and Cythera sat on the other side of the table. Cythera got his details then began the interview.

"Hugh, you're a part of the White Ridge pack, is that correct?" Cythera said.

"Yes. I've been in the pack ten years."

"And if you don't mind me saying, you appear to be the smallest. You are the bottom ranked werewolf?"

"I am. It's not the easiest position, but the other werewolves leave me alone or tolerate me. It's a privilege to be a part of Decker's pack. He had no hesitation in accepting my request to join."

"Which pack were you in previously?"

"Does it matter? I'm not here to talk about my history. I'm here to make sure my alpha goes free and the killer is caught. That's me."

"I need to get a full picture of your background. Discover the influences that turned you into a killer, if that is what you are."

He chewed on his thumbnail some more. "I tried several packs, but they didn't work out. A lot of packs are more aggressive than Decker's. Some of the werewolves took their frustrations out on me."

"That must have been hard," Cythera said.

Glenda shrugged. "It's how werewolves operate. You didn't take it personally, right?"

"I didn't. But I didn't like it. For a while, I was affiliated with no pack and tried to make a go of things on my own. That got me in even more trouble. Werewolves chased and almost killed me. Then I heard Decker was looking to expand his numbers, so I requested to join. He made it clear I'd never be a high-ranking werewolf, but I didn't care. It was enough to have a safe place with werewolves who supported me. And I do the same for them. I always protect my alpha."

"Including lying about killing Emron?" Cythera said.

"It wasn't a lie. I did it."

"Forgive me for saying this, but you're the smallest in the pack. How were you able to defeat a prime werewolf?"

A flush of color crept up Hugh's neck and onto his cheeks. "I got a lucky strike. I'm small, but I'm still strong and fast. And I've learned plenty from Decker since joining his pack."

"What weapon did you use to kill Emron?"

"An axe and a sword." There was no hesitation.

"Everyone knows what weapons were used," I muttered. "It's all people are gossiping about in Crimson Cove."

Zandra nodded. "I expect all the other werewolves are saying the same thing."

Cythera's gaze flicked over Hugh. "I estimate Emron was three times stronger than you. He'd have overpowered you when you struck him with the axe. How did you defeat him?"

"I... I surprised him. And he wouldn't see me as a threat, so he had no reason to be on his guard."

"There was no evidence of a fight," Cythera said. "Emron wouldn't have let you attack and not retaliated."

"Sometimes, being bottom of the pack has its advantages. Not many, but one thing about my position is nobody notices me. It's simple to slip in and out of a situation. I don't give off tense or threatening vibes for other werewolves to pick up. If they're not looking for me, they don't see me. Emron was the same. He was only interested in those with the greatest power, since they were his biggest threat. I'm a threat to no werewolf."

"How did you get into his tent?" Cythera said.

"He had the door open, so I walked in."

"Then what did you do?"

Hugh lifted his chin. "Stuck the axe in his shoulder and used his sword to take his head off."

"Did you use any magic or potion so he was immobile?"

"Like I said, I got lucky. It was me. Decker had nothing to do with this. My alpha is innocent."

Cythera exchanged a glance with Glenda, who lifted one shoulder then shook her head. "While your loyalty to your alpha is admirable, we know it wasn't you."

Hugh sat up straight in his seat. "It was! I did it. I kept quiet in the hope someone from Leon's pack would get the blame. They were the ones being hostile during the negotiations. It made more sense you'd look at them, not pin it on my alpha."

"We're not pinning anything on him. We know it was Decker," Cythera said.

Hugh's eyes narrowed and his hands clenched into fists. "Why don't you believe me? Let him go, and I'll take his place."

"Thank you for your time, but you're free to leave." Cythera went to stand, but Hugh grabbed her arm.

"I thought I could get away with it, but I'm willing to take my punishment for the good of the pack."

Cythera eased her arm out of his grip. "The reason you're not being charged is because we have evidence Decker was in Emron's tent. We found his fur and blood at the scene."

Hugh rocked back in his seat as if someone had shoved him. He stared openmouthed at Cythera. "It couldn't have been him. Decker wasn't there."

"How else did his blood and fur get into the tent?" Glenda said.

"Decker was... he wasn't... he was... I can't say. It's forbidden." Hugh gripped his jaw and wobbled it from side to side.

"Your alpha has forbidden you to say where he was?" Cythera's eyes gleamed. "Because he wanted to ensure no one in his pack revealed the truth?"

"No! It's not that." Hugh's gaze grew frantic. "It has nothing to do with murder. That evidence shouldn't have been in the tent."

"Yet, it was."

"Wait! Wait! This makes no sense. Leon and Decker knew not to speak with Emron outside the official negotiations, or it could ruin everything. Emron spent the same amount of work and social time with each pack. It was all arranged."

"They didn't have a fight or come to blows recently?" Cythera said. "That would explain why Decker's blood was at the crime scene."

Hugh sighed. "No. Decker is a werewolf of honor. He respects boundaries. Unlike Leon. Decker would never go after Emron. He's got too much to lose. It was me."

"Given that the axe and sword had no incriminating prints, we have no proof other than your word that you did this," Cythera said.

"Isn't that good enough?"

"Not when the evidence points to another werewolf, and you've already revealed you'd do anything to protect your alpha."

"I had to step forward. When I heard you'd brought Decker in and he was your prime suspect, I couldn't sit back and let anything bad happen to him. If I'd known that was your plan, I'd have confessed sooner."

"They're going in circles," Zandra said. "Hugh will keep saying he did it. The angels will keep saying there's no evidence, and then we'll get the speech about protecting the alpha again."

"And I expect the angels are hearing the same story from the other werewolves," I said.

"Let's get out of here, shall we?" Zandra said. "We're learning nothing new."

We watched the interview for a few more minutes and then quietly left the room.

Finn was coming out of an interview room with another protesting werewolf. After he dismissed the wolf, he walked over to us.

"Let me guess, they're all saying they're guilty of murder?" Zandra said.

"Yep. I've spoken to two werewolves. They tell the same story, although the details are vague. They all know the murder weapon used, though, and are claiming they did it."

"Same with Hugh," I said. "They're willing to sacrifice their freedom for their alpha."

"It's what werewolves do," Finn said. "We have to interview them all since they've confessed, but we won't get anywhere. Cythera will eventually charge Decker with murder. All this has done is buy him time."

I hopped on the desk and investigated a pile of paperwork. It was nice thick paper and felt good under my toe beans. "The evidence points toward Decker, but we should speak to Leon, see if he knows anything. He'll have a complicated situation on his paws, now the negotiations are suspended."

"Why bother when the evidence points to Decker?" Zandra said. "The angels have everything they need to close the case."

I flicked my ears. "Just curious."

Finn grinned. "You know where curiosity leads?"

"To glory." I hopped off the desk. "I want to make sure nothing's been missed. We don't want an innocent werewolf going down for a crime he didn't commit."

"It feels like an open and shut case to me," Finn said. "Although I'm in for a long night if these werewolves keep saying they did it."

"Good luck. Catch up tomorrow?" Zandra said.

"Sure. I'll be the exhausted angel with bags under his eyes, mainlining coffee and forgetting his own name after a night with these feisty furballs."

She patted his arm. "I'll bring you a thermos of something strong."

We left the angels and the werewolves to bicker and headed home.

"You really want to speak to Leon?" Zandra said.

"No. I'd be content never to see him again, but this murder feels too tidy."

"It's hard to have a neat murder. Your kitty senses tingling?"

"A little. Werewolves are cunning. And that evidence is a parcel of convenience. A gentle question or two to make sure the angels have the right guy would be useful. And Decker mentioned being set up. There could be something behind that."

Zandra walked in silence for a moment. "Whatever helps you sleep."

"And whatever gets the werewolves out of Crimson Cove quickly." Angel Force would eventually get the job done, but with help from me, it would be done much faster.

Chapter 9

Camp werewolf

We were up early the next morning, and after a speedy breakfast of dried fish for me and a granola bar and coffee for Zandra, we were out the door and on the road before Vorana and Sage were up. Our destination was Leon's camp in Crimson Cove woods.

"Leon won't appreciate us poking around and suggesting he killed Emron." Zandra ambled along, picking granola out of her teeth.

I was also working on getting a small piece of dried fish from my back teeth. I kept getting wonderfully faint hints of intense salmon. "He'll hate it, but I keep coming back to that conversation we had about motive. Why would either alpha risk everything by killing the negotiator who was helping find the solution to their warring?"

"A second of madness? Or a loss of control?" Zandra said.

"But werewolves are unique. It's the pack bond. It's like what we have. We always think of each other, just like the werewolves do when they make a decision. It's never about the individual but more about what the pack would gain or suffer."

Zandra arched an eyebrow as she looked down at me. "I always know how grumpy you get if I forget to refill the treat jar."

"If the jar gets empty, that's tantamount to animal cruelty. You know better than that."

She chuckled. "As if I'd ever do anything so cruel. You have a point, though. Both alphas have thriving packs. Something must have gone wrong to make one of them kill Emron."

"And we'll make that clear when we speak to Leon. But it also opens the question as to why Decker would act that way. What would his pack gain from him taking out Emron? Maybe Leon knows the answer."

We entered the woods and walked along the path toward the main campsites. There were several campsites in the woods, and the packs occupied the two largest.

I lifted my booping snooter and inhaled deeply, my eyes narrowing as I stared into the foliage. "Don't react, but we're being watched. Although a more accurate description would be stalked."

"The werewolves are on to us?" Zandra kept walking, her arms loose by her side.

"They smelled us coming."

"Do you consider them a threat?"

"Werewolves are always a threat. I'll keep watch and make sure they do nothing foolish."

As we continued through the woods, there were signs the werewolves had been rampaging. Bushes were crumpled, tree branches gnawed, and there were large paw prints in the damp soil.

A werewolf stepped onto the path in front of us. His fur was a dense black, and he had a white bib and white front paws. His head was lowered and his hackles raised as his amber eyes gleamed at us.

"Greetings. I'm Juno, and the wonderful witch beside me is Zandra Crypt. We're here to speak to Leon. We come in peace."

The werewolf growled.

"There's no need for snarls. We're working with Angel Force to investigate Emron's murder." It was sort of the truth, since Finn had asked us to lend a hand.

Another werewolf stepped onto the path and joined his pack mate. He was a similar size, but his fur was speckled black and white.

There were several growls and grumbles as they communicated with each other.

"Unfortunately, I don't speak werewolf, but I assure you, we're not here to make trouble," I said.

"This'll take ten minutes," Zandra said. "Your alpha must be interested in an update on the investigation."

The werewolves grumbled among themselves some more.

"You can't be here."

I turned and discovered a guy wearing only jeans, his perfectly sculpted abs on display.

"This is our temporary territory while we're here. You're trespassing," he said.

"Sadly, you're wrong," I said. "Crimson Cove woods is open to all. And while I appreciate werewolves are territorial, you have no claim over this land."

The two werewolves and the guy growled.

Zandra lifted her gaze to the sky and crossed her arms over her chest. "Don't make us late for work. All we want to do is talk to Leon."

"Our alpha can't be disturbed. He's busy. Leave," the half-naked guy said in a growly tone. "We won't tell you again."

Although it was sensible to be cautious around werewolves, I'd been nothing but polite, and although Zandra radiated tension, she'd kept her sharp tongue hidden. Therefore, it was time to show these werewolves who the true alpha was around here.

I hopped onto Zandra's shoulder. "Are you ready to teach these misbehaving puppies a lesson?"

"I thought you'd never ask." She cracked her knuckles. "You guys brought this on yourselves."

The half-naked guy was just opening his mouth to issue another growly command when Zandra whacked him with an immobilization spell. While she tackled him, I shot a powerful knockback spell into the two four-pawed werewolves.

They howled as they flew backward.

I wriggled my paws. My magic was being gloriously majestic.

One werewolf made a valiant attempt to lunge at me and Zandra, but he was whacked off his paws by another spell. It felt good to have some of my power back. I'd been working on an almost empty magical tank for too long.

Thanks to the rediscovery of my hidden power right here in Crimson Cove, I could sense things were changing for the better.

"You'll regret this," the immobilized werewolf grumbled.

"Regrets are pointless," Zandra said. "Now, which way to Leon's tent, so we can have a friendly chat with him?"

He growled.

"We'll find him ourselves. The smell of damp dog will give him away." I zapped the two shaggy werewolves one more time as a warning not to get cute and chase us.

They wisely stayed on the ground, their bodies shivering from my magic.

"Any more furballs we need to watch for?" Zandra's step was brisk. She knew she'd pushed her luck by taking on those werewolves.

"All good. They must have been the patrols keeping an eye on things."

"Let's make this quick. When those wolves return to camp and report what happened, Leon may not be so friendly with us."

"I doubt they'll say anything. After all, they'll feel embarrassed after being bested by such a tiny witch and her gorgeous, adorable familiar."

Zandra tickled under my chin. "Adorable and lethal. Those spells you whacked out had power. It's why we make such a great pair."

"I couldn't agree more."

Five minutes later, we entered an elaborate Persian festival. The tents, if you could call them that, were enormous multi-colored domes, more like small circus tops. They were vibrantly colored in deep purple, and red flags showing the werewolves' coat of arms waved in a lazy breeze.

"Talk about super glamping," Zandra muttered.

"The biggest tent must belong to Leon," I said. "Let's try there."

Two werewolves standing on two feet and with not a fur in sight emerged before we got within touching distance.

"Boss, we have unexpected visitors," one of them said.

A moment later, Leon poked his head out of the tent opening. "Huh! How did you two get in here? We're on lockdown while we deal with a few things."

"We had a friendly word with your guards, and they realized it made sense to let us through," Zandra said.

"Greetings," I said to the watching werewolves. "I'm Juno, and this is the magnificent Zandra Crypt. We're working with Angel Force to investigate Emron's murder, and we have questions for you."

"We've met before." Leon studied us from under thick eyebrows. "I know Angel Force is letting in all kinds of supernaturals, but I thought you had to have a little angel in you to join." He emerged from the tent. His blond, surfer style hair was messy and his jeans unbuttoned, his checked shirt open to display yet another fine set of abs.

Although werewolves could be difficult to deal with, they were always a pleasure to watch.

"We freelance for them sometimes," Zandra said. "We actually work at animal control with Barney Hoffman."

"I get it. The angels and animal control keep watch on us. Make sure we don't get too wolfie and go insane."

I looked around the camp. More werewolves had appeared. "We're not here to make trouble. We just want to get to the bottom of this murder."

Leon waved his hand. "Everyone go about your business. I'm sure this sweet little witch and her adorable fluffy won't cause problems."

Zandra's shoulders hitched, but she kept silent as the werewolves melted away, although I was certain they'd listen to every word we were about to say.

"Coffee?" Leon said. "We were out running most of last night and then dealing with the Emron situation, so I've had little sleep."

"Coffee would be good, thanks," Zandra said.

Leon clicked his fingers, and Nico dashed over, his posture hunched as he passed around mugs and served coffee from a sturdy tin pot. He kept his gaze down as he served Leon and only glanced at Zandra for the briefest of seconds before rushing off again.

Leon drank down half his mug in one go. "I'm not sure what I can tell you that the angels don't already know."

"What was your opinion of Emron?" I hopped off Zandra's shoulder, settled on a tree stump, and curled my tail around my paws. She pulled up another slab of wood and perched on the edge.

Leon's face creased for a second, and he ran a thumb across his chin stubble. "I wasn't a fan. The guy had an ego like he was the overlord alpha, but I get why he carried himself that way. He was everyone's go-to werewolf when negotiations got difficult."

"Does that mean you didn't like him?" Zandra said.

"I accepted his position and his skills as a negotiator. I was aware of his track record of getting results and preventing skirmishes from getting out of hand. That was why he was here." Leon glanced around. "Nico, breakfast. You two want something?"

"We're good," Zandra said.

Nico dashed over with a huge tin tray of cooked meats.

I licked my lips and tried not to drool. My dried salmon breakfast suddenly seemed inadequate.

Leon chuckled and tossed me a strip of beef. "Help yourself. I've got plenty."

I accepted his gift with a nod of gratitude and tucked in. It was sublime. Medium rare, with a faint peppery hint.

Zandra smirked at me as she sipped her coffee.

Leon finished his first hunk of meat. "I understand why Angel Force is being thorough. After all, you don't want to get things wrong with the werewolves. From what I understand, there's evidence to show who killed Emron."

"How would you know that?" Zandra said.

"Because small town gossip is useful, and my werewolves never miss that kind of information." Leon chewed on another chunk of meat, the juices sliding down his chin and into his blond scruff.

"If you ask me, this crime is evidence Decker was getting sloppy. I suggested several times he step aside and let a real alpha rule his pack before things blew up. Too late now."

Although there were no werewolves in sight, there was a grumbling of agreement from the nearby trees.

"What was Decker doing that you didn't agree with?" I said.

Leon tossed me more meat, which I caught in the air. "He was getting soft and overindulging his werewolves. And he was too slow in growing his pack. Decker prefers natural born werewolves as opposed to changing someone. But when an alpha gets afraid to bite, it shows their time is up. They should clear the path."

"For someone like you?" Zandra said.

"For me."

There were more grumbling agreements from the shadows.

"From what I've seen of the way Decker runs his pack, he's a fair alpha," I said. "And it's always tricky turning someone into a werewolf with a bite. You get more fatalities than successful changes."

"True. Which is why only a few of us can do it and why only a few of us get to rule a pack as successful as mine," Leon said. "But Decker's been making mistakes. It was an idiot move to leave behind evidence. I don't know. Maybe he did it deliberately. He knew he was failing but didn't want to look like a coward by giving me his position and pack."

"He can't give it up. It has to be taken from him," I said.

Leon shrugged. "That's what I meant. Decker doesn't have the stomach for a fight. He's failing, so he arranged this."

"You really think Decker did it?" Zandra said.

"I'll leave it to the angels to decide if his blood and fur at a murder scene tell the whole story." He shook his head. "I knew something like this would slam him off his feet."

Zandra tensed, and my toe beans tingled. "How do you know what the evidence was?"

Leon's expression grew smug. "I have my sources. And like I said, my werewolves miss nothing. Decker panicked because the negotiations weren't going his way and lashed out at Emron. Did you know he'd asked to have a replacement negotiator put in place? They denied his request."

"I didn't know that. Why would he do that?" Zandra said.

"It was a stalling tactic. Decker hated the way the negotiations were falling. He thought someone else would be easier to win over. And he was denied the request because Emron was the best in the business."

"Are you saying that because Emron was supporting your negotiation plans and not Decker's?" I said.

There were several grumbles of disapproval from the listening werewolves.

Leon raised a hand, and the grumbles stopped. "It had nothing to do with that. I was simply right. My plans made the most sense, and Decker hated that.

He was causing trouble and slowing things down. Requesting Emron be taken out of the negotiations was another way of getting more time to figure out a new angle."

"You think, because Decker didn't get what he wanted, he murdered Emron?" I said. "Even though he's lost everything by killing him."

"It's more evidence to show he's lost his edge. He no longer deserves the alpha role."

We were quiet for a moment. I chewed my meat while thinking through this new information while Zandra sipped her coffee.

"Does this mean the negotiations are over?" Zandra said. "What will happen now?"

"That's easy. I'm the only alpha left standing. Decker can't rule once he's convicted, so I'll claim his territory and his pack. They're adjacent to my territory, so I'll get the first option to take over. It's only fair."

"That's convenient for you," I said. "Emron's dead, Decker looks guilty, and you get everything you want."

Leon growled. "Be careful what you say. I'm being hospitable because I'm in a good mood, but that can vanish. Sure, this situation has ended in my favor but not because of anything I've done. I wanted these negotiations to succeed. I was as tired of fighting as Decker."

"Yet you were the one who instigated it," I said.

"Who's been telling you lies?" Leon grinned, although it looked closer to a snarl. "Perhaps I was a little less friendly than Decker but only because I could see I'd be the better alpha when I merged the packs. I had an expansion plan and targets to hit to create new werewolves. Decker was cruising and getting lazy as he aged."

"Decker isn't old. He's a prime werewolf, just like you," I said.

"That was the wrong choice of words. He's mellowed. You can't relax when you're at the top, because there's always someone snapping at your heels."

"His pack won't join you easily," Zandra said.

Leon shrugged. "If they resist, they die. It's my right to rule. It's a simple concept and one they understand. They know the consequences of disobedience."

"Did you know each member of Decker's pack has confessed to the murder?" I said.

"I'm not surprised to hear that. Mine would do the same if the situation was reversed. Werewolf loyalty can't be beaten." Leon raised his mug and scowled into it. "Nico, more coffee. I swear, that werewolf. I don't know why I keep him around. He's worse than useless."

"Sorry, sorry, sorry." Nico dashed over, freshened both mugs, and then slunk away.

Leon shook his head. "I've never had a more pathetic bottom in my pack. I keep expecting one of my werewolves to deal with him."

"You mean kill him?" A shudder ran down my spine. I knew of the brutal nature of werewolves, but it still gave me an unpleasant shock to witness it.

"He's soft. It's not so much his size that's the issue, simply that he doesn't have the werewolf instinct.

He was bitten by accident. Nico stumbled into two of my werewolves fighting, was dumb enough to think they were large dogs, and intervened. We assumed he'd die. So I was amazed when he was still going three weeks later. We snuck him out of the hospital and initiated him into our ways."

"That shows Nico has a fighting spirit," I said. "You want that in a werewolf, no matter their status in the pack."

Leon's top lip curled. "Maybe. I just don't know about him." He brushed his hands together. "Now, I've told you everything."

"You haven't told us your alibi," Zandra said.

"The angels know where I was. And since Decker is under arrest and not me, you can assume it's solid."

"Indulge us," I said. "Then we'll leave."

Leon sucked air through his teeth. "We'd taken over the pizza parlor that night. We convinced the guy who runs it to stay open late. I was there with my pack. You're welcome to ask them, but they'll all tell you the same thing. There were plenty of witnesses who know where I was when Emron lost his head."

There were soft growls of agreement.

"Now, unless you want to help with the details of the pack merging ceremony, you need to leave."

Zandra set down her mug and stood. "Hold off on that. Decker's pack remains loyal to him."

"I'm sure they will, despite his guilt. But the Wolf Council will strip him of his title. This act was malicious. We all understand the rules of violence and retribution, and there's a time and a place to end another werewolf's life, but by murdering Emron, Decker has to pay."

As one, half a dozen werewolves appeared around the tent.

"Here's your escort. Thanks for dropping by," Leon said.

"We're good. We know the way out," Zandra said.

"Always happy to work with Angel Force and animal control. We're on the same side and want the best for the supernaturals. Just as you look out for each other, I look out for my wolves." Leon gestured at the waiting werewolves. "I'll support Decker's werewolves during the merging. You have nothing to be concerned about."

The werewolves took a step forward.

I hopped onto Zandra's shoulder. "Time to go," I whispered into her ear.

She nodded slowly, said goodbye to Leon, and turned and left. Although her pace was slow and steady, tension radiated from her shoulders. We knew how close we'd come to Leon turning from friendly to feral.

We waited a full five minutes before speaking. After all, werewolf hearing was acute.

"I do not like or trust that guy," she whispered. "He knew too much."

"I agree. Despite Leon saying he wanted the arguing done, he's gotten everything he wanted. Two packs and an expanded territory without shedding blood or losing werewolves." I kept a watchful eye for any stalking wolves. "The guy seems power mad. This friendly act could be a front. Leon hated the negotiations and saw things weren't going his way. This was the simplest solution. Kill Emron and win the werewolf lotto."

Zandra huffed out a breath. "Yeah, but how will we prove that?"

Chapter 10

A questionable werewolf

"I'll put the last of the equipment in the van, then we'll head home and grab dinner." Zandra stacked three clean cages in the back of the van.

My stomach growled in anticipation. It had been a busy day at animal control. We'd checked half a dozen licenses and three new adoptions to ensure the rehoming was going well, and searched for several reported sightings of a devil-horned hill beaver. All that work made me ravenously hungry.

"I'd ask what you want, but you'll say fish." Zandra appeared around the side of the van, where I perched on the hood, and grinned at me.

"You know me so well. We could treat Vorana and get pizza on the way home. I've been thinking about gorging on a seafood medley pizza ever since we discussed it."

"Vorana prefers home-cooked. To be honest, I prefer her home cooking, too. I never thought I'd say that, but she makes veggies taste amazing."

Zandra had been a takeout queen when we'd met. She was much like her older half-sister, Tempest, in that respect. But living in the home of someone who was an amazing cook changed things for the better. And my stomach was grateful for that.

I wrinkled my booping snooter as Katrine strode past with a face like a slapped behind. She was followed by Nico, Hugh, and a small, mousy-haired female I'd never seen.

"I will have my audience with Leon." Katrine kept walking, setting a remarkably speedy pace, given the six-inch heels she wore.

"Of course. Whatever you need. But it's not that simple." Nico was crouched slightly as he scurried behind her. "Given everything that's happened, Leon is busy. He'd kill me if I interrupt him."

"He's not busy enough to avoid me." Katrine kept walking. "Make it happen, or you'll regret it."

"What's gotten her so riled this time?" Zandra leaned against the van and watched the argument as they continued into town.

I'd already hopped off the hood and followed the small group. "Let's find out. It could be important. Something to do with Emron's murder, perhaps?"

"We're still pursuing that?" Zandra pushed away from the van.

"I have a feeling in my gut this murder isn't as simple as it seems. Decker hid something during his interview. It had something to do with his alibi. Come on, let's go see what they have to say."

Zandra didn't protest as she followed me. "Are you sure that's not just hunger you're feeling?"

"It's both. This won't take long. The speed Katrine is going, she'll be across the other side of Crimson Cove and into the next town in less than an hour. Maybe she won't come back."

"Something has annoyed her. Although, maybe that's her default position. She always seems so grouchy."

We kept back, so we couldn't hear the rest of the conversation, but I could tell Katrine was furious as she waved her arms around and glowered at Nico. Neither Hugh nor the female who stuck close to his side had much to say, but Hugh kept shooting Nico a supportive look and nodding at him.

Katrine abruptly stopped and turned to Nico.

Zandra ducked into the doorway of a store. "If I get any closer, I'll get seen eavesdropping. You go see what you can hear and report back."

I nodded and hurried closer, keeping near the wall and crouching low to make myself as small as possible. Once I was within earshot, I ducked behind a recycling container.

"You're wasting my time, and that's valuable. I demand to see Leon."

"I understand. And I'm sure he'll want to see you, too. It's just—"

Katrine cut Nico off. "If you know he wants to see me, then make it happen. Take me there now. He'll want what I have, but he must agree to my terms. I won't be messed around. I can get other offers."

Nico stooped low, his back hunched and gaze on the ground. "I'll do my best. I know this is important to you."

"And him!" She swatted the back of Nico's head. "You're pathetic."

"Leon has a lot on his mind," Hugh said so softly I barely caught the words. "He's planning to merge the two packs as soon as Decker is charged with Emron's murder."

Katrine sniffed. "Maybe so, but this is even more important. The way you're acting suggests you think I'm lying. You've seen the results. I gave this sniveling moron a copy to pass on to Leon."

"Yes! And it's wonderful news."

The quiet woman who stood with Hugh moved so she was behind him. It looked like she wanted to be anywhere but in the middle of this argument. She was stooped, just like Nico, and staring at the dirt, her hands clasped in front of her.

"I'll go myself. I don't need an invitation." Katrine went to move off, but Nico caught hold of her arm.

"It'll just be a few more hours. You need to be patient."

She shook his hand off her arm. "By then, I'll have found a better deal. You know my terms. There'll be another werewolf prepared to meet them. I only offered this to Leon because I know how much he'd love to rub Decker's nose in it."

What did Katrine have that allowed Leon to get one over Decker?

"Bear with us," Hugh said. "We can get something figured out."

Katrine jabbed a finger at him. "Don't think Decker has any rights in this."

"I... I didn't mean that. But he can't be left out of such an important decision."

"He's in a cell about to be charged with murder. He's not a part of this deal. He can't offer me anything of value."

"But... I mean, we can arrange something."

"Like you did, going around town and telling everyone you murdered Emron to protect Decker? That worked well. And I don't hear you yelling about being a killer anymore. Lost your nerve?"

He lowered his head. "I had to protect my alpha."

"More like you got scared. You're a pathetic coward, just like Nico." Katrine dismissed him with a wave of her hand.

Hugh glanced at the female beside him. "Yeah, that's me."

The ground beneath my paws rumbled, and a few seconds later, an enormous, wet tongue licked me from head to tail. I squirmed away and hissed, flipping around with my claws out.

Archie stood in front of me, his tongue hanging out and his tail wagging. "Are you playing hide and go seek? That's one of my favorite games. The vampires play it with me for hours. They're so good at hiding, mainly because they turn into smoke or bats. But I can still hunt them. Remus always tells me how magnificent I am when I win. Can I join in? Who you playing with? Zandra? Mack? Sage?"

I glanced around the recycling container, relieved to see the argument was still continuing and Archie's clumpy-footed arrival hadn't revealed my location. "Greetings. It's not a game. I'm on a mission."

"One of your kitten impossible missions? You should have said. I'd have joined in. What we doing?" He crouched, his eyes narrowed.

"It's covert surveillance. And right now, you're being the opposite of covert. Could you make yourself smaller?"

Archie studied his long front legs. "I'm not sure how. And I'm bigger these days because of the amount of food Remus feeds me. I get six meals a day and snacks."

"And I'll continue to feed you, you magnificent beast, for as long as you desire it." Remus appeared out of the shadows. He was dressed from top to toe in pale lilac velvet with a frilled white shirt and a matching top hat. He carried a long black cane with a silver end.

I looked him up and down. "Love the outfit. Have you been here this whole time?"

"I don't lurk in the shadows like a common vampire waiting for my next feast. We were out for a stroll when Archie said he smelled you and wanted to know what you were up to. Of course, I can never say no to my wonderful hellhound. He ran on ahead, and I took the direct route on the wing."

I glanced at the argument again. "Perhaps we could pick this up another time?"

"And leave you to have all the fun while you snoop on those werewolves?" Remus shook his head as he waggled a finger in the air. "That hardly seems fair. I hate missing out on gossip."

Katrine turned suddenly and marched away, leaving Nico, Hugh, and his female friend staring after her.

I glanced up at Remus. "Have you heard about the werewolf being murdered?"

He nodded. "A sad business. I'm never impressed with the way werewolves conduct themselves. They're all muscle and no manners. Of course, I'm tolerant of all, but even I have limits when it comes to bad manners."

"So do I," Archie said. "But everyone's a friend until they show themselves to be an enemy. Isn't that right, Remus?"

He petted Archie on the head and fed him a treat from a small purple satchel slung over his shoulder. "Whatever you say, my little ball of fluffy wonderment."

"Remus has been teaching me about seventeenth century poetry, and I've been teaching him about how to be good and kind to everyone. I read about it in a book."

"I'm glad you're both learning useful things." My gaze was still on Katrine. "While you're here, I could do with some help. I'm working with Zandra on the werewolf issue, but it's getting messy."

"It always does when the wolves run free. I heard the angels made an arrest," Remus said.

"They did. And although there's evidence to show guilt, I'm not sure they've got the right person."

"Ooooh! You are on a mission," Archie said. "Let's help, Remus. I love being involved in Juno's adventures. She always takes us to such fun places. Can we help? Say we can. I wanna."

"As charming as Juno is, she frequently puts you on death's path, my adorable bundle of fluffy magnificence. I'm not sure I approve of such a risk. I could never lose you."

"I'm almost impossible to kill, so I never mind wandering death's path," Archie said. "And I love hanging out with the magical misfits. I fit right in."

Remus tapped his cane on the ground several times. "I must admit, I want to know what troubles the visiting werewolves. If we can be of service, while ensuring this problem disappears, then I'm happy to indulge you. Only because Archie asked, you understand."

Archie lifted his front paws off the ground and slammed them on Remus's shoulders. The vampire barely moved, despite the enormous weight he'd just been handed. He simply chuckled as Archie enthusiastically licked his face.

"Best day ever," Archie said. "Juno, what do you need me to do?"

"I was hoping to have a conversation with Nico and Hugh. Katrine is after something, and she's got a secret she wants to share with Leon. Or make a deal with him. I'm uncertain about the specifics. I was thinking—"

"Say no more. I'll get what you need." Archie torpedoed toward Nico and grabbed him around the throat.

"Ah. That's not what I meant." I cringed as Archie body slammed Nico to the ground.

Remus chuckled. "Archie has a straightforward way of doing things. He needs clear instructions to make sure nothing goes awry. But he's always enthusiastic, so even if things don't go to plan, I never scold him." He crouched beside me as Archie and Nico tussled. "And I must thank you again for bringing me together with Archie. I didn't realize my life was incomplete before such a wonderful creature joined me. I can always trust Archie, and he'll always be there for me."

"You're welcome. I hope you'll always be there for him, too."

"It's the promise we made to each other. I've always had a deep and sincere bond with my vampires, but I never thought things could be better with another creature. How wrong I was. Archie is a wonderful being." Remus pressed a hand to his heart.

The soft expression on his face made me smile. "Does that mean you owe me a favor?"

Remus stood and dusted off his knees. "From one powerful supernatural to another, I consider you an ally, and we'll leave it at that."

I could handle having a friend as powerful as Remus on my side, so I lifted a paw, and we shook on it.

"What's going on?" Zandra dashed over. "We're supposed to be keeping a low profile, so we don't get two werewolf packs eating us."

"Archie wanted to help," I said. "And I needed to find out what Nico and Hugh were talking to Katrine about."

"And my wonderful hellhound took his usual direct approach. And here we are. Nico is being brought to you," Remus said.

Nico had stopped fighting Archie. One arm hung limply by his side, and he dragged one leg behind him. Hugh and his female friend followed a short distance behind, but they hadn't attempted to fight Archie off. Sensible choice.

"I got him for you." Archie wagged his tail. "He didn't want to come, though. He kept telling me to get off and leave him alone."

"Thank you, Archie. You could have asked him to join us, though. I know Nico." I inspected Nico's injured leg. The wounds would heal. Werewolves restored themselves remarkably quickly.

Archie kept wagging his tail. "Would you have come if I'd asked you to?" He looked at Nico.

Nico touched his injuries and winced. "It depends. What do you want to talk to me about?" His gaze went from Archie to me then to Zandra and Remus. His eyes flashed amber when he recognized the vampire. "I want no trouble. We're not here because of any vampire issue."

Remus raised his hand. "Relax. I was simply enjoying a walk with my hellhound when we encountered our friends in need. I'm certain, much like you, you never abandon your friends."

"Oh, no." Nico glanced back at Hugh, who had one arm around the small female's shoulders. "It's just Leon said to keep away from the vampires in Crimson Cove. They're trouble."

"True. We're troublesome if werewolves come for us, but we're showing respect and keeping out of your way while your negotiations happen. Although, because of your recent loss, I understand they may be over now." Remus canted his head. "I trust that won't be an issue for my hive."

Nico and Hugh shared a look but made no comment.

"No problem," the female whispered.

"Nico, what was Katrine arguing with you about?" I said. "She had something urgent to tell Leon."

He nodded. "Err... yeah, you could say that."

"Does it have anything to do with what happened to Emron?" Zandra said.

Nico hesitated and shared another worried look with his friends.

"We need to know. It could be connected to the murder," I said.

"No. At least, not that I can figure out." He drew in a breath. "Katrine wants an alpha role in her own pack of submissive werewolves, a monthly payment from my pack, and for it to be known to all she's under Leon's care."

"That's some list of demands," Zandra said. "I get she has a privileged position because she was Emron's girlfriend, but why would Leon give her all that?"

"Is she blackmailing him?" Remus said. "So cheap."

"Did she see Leon kill Emron?" I said. "She knows his secret, so is demanding he pay to keep her silent."

"No, nothing like that. It's got nothing to do with Emron." Nico rubbed the back of his neck. "Katrine is pregnant with Decker's pup."

Chapter 11

Congratulations!

"Katrine was involved with Decker?" I said. "I thought she was Emron's girlfriend."

Remus tutted and rolled his eyes to the heavens. "I'm not surprised to hear this. Werewolves have such salacious appetites. They'll hump anything if it stays still long enough."

"We should get going," Hugh said. "I need to get Valerie settled in, and Leon will miss you before too long."

Nico nodded. "I'm late getting his food. He'll punish me if I'm not careful."

"He'll do that, anyway." There was a note of bitterness in Hugh's words.

"We need more information," I said. "How did Katrine get pregnant with Decker?"

"Juno, I'm certain you don't need a diagram to understand how a werewolf pup is conceived," Remus said. "It's simple. You insert—"

"Not that! I didn't know they were seeing each other. It must be recent. Katrine's not showing."

Nico stepped back, eyeing Archie. "I don't want more trouble. We really need to leave."

I glanced around. The street had grown quieter as the evening drew in, and there were more werewolves in evidence. We could do without attention being drawn to us.

"May I make a suggestion?" Remus said. "My instincts tell me this is a delicate conversation and best done in privacy. You're welcome to a private booth at my bar. It's near here, and we serve wonderful food. And I've heard Juno's stomach growl several times. Zandra, it's never good to let our familiars become hungry."

"We were on our way to dinner when we got involved in this," Zandra said.

"No matter. My bar is available to you, as is the food. No charge. You'll be my guests."

"We don't have time." Nico inched away. "There's so much going on with the packs. Leon is demanding the merging ceremony take place the second Decker gets charged."

"Pack merging ceremonies take months," I said. "The werewolves from the fallen pack need time to form bonds with their new pack, and the alpha must induct each werewolf into the rules and ensure they pass certain tests. If it's done quickly, things go wrong."

"And werewolves die," Hugh muttered.

"Leon is done waiting. He said the negotiations took too long. He wants to get back to our territory and work on the expansion plan. It makes sense to do it fast." There was no conviction in Nico's words.

"You can spare my dear friends half an hour." Remus flashed his fangs and rested a hand on Archie's enormous head. "Or do you want my adorable four-legged friend to assist you in finding your way to free food and drink?"

Nico gulped. "No."

"So, let's do this the nice way over fine food and cocktails, rather than Archie dragging you into an alleyway and torturing the information out of you."

"Less on the torture," Zandra murmured.

Nico's breath came out in tiny spurts. "Cocktails would be great."

"Excellent. I'll lead the way. You chat among yourselves." Remus strode off with Archie, whistling a tune as he twirled his cane in the air.

Zandra leaned in close to Nico. "Archie would never torture you. He looks terrifying, but he's a softie. This won't take long. We're still figuring out what happened to Emron, so any information you can give us would be helpful. We have to make sure we've got the right person for this murder."

Nico shrugged, and Hugh nodded.

"We're not being difficult." Hugh walked alongside me and Zandra. "It's such a tense time for the packs, though. One wrong step or wrong word spoken to the wrong person, and this'll descend into chaos."

"This conversation will only be between us," I said. "Leon doesn't have to know."

Nico heaved out a sigh. "Leon knows everything. He has eyes and ears all over the place."

"Not in my club," Remus called over his shoulder. "And it's a vampires' only night. Any werewolf who comes in without my permission will be torn to pieces. Keep up. Cocktails await."

Nico, Hugh, and his female trudged along with me and Zandra. None of them seemed inclined to make conversation.

"Greetings. We've not been properly introduced," I said to the shy female. "I'm Juno, and this is Zandra Crypt, my wonderful, bonded witch."

She nodded, her gaze skittering to Hugh. "Valerie Bishop."

"You're Hugh's..."

"Sister," he said.

Valerie chewed on her bottom lip, her gaze never staying on one thing for more than a second. "I sprung a surprise visit on him."

"Are you staying long?"

She hunched, making it clear she didn't want the conversation to continue. "I'll be gone soon. I wouldn't... no, I'll get out of here as quickly as I can. I don't want to get in the way."

"You're not. We'll make things right." Hugh's hand tightened on her shoulder.

"Stay for as long as you need," I said in a soothing tone, sensing Valerie had trouble in her life. "All supernaturals are accepted in Crimson Cove. I'm sorry you showed up during such a difficult time."

She nodded but did not try to continue the chat.

Other than Remus pointing out interesting landmarks as we walked the short route to his bar, the rest of the journey continued in silence. Nico and Hugh stayed in subservient positions, while Valerie did her best to make herself invisible.

Remus went in first, and within thirty seconds, he'd arranged a private room we could access from a side entrance in the building.

We walked along a warmly lit corridor, turned right, and entered an opulent room decorated with deep green and gold wallpaper, black wood flooring, and plump, comfortable couches dotted around.

"Make yourselves at home," Remus said. "Refreshments are on their way."

Rather than leaving, he settled in a chair, crossed one leg over the other, and sat Archie beside him as if waiting for the main performance to start.

Zandra picked a seat, and I joined her on the arm of the chair. After a few seconds of looking around, Nico, Hugh, and Valerie settled on the same couch, huddled as if anticipating a firing squad was about to enter the room.

There was a knock on the door, and two servers entered, one carrying a tray of brightly colored cocktails festooned with fresh chunks of fruit and paper parasols. But it was the other server who had my attention. She carried two huge silver platters heaped with food. Among that feast was the aroma of fish.

Once the servers had set out the treats, they left and closed the door.

Remus gestured at the food and drink. "Help yourselves. I asked for the steaks to be extra rare. Or there's chicken. And fish. I find discussions go much better when everyone has a full stomach." He picked up a glass of red. Definitely not claret.

Valerie eyed the plate of chicken wings and licked her lips.

"Go ahead," Hugh said softly. "I know you haven't had much today."

The second Valerie grabbed the chicken wings, it became a free for all. I dived into the plate of salmon, Zandra grabbed a burger, and Archie hoovered up three steaks one after the other. Nico and Hugh also chose two extra rare steaks and a giant bowl of chips.

Remus sat back with his drink, amusement on his face as he watched us take our fill. Some vampires had a thing about watching people eat.

Ten minutes later, my stomach was so distended I could barely move, but the feast had been worth it. The salmon was melt in the mouth perfection. I expected nothing less from Remus. He always treated his guests well.

"Wonderful. I so enjoy seeing people indulge," Remus said. "And werewolves always have huge appetites."

"In every respect," Nico said quietly.

"What do you mean?" Zandra said.

Nico glanced at Hugh, and they shared a nod.

"We know you want to solve Emron's murder," Hugh said. "But there are some things we can't talk about. Our alphas forbid it."

"Emron wasn't an alpha to either of you," I said. "Have Decker and Leon forbidden you from revealing something about the murder?"

Nico shook his head, but Hugh stayed silent.

"Decker hid something during his interview," I said. "He's a lousy liar."

"That's because he values honesty above everything else. Don't try to get the information out of me, though. I literally can't speak about it," Hugh said. "But it has nothing to do with his guilt. I know he didn't do it."

"What can you talk about?" Zandra said. "Things look bad for Decker. We need to find something to help him if he's innocent."

The werewolves were silent.

"We can talk about what we thought of Emron," Nico finally said.

"That could help," I said. "I've heard he had an ego."

"He did. But then, he was a werewolf. Although many respected him, neither of us liked his methods," Hugh said.

"What methods are you talking about?" I wasn't forgetting Hugh had a secret Decker ordered him to keep, but I'd figure out another way to get it, since he'd been alphaed into silence.

Hugh caught hold of Valerie's hand. "Emron curried favor with other werewolves by offering them his girlfriends."

Zandra grimaced while Remus shook his head.

"It's an old tradition Emron liked to use," Nico said. "Werewolves have big appetites for food, fighting, and... bedroom fun. And there are so few female werewolves that match their energy, so when one is interested, they take advantage. It's all consensual."

"Or they've been brain-washed into thinking it's not a problem," Remus said.

Hugh and Nico looked away.

Valerie nodded but then took more chicken wings and focused on them.

"Apart from Katrine," Hugh said. "She was always willing to be a part of Emron's negotiations. She enjoyed baiting men against each other. She'd get with one and compare him to someone else she'd been with."

"Werewolf egos would have hated that," Zandra said.

"The fights got ugly," Nico said.

"This is like a soap opera. Please, continue," Remus said. "This is the female I saw you with earlier? The angry one with the expensive taste in footwear?"

Hugh nodded. "She was involved with Emron for years. She even helped him rise through the ranks. Although I don't know for certain, she may even have suggested he be a part of this negotiation."

"Why?" I said. "To get access to the alphas?"

"Most likely for the accolade. When Emron shone, so did Katrine. He'd have become a legend if he repaired the feud between our packs."

There was a lull as we digested this information.

"Sometimes, female werewolves act like they're happy to do something, but it doesn't mean they are. Maybe Katrine isn't so different." Although Valerie's voice was quiet, her tone was firm.

Hugh patted her shoulder, regret on his face. "Of course. Sorry. The accolade comment was dumb. I wasn't thinking. But I know Katrine. It's how she operates."

Valerie didn't seem happy with that response as she picked the last strands of chicken from the bones.

"You said Katrine is pregnant with Decker's pup," I said. "Have they been involved for long?"

"Five seconds, if that. Decker has other... attachments. That's all I can say." Hugh moved his jaw from side to side as if it hurt to speak. "Katrine offered herself to Decker all the time, but he refused her. One night, he'd been drinking, and Katrine was persistent. He'd been having trouble with his other... attachment, and I reckon he had a weak moment."

"That's all it takes. Or at least, so I hear." Remus grinned over the top of his glass.

Hugh nodded. "True. Katrine is now claiming the pup is Decker's."

"That's the reason she wants to see Leon?" I said.

"She's offering Leon her pup in exchange for everything she desires."

"Oh, this is too much," Remus said. "I should write this down. It would make an incredible movie script."

"Remus, you're not helping," Zandra muttered.

Hugh frowned at him. "Leon will get Decker's pup to raise as his own."

I swallowed my revulsion. "When Decker finds out, and he will because Leon won't be able to resist telling him, it'll send him insane."

"It would cause a war," Zandra said. "Possibly the war to end all werewolves."

"And drag other supernaturals into the mess as well." Remus no longer smiled as he saw the seriousness of this situation. "Decker won't allow his pup to be raised by another werewolf. Werewolves are insanely protective of their offspring."

"It would be a nightmare, but that's what Katrine wants. She gets a thrill out of men fighting over her. Imagine how she'd be if she started the next werewolf war," Nico said. "And since she's the pup's birthmother, she'd be untouchable. She'd become even worse. Katrine delights in hurting people and ruining what they have."

"Has she always been like that?" Zandra said.

"Since I've known her," Hugh said. "Katrine always goes to our elite parties and events. Decker gets invites to most of them and always takes his pack, so we've seen her in action."

"She's not a full werewolf, though," I said. "How did she get so much power over the werewolves?"

"She's a hybrid of werewolf and coyote, mixed in with something deeply creepy. And she's got power because she knows who to be seen with. Emron included. Katrine knows the value of connections."

"And she's stunningly beautiful," Remus said. "That plays to her favor."

"Although she's not a full werewolf, she behaves like she is. Emron recognized her ambition and connections and knew they'd be suited," Hugh said. "He considered her an asset, despite her terrible behavior and sense of entitlement. And now the pup..."

"They sound like terrible people," Remus said. "Vampires would never behave so badly."

I was tempted to give him a short history of all the gruesome things vampires had done over the centuries, but Remus wasn't oblivious to the truth, even if he didn't like to study it too closely.

Nico opened his mouth but said nothing.

"Go on," I encouraged. "What you say between these walls goes no further. It'll never get back to Leon."

Nico sighed. "I thought Emron was a douche."

"He was," Hugh said. "I didn't trust him."

"Why not?" Zandra said.

"He always made out he was doing the best for others, but he didn't fool me. As a bottom of the pack werewolf, I could slip in and out of situations unseen, but I paid attention when I did. Emron always worked a situation so it benefited him. Just like with Katrine, he cared nothing for her, only what she got from pillow talk with other werewolves."

"Although she used him right back," Nico said.

"Did Decker find out Katrine used him to get pregnant?" Zandra said. "Was that her plan? He'd be angry about being tricked. Angry enough to kill Emron if he thought he was in on the scheme."

"Decker wouldn't do that," Hugh said. "That never happened. He has no clue Katrine is pregnant."

I sat up straight. "The pregnancy could be a happy bonus. One Katrine will exploit. But what if there's more to this?"

"What are you thinking, Juno?" Zandra said.

"What if the evidence at the murder scene was planted, just like Decker suggested? I doubt Katrine is placid in the bedroom, so it would have been easy for her to draw blood and get some of Decker's fur during a heated moment. What if she got what she needed, whether working alone or with Emron, and framed Decker?"

The werewolves exchanged a look.

"Would that be possible?" I said.

Nico nodded, although Hugh's gaze remained fixed to the ground as he clasped his sister's hand.

"She's devious enough to try. But why frame Decker?" Nico said.

I looked at Zandra. "That's what we need to find out."

Chapter 12

Ginger tea and sympathy

I wandered along beside Zandra, breathing in the pleasant early morning air the next day and wondering how soon it was acceptable to request a second breakfast.

After making inquiries to discover where Katrine was staying, I hadn't been surprised to learn she wasn't sleeping in a tent. From her designer clothing to her expensive manicure, she was high maintenance, and even a fancy marquee style tent like Emron had used wouldn't have been suitable for her.

We'd tracked her to the recently opened hotel, the Sleepy Stardust Sanctuary, run by Lizzie Briar. It had been late when we'd learned where Katrine was staying, so we decided to continue the investigation this morning.

Zandra drew in a breath. "I'm still unsure about Katrine's motive for framing Decker. Why not use her pregnancy as leverage to get whatever she wanted from him? Decker's wealthy, and werewolves do anything for their offspring. He'd have offered her the world."

"Perhaps the pup isn't his," I said. "Katrine was in a relationship with Emron, only managed to get into Decker's bed once, and by all accounts, she enjoyed the company of other werewolves, too. No judgment. Just stating the facts."

"Would she take a risk and lie about who the father is? Decker will know the pup isn't his once it arrives." Zandra took a sip from her thermos coffee mug. "I wish she didn't have such a great alibi. She's got a good motive for wanting Emron gone. I expect he didn't mind her getting it on with other werewolves so long as it benefited him, but this pup changes everything and puts her in a position of power. He'd have hated that. They could have argued about it."

"I didn't know him well, but he was clearly a werewolf who loved being considered one of the best."

Zandra kicked a stone along the ground. "Katrine may not be the killer, but she had an opportunity to plant the evidence since she discovered Emron's body."

"Not impossible but unlikely. It suggests she knew Emron was about to be killed," I said. "And she'd have needed the evidence on her and to be certain Emron was dead by the time she returned from her doctor's appointment."

"So Katrine's working with someone else," Zandra said. "She must have loads of werewolves wrapped around her little finger. And with a pup on board, she's a valuable commodity. What's to say there isn't another werewolf lurking and watching what's going on?"

"If that's true, our suspect list will become longer and deadlier. Let's start with Katrine and see what she has to say."

We arrived at the Sleepy Stardust Sanctuary and walked through a set of open doors and into a jasmine-scented oasis of cream and white with an accent hint of pale blue.

Lizzie Briar greeted us with a smile. She was a petite half-elf, with adorable pointed ears and short green hair that she spiked into points. She was even newer to Crimson Cove than we were but always had a sunny smile and a warm greeting if ever our paths crossed. "Good morning. Do you need a room?"

"We'd like to speak to one of your guests. Katrine Nominski," Zandra said.

Lizzie tensed, and the sunny smile dipped behind a cloud. "Are you two friends?"

"No, definitely not friends. We're working with Angel Force on the investigation into the werewolf murder. I expect you've heard about it," I said.

"Oh, sure. Who hasn't? What a horrible business." Lizzie tidied the information brochures in front of her.

"Katrine was connected to the victim. We have a few questions for her. Mind if we go up to her room?" Zandra said.

"Sure. You're braver than me if you do. Since Katrine checked in, she's been demanding. Different pillows, a new feather duvet. She didn't like the breakfast, the water wasn't hot enough, then it was too hot. I've been bending over backward to accommodate her. I'll be glad when she checks out."

"She'll be gone soon," I said. "Especially if we discover she's involved in Emron's murder."

Lizzie's mouth dropped open, and Zandra cast a warning look in my direction.

I made no apologies. Katrine was a nuisance, and everyone wanted her gone. "Which room is she in?"

Lizzie snapped her mouth shut. "Up the stairs, turn right, and it's room eight. Best of luck."

We headed up the stairs, and as we approached the hotel room, a sour smell reached my booping snooter.

Zandra knocked on the door. "Katrine. It's Zandra Crypt and Juno. We've got questions for you."

There was no reply, although the unpleasant smell remained. I pressed my booping snooter to the gap below the door. A weak retching sound reached my ears. "She's here but otherwise occupied. I suggest a gentle unlock spell to get us in and see if we can be of assistance."

"You sure? We know how difficult she can be."

"I expect she'll appreciate the company, given her current situation. We're about to find Katrine looking less elegant than usual."

Zandra tilted her head and raised her eyebrows as she spun out a spell. The door clicked open, and she pushed it.

The sour smell intensified, and Zandra covered her nose and mouth with one hand. "Morning sickness?"

"Let's head to the bathroom, see if she needs anything."

We had no trouble locating the bathroom, since the retching sounds continued.

Zandra tapped on the door. "Hey, Katrine. Do you need anything?"

"Go away. I didn't order room service." She retched again. "Urgh! Make this stop."

"We're not room service," I said. "We're here to talk to you about Emron."

She groaned. "Leave."

"Do you need some water?" Zandra looked down at me. "What helps morning sickness go away?"

"Not getting pregnant from a one-night stand."

"Not helping."

"Ginger worked for me."

Zandra's eyebrows shot up. "Huh! You've had kittens? Do you still see them?"

"Um... not sickness from morning sickness. I meant the general feeling of nausea. Ginger snap cookies or crystallized ginger. Even ginger tea is acceptable." That was a landmine I'd almost stepped on and detonated chaos around me.

"Oh, sure." Zandra stepped away from the bathroom and looked around the bedroom. "There's no ginger anything in here."

"Mints?"

"Hang on. I might have something." She came back with a packet of mints. "Katrine, try one of these. They'll help you feel better."

"Why are you still here? I'm sick."

Zandra posted the mints through a gap in the door. After a second, they were grabbed out of her fingers. "We need to talk about Emron. It's important to the investigation. When you're feeling better, come out and we can work through our questions."

There was silence for a moment. "Who are you again?"

"Greetings. I'm Juno, and my wonderful witch is Zandra."

The door opened wider. Katrine sat by the toilet bowl, her legs out in front of her. Her skin was gray as she sucked on a mint. "Never get pregnant. It's the worst feeling in the world."

Zandra shrugged. "Thanks for the advice. About Emron—"

"You're not angels."

"Animal control," Zandra said. "We're working with Angel Force because this case involves werewolves."

Katrine waved a hand in the air then pushed another mint into her mouth. "I'd never have gotten knocked up if I'd known it would be this bad." She pressed a hand against her stomach.

"It'll be worth it," I said. "The werewolves will celebrate a new pup coming into the world."

"That's the plan." Katrine slowly got to her feet. She flushed the toilet, splashed water on her face and the back of her neck, and ate another mint. "Make this quick. I'm going back to bed."

"We're sorry for your loss." Zandra stepped aside to let Katrine into the bedroom.

"My loss?"

"Emron. You were together for a long time. Given your condition, it would have been nice to have him around to support you."

Katrine shuffled onto the bed and rested back on her pillows. "I've been around werewolves all my life, so I'm used to violence and death." Her gaze flickered over us. "It was kind of a shock the way Emron was killed. I kicked his head when I walked into the tent. It was lying by the door. Messed up my favorite pair of heels. Nasty."

"That must have been stressful," I said as levelly as I could. Trust this conniving creature to be more concerned with the loss of a pair of designer heels than her long-time squeeze. "You need to avoid stress while pregnant. It's bad for the pup."

"Werewolves and stress go together like peanut butter and jelly." Katrine pressed a hand to her stomach again. "Even the thought of food turns me green." She sank lower onto the bed.

"I suppose you'll stay with Emron's family?" I said after a quick glance at Zandra, who looked like she wanted to bring up her breakfast after learning about the head kicking incident. "They'll help you with the pup."

A small smile played across Katrine's lips. "Something like that. Although, as I'm sure you're aware, my relationship with Emron wasn't typical."

"You were romantically involved, though?" Zandra said.

"To begin with. I enjoyed his company, but I loved his position more. Well, his potential. He wasn't top negotiator with the werewolves when we met, but

I saw the werewolf he could become, so I made it happen. He got to the top because of me."

"It was more of a business arrangement?" I said.

"It evolved, so I guess you could call it that. I made Emron look incredible by being on his arm, and I used my unique charms to ensure he had valuable information, so his position was secure. It worked for both of us."

"How long had your relationship been like that?"

She quirked an eyebrow. "You want to know if I was still sleeping with Emron? You have doubts this pup is his?"

"From what we've heard, it definitely isn't his," Zandra said. "You're saying it's Decker's."

Katrine shrugged. "I'm not hiding that information. I wish I'd never bothered with Decker, though. I should have picked an easier target. Still, what woman doesn't love a challenge?"

"Why is that?" I said. "Decker didn't like you?"

She sighed and adjusted the bed covering. "Well, for one thing, the idiot is about to be charged with murder. He also denies sleeping with me when it absolutely happened. Maybe he had a few too many to drink, but no one forgets a night with me. And he's uptight. Decker never kicks back and has fun. It was no big deal, us being together, but he made out like it was disgusting and he was ashamed. It's a badge of honor to be seen with me. A gold star if you get to share my bed."

"So, you wanted to teach him a lesson?" I said. "Is that why you're in negotiations with Leon to hand over the pup to him?"

Katrine scowled at me. "Since you already know the answers, why bother coming here? Go bother someone whose stomach isn't kicking itself to death."

"We need to know how far you'd go to teach Decker a lesson." Zandra crossed her arms over her chest.

"Far enough. And it's no less than he deserves. He could have had me. Me! I'd have given him everything. I have money, influence, and connections. But he turned me down. For what?"

"To keep his dignity intact and not worry about finding a silver knife in his back when you got angry. Does Decker know you're saying the pup is his?" I said.

She flashed her shiny teeth at me. "As far as I'm aware, he doesn't know. And his werewolves aren't able to see him, so unless the angels have blabbed, Decker knows nothing."

"But you want him to know you'll sell his pup like it's the latest business to float on the stock market," I said. "Why? To get a reaction?"

"Maybe. It would be fun to watch the fallout."

"If you call war fun."

Katrine shrugged again. "It won't happen. Not now he's locked up. He's powerless and therefore worthless."

"Since Decker rejected you, you wanted revenge," Zandra said.

"What female with an ounce of common sense wouldn't want that? No one uses me and then makes out like nothing happened."

"Maybe you got that revenge by framing Decker for Emron's murder," I said.

Katrine's mouth dropped open, and her gray skin turned white. "How would I have done that?"

"You got the evidence you needed to plant during your conception encounter."

She shook her head vigorously. "It would have been dumb to take Decker out of the equation when I was working on the deal of a lifetime. You're wasting my time if that's your line of thinking. Are you sure you work with the angels? You're not some dumb reporter looking for an angle? If you are, which paper do you work for? I don't give information for free."

"We're not journalists," I said. "You won't get any money out of us. This is all about your petty need for revenge against the one werewolf you couldn't have, despite using all your charms to win him over. It doesn't feel good to be turned down by someone you want, does it?"

Katrine sucked on another mint. "It's so rarely happens that it was a shock. I still didn't frame Decker for Emron's murder."

I glanced at Zandra. Katrine had been stunned by our theory. If she'd been involved with framing Decker, she'd be much smugger and wouldn't be able to resist dropping hints at how incredible she was.

Zandra half-shrugged and flashed up her eyebrows.

Katrine settled her hands on her stomach. "For all my problems with Decker, and the fact I'll never forgive him for rejecting me, he insisted on doing right by his werewolves. And he wanted the negotiations to succeed. He had no reason to make them fail, and that's what happened when Emron was murdered."

I tilted my head back. Interesting. Would Katrine support Decker's innocence if she'd framed him? Or was this a trick in her purse of treachery?

Doubt flickered through me. Were we looking at this the wrong way? There was no mystery to solve. Decker hadn't been framed, he'd just made a grievous error that had changed the course of his pack's future forever.

"If it wasn't you—"

"It definitely wasn't me. I didn't kill Emron, and I didn't plant evidence," Katrine said. "I know my alibi's been checked. You've got nothing on me."

I raised a paw. "Let me finish. If it wasn't you, and Decker is protesting his innocence, who do you think murdered Emron?"

She took a slow inhalation, and a devious smile crossed her face. "Have you spoken to Emron's wife? That sour-faced old hag has wanted him dead for years."

Chapter 13

First date nerves

After getting details from Katrine about where we'd find Emron's wife, Grace, we left the hotel and headed to work.

As much as I wanted to resolve this murder and get back to the important tasks of matchmaking my witch, making sure her ghoul mother behaved, and spending time with Sammy over a fish supper, duty called. And animals in need were waiting.

We'd been so busy all day doing home checks and patrolling an area looking for a misbehaving tulip-nosed musk rat, I'd barely had time to consider Emron's murder. But it lingered at the back of my mind. Every time we questioned a suspect, a new layer of complexity was added.

Was that the problem? We were looking for complexity where there was none. The evidence pointed to Decker as the killer. Some suggested he'd lost his edge and was getting lazy. Maybe he didn't want to be an alpha anymore but was unable to step down. By killing Emron, he ended the negotiations, his reign as alpha, and got what he wished for. Well, maybe not exactly. After all, he'd spend his life in jail. That was if he was fortunate and the Wolf Council looked kindly on his actions. They often prescribed death when murder was committed.

Zandra leaned back in the driver's seat of the van, pulled out her mobile snow globe and checked it. "Still no word from Finn. I figured he'd respond after our chat with Katrine. And I was hoping we could see Grace after work. I'm done with this werewolf business, but until this murder is cleared up, neither pack is going anywhere."

"Which means limited access to the fine food in Crimson Cove. That's unacceptable. It'll be good to have the place back to its usual peaceful self. Well, peaceful-ish."

"And I'm neglecting Adrienne and Joel. I'm either busy with the werewolves or busy with work. There never seems time for much else. I don't want her thinking I'm unhappy she's back."

"Your mother understands. And she's happy setting up home with Joel on Cannibal Bill's land. She's volunteering at Finn's sanctuary, too, and they've been helping Cannibal Bill build outdoor pens for his free roaming food. Adrienne's too busy to miss you."

"I want to keep an eye on her, though. You know, make sure the ghoul thing doesn't get too intense. And I'm still figuring out what relationship we now have. It's never been simple between us."

"I know. But Adrienne is doing well. If it weren't for the deathly pallor and slight shamble to her step, you wouldn't know she was a ghoul. Joel, not so much. Adrienne really is something else."

"Yeah, don't I know it." Zandra checked her mobile globe again.

I hopped onto her shoulder from my comfy passenger seat. "Is something else worrying you?"

"Who said I'm worried?" Zandra stared at the globe and shook it.

"Our bond. What aren't you telling me?"

"It's nothing."

"It's definitely something. I've been watching you this afternoon. You've been tugging on your hair, muttering to yourself, and pacing whenever we've had a spare moment. You're not worried about this murder, are you? We'll figure out what happened to Emron."

She set down her mobile globe. "It's not that. Although, I still have no clue who killed Emron. And I definitely want the werewolves gone. It's just... Randal sent me a message earlier today."

"Has he got more tech he wants to show off?" Ever since Randal started the system upgrade at animal control, he'd found reasons to show Zandra his latest bit of technology. It was an odd flirting method, but it worked on my wonderful witch.

Zandra picked up her globe again. "He's asked me out for dinner tonight."

I was so surprised, I almost fell off her shoulder. "I knew you two liked each other. I sensed it the first time you met. Of course, he'd instantly fall in love with you, but I wasn't sure what you felt for him. How do you feel? Do you like him? Could there be a future for you as a couple? And what about—"

"Relax! This is the reason I've said nothing to you. Besides, it's more of a friend date than anything else."

"A friend date? Is that how he described it when he messaged you? He wants to take you out as a friend?"

"Well, no. Not exactly that."

"Let me see the message."

"It's private!"

"It's bothering you. And I know what you're like. You read into things. The message. Now."

Zandra grumbled under her breath as she opened the message for me to read.

Hey, Zandra. I expect you're busy tonight, but if you're not and you want to, how about dinner? It would be great to catch up outside of work. What do you think? Randal x.

"I don't see the word friend in any of that," I said. "It's a date."

"Is it?" She stared at the message. "I mean, I like him. He's funny and smart. But I'm so busy. I don't have time to date."

"You absolutely do. And you must. Now, what will you wear? Of course, you need to go home, shower, wash your hair, maybe a slinky red number?"

"No! No slinky anything numbers. This is a casual burgers and beer date."

"Burgers and beer on a first date." I shook my head. "You can do better than that."

"We're going to the bar next to Torrin's workshop. We want to keep it casual. Nothing intense. No expensive dinners or romantic walks. We're testing the water. See if this is something we want."

"Do you have doubts about Randal? Is it something he said? Turn him down if you don't want to date him." My mind worked on overdrive, mentally pulling through Zandra's limited closet to see if there was anything suitable she could wear for this casual sort of date with a friend who might want to be more than a friend. When did dating get so difficult?

"Nothing he's done has made me doubt him. It's more that I'm not sure I'm ready."

"Is it because you still have feelings for Finn and Torrin?"

"Juno! You were the one pushing me toward them. I like those guys, even though they can be jerks and they hide things from me when they shouldn't, but I was never into them like that. I've only ever seen them as friends."

I considered her words. "So, we focus on Randal."

"How about I focus on Randal, and you focus on your own relationship? How are things with Sammy?" Zandra slid out of the van, locked it, and strolled away from animal control with me still on her shoulder.

"We're as perfect as we can be. How about we double date? I'll bring Sammy, so we can keep an eye on things."

"What do you want to keep an eye on? It's burgers and beer, not moonlit serenades and inappropriate declarations."

"I want to make sure things go smoothly." As wonderful as my witch was, her dating experience was limited. She'd avoided the awkward teenage years of intense dating and falling in love with the first person she lusted after. And as uncomfortable as those formative years could be, they were important. I wanted to make sure Zandra got things right and found happiness without being messed around by a loser.

"It'll be smooth," Zandra said. "Well, maybe not smooth. I get tongue-tied around Randal."

"And he stutters every time you look at him. It's a match made in heaven. I'm surprised I never noticed before."

"Because you were too busy setting me up with Finn and Torrin."

I sniffed. "Perhaps. You'll barely notice we're there. We can sit at a separate table. Close enough to listen to the conversation, of course. I don't want there to be awkward silences."

Zandra huffed out a breath. "You can join us. But no poking your nose in and messing this up for me. I like Randal. He's different from other guys I've dated. I want that. Someone stable."

"My booping snooter will stay firmly fixed on my food." Although there'd be plenty of sideways glances to ensure things went well and I didn't need to offer handy conversation starters. "Now, what will you wear?"

An hour later, we were at the bar. Randal was late.

I bit my tongue so as not to criticize, but I loathed tardiness. It suggested a selfish nature. If a person made you wait for them, it showed they considered your time less important than theirs.

My gaze drifted over Zandra's outfit. I'd convinced her to wear black jeans and a black tank top with a few sparkly shimmers on it. It was clean and understated. That was the best I could hope for from my witch. Her fashion eye had been gouged out and replaced with a desire for practicality and to wear things that never needed pressing.

I'd had a quick groom to ensure my fur was pristine, contacted Sammy, and was thrilled he was sitting beside me as we waited for Zandra's late date to show, so I could give him a piece of my mind about keeping my witch waiting.

Zandra checked the time again. "Five more minutes and I'm grabbing takeout and we're going home."

I made reassuring grumbles as I rested my paw on her leg.

The main door was shoved open, and Randal stumbled in. He looked around, saw us, and dashed over. He stank of smoke, and his hair was crispy at the ends. There were also several burn holes in his superhero emblazoned T-shirt.

Zandra jumped from her seat. "What happened to you?"

Randal looked at his clothing and brushed flakes of soot off his dusty jeans. "Sorry I'm so late. I was about to leave when there was a power outage. I checked the systems and discovered a group of non-magicals had wandered into my wards. I'd set up equipment to monitor the new uploads on the edge of Crimson Cove. I don't know how they did it, but they blundered through the wards and messed with the equipment."

"That's awful." There was a smile on Zandra's face. "I figured you'd stood me up."

"No! And I got here as quickly as I could. I had everything planned, but I ran out of time. I had to get the non-magicals out of the way, fix the wards and equipment, and set up new spells they wouldn't break through." Randal snagged his fingers in his burned hair and winced. "In my hurry to get it all done, I stuck my hand on something I shouldn't. This is the result."

"It's a unique look," I said. "Zandra won't forget this first date."

Randal's cheeks flushed. "I made a mess of things. And I left behind the flowers I'd gotten you."

He went up in my estimations, and his lateness was forgiven. After all, he'd been saving Crimson Cove from pesky non-magicals and gotten my witch a gift. And although she wasn't a flowers kind of person, the intention was well meant.

"How about we order?" Zandra eased back into her seat. "You can tell me all about it. It sounds like an eventful day."

"It wasn't the afternoon I had planned. Sorry, again. I didn't want you to think I'd forgotten you. That would never happen. I was looking forward to tonight." Randal pulled out a chair and dropped into it. "And I'm starving. I used a battleship's worth of magic getting everything fixed quickly so I could get here fast."

"Let's grab drinks and check out the menu." All Zandra's tension had disappeared, and she was still smiling. She was pleased to have Randal here, despite the curious looks his singed appearance gathered.

"Perhaps we should leave you to it?" I was prepared to leave the lovebirds to get to know each other. Although, I wouldn't be far away.

Randal shook his head. "You're fine here. Although you might get bored with our chat about wards and magic." He reached over and tickled Sammy under the chin. "Unless you have a romantic evening planned for your lady."

Sammy purred and leaned against his hand. "No romance planned." He glanced my way. "Unless you want some."

"I'm happy to have a romance-less date if you are." I smoothed a paw down Sammy's side to show I was teasing.

Again, Randal zoomed up in my estimations, since he was happy for me to be around. Which I always was. And he liked Sammy, which gave him bonus points. This tech mage was proving appealing.

The main door to the bar opened again, and my happy mood faded as a group of non-magicals wandered in. The place went silent as they headed to the bar and ordered drinks. Not that they noticed they were under scrutiny by a room full of people who could kill them with the flick of a wrist.

"What are they doing here?" Randal whispered. "Everywhere I go, there are more non-magicals creeping through the cracks. And they're not affected by the magic. I've seen that same group around for days."

"I don't get it." Zandra watched them lounging by the bar. "They shouldn't be able to wander in and out of places. Finn said some of the non-magicals have seen the angels' wings."

"No way! This is serious. There must be a problem with the magic in Crimson Cove if they can see our true forms. Most of us pass for pretty normal, but angels, pixies, elves, changed werewolves, they'd struggle. What's going on?"

"Hey, guys. What'll it be?" A friendly-faced waitress stopped at our table.

"I'll have the witch's brew," Zandra said, "and a double cheeseburger with a side order of curly paprika fries. A salmon burger for you, Juno?"

"Make that two," I said with a nod to Sammy.

"What's witch's brew?" Randal peered at the menu.

"It's the local ale," Zandra said. "It's good. It's got a kick. Tastes of honey, so be careful to pace yourself."

"I'll have that, too," Randal said, "and the enchiladas with a side order of roasted squash."

"Coming right up." The waitress headed away and put the food order in.

"I didn't know you guys were coming here tonight." Torrin strode over, a half-empty glass of beer in his hand and a lazy smile on his face.

I shook my head at him, hoping he'd get the hint now was a bad time for a chat, but he ignored me, his gaze roaming from Randal to Zandra.

"Oh, yeah. You know, just catching up," Zandra said.

"Fun! I'm unwinding after work." Torrin gestured over his shoulder at the workshop he had next door. "It's all go. Someone always needs something fixing. I shouldn't complain. It keeps me busy and out of trouble."

"I expect it does," Zandra said slowly. "Perhaps we can catch up another time, though."

"Don't mind talking shop in front of me. I've been hearing all about that dead werewolf. Are you working on that with Finn?" Torrin set his glass on the table.

"We are. We're off duty at the moment, though," I said.

Torrin shook his head. "I can tell the werewolves are anxious. It's making my dragon side itchy. All that testosterone and repressed killing urge in the air is bad for me. You close to figuring it out?"

"Getting there," Zandra said. "I'll swing by your workshop another time, and we can talk about it. Just not right now."

Torrin's gaze went from Zandra and then to Randal. He scratched his chin. "Oh! My bad. Is this a date?"

"Got it in one," I said. "Now if you don't mind..."

"Really? You two are dating?" He waggled his finger between Zandra and Randal. "Weird. I don't see it."

"You should try," I said. "Over by the bar, far away from our double date."

Torrin moved from scratching his chin to the back of his neck. "You two are official? How did I miss this happening?"

Randal cleared his throat. "This is our first date."

"Crud! I'm a jerk. I had no clue. Interesting." Torrin picked up his glass and took a swig.

"It would be even more interesting over by the bar," I said.

"Yeah, sure." Torrin stared at Randal for a second. "Huh! Didn't see this coming. I'll leave you to it. Enjoy your evening." He wandered away but glanced over his shoulder several times and shook his head.

Sammy looked at me and winced.

I mirrored his gesture.

After a long silence, Randal pulled back his shoulders. "So, where were we?"

"Wondering why the non-magicals are hanging around Crimson Cove." Zandra tugged on the ends of her hair.

"Yes! Right. It's a puzzle."

"Yep."

The silence descended again.

I slipped off my seat, and Sammy joined me on the floor.

"I want this date to go well. Zandra likes Randal. We need to make sure there is no more interference," I whispered.

"Sure. How can I help?" Sammy said.

"You head off anyone who tries to bother Zandra. I'll give her prompts for useful topics of conversation. They're lost, and I don't want Randal to get away if Zandra wants him as her mate."

"Should I use magic to block people? You know my power can be twitchy when I'm nervous."

"Whatever means necessary to keep the pests away and stop this date from being ruined."

Footsteps approached, and I tensed, but it was the waitress with our food and drinks. That was an acceptable intrusion.

"Hey! I didn't expect to see you two in here."

My head shot around, and I recognized Finn's boots. I wriggled out from underneath the table. "Greetings, Finn. I figured you'd still be working on the murder case. Solved it already?"

He huffed a laugh through his nose. "Not a chance. I just stopped by to grab food. I'm glad I saw you, Zandra."

"If this is about the murder, we can pick it up tomorrow." Zandra nodded at Randal.

"Sorry, but this can't wait. Not since your message helped me out." He grinned at Randal. "I hope I'm not intruding."

"You are," I said. "We were about to enjoy a delicious meal. And this is a double date." If I spelled things out in simple language using no more than two syllables, Finn would understand he needed to be somewhere else.

"Oh! Sure. And that makes me feel bad." He grabbed a spare chair from an empty table and straddled it. "The thing is, I've been doing some digging into Emron's wife, and you're onto something. I hoped you and Juno could come with me to interview her."

Zandra's eyebrows shot up. "When?"

"Now. Grace is available this evening, and she said she wanted to get things sorted quickly."

Zandra looked at her untouched food and then at Randal. "This evening is jinxed."

He nodded. "It feels that way."

Finn shrugged. "Murder suspects don't wait around. I could go alone, but I'd appreciate expertise from animal control. I could try Barney—"

"No! Barney's stressed enough as it is," Zandra said.

"How about Glenda?" I said. "Being a werewolf, she wouldn't blunder into any difficult situations with Grace. And she's been acting as a neutral liaison for the packs during the interviews."

"Glenda's had a few run-ins with Grace, so bad idea." Finn's expression was full of apology. "I'm sorry about ruining your date, but the werewolves don't play nice, so we can't wait around. They're all getting agitated the longer they stay in Crimson Cove."

"And agitated means bloodshed for werewolves." Zandra pushed back her chair. "Sorry, Randal. Another time?"

Randal nodded, and although he was smiling, there was disappointment in his eyes. "Of course. Whenever you like. You know where I am."

Finn clapped his hands together. "Excellent. Let's go see what the scorned wife has to say about beheading her cheating hubby."

Chapter 14

A werewolf scorned

Finn was driving an official Angel Force vehicle. Unsurprisingly, it was white. Zandra was in the passenger seat, which left the back seat free for me and Sammy.

I snuggled close to him, trying not to be morose about the delicious food we'd left at the restaurant. We should have gotten it packed for eating on the road. Although that would have been an even bigger snub for Randal, to take the food and leave him with nothing.

"Do you think Finn is jealous of Randal?" Sammy whispered in my ear.

"Why wouldn't he be? Zandra is wonderful, and she wasn't on a date with him." I licked Sammy's cheek.

"He must still have a crush on her."

"Of course he does. But I can't let that get in the way of my witch's happily ever after with Randal. They were just getting to know each other when Torrin blundered over and insulted Randal, and then Finn forced werewolf murder on the date."

"You think they're working together to stop Zandra and Randal from becoming an item?"

I paused in my grooming. "I hadn't thought about it. Would they be that devious?"

Finn cleared his throat. "I hate to be accused of being an eavesdropper, but angels have excellent hearing."

Zandra glanced over her shoulder. "What are they talking about?"

I caught Finn's grin in the rearview mirror. "They want to make sure you're happy."

"I'm happy enough." Zandra twisted in her seat. "Don't stir trouble, Juno. Let's focus on the murder."

"I never stir." Maybe I let things gently simmer from time to time to see what would bubble to the surface, but I'd need to watch Finn and Torrin to ensure tonight was bad luck and not a carefully timed sabotage.

"Hey, have you got any cute single friends to fix me up with?" Finn said to Zandra. "Since you're dating Randal, I need to look elsewhere for a girlfriend."

"You considered me girlfriend material?" Zandra choked out a laugh.

"Why not? I like you. You like me. We're both single. Well, I am."

"Uh, sure." Zandra's bottom lip jutted out. "Vorana and Sorcha are single."

"Yeah, but they're my friends. I don't see them in a romantic light. Not that they aren't gorgeous and fun to be around, but you know what it's like. Once you've been friend zoned, there's no going back." He waggled his eyebrows, giving me a wink.

"I'll give it some thought," she said. "Do you have a type?"

"Smart, determined, funny, hard-working, preferably brunette." He caught my gaze in the rearview mirror again. I had yet to decide if Finn was teasing.

"So, how will we handle this interview?" Zandra said. "Did you dig up any dirt on Grace?"

"She's squeaky clean. Grace comes from a long, ancient line of werewolves. Her family established the Golden Pentacle pack almost a thousand years ago. She even had a great grandfather who served as overlord alpha for a time."

"I've heard of them," Sammy said. "They're one of the most long-lived and successful packs around."

"You got it," Finn said. "Practically royalty. Only a level below the werewolf overlord. Everyone listens when they talk. And all the packs want alliances with them."

"Grace's marriage to Emron was an alliance, wasn't it?" Zandra said.

"It was. She married young, so I doubt she had any choice in the pairing."

"I heard Decker and Leon were interested in matching with Grace."

"Interesting. I didn't know that. You think there are old grudges resurfacing after all this time?"

I shook my head. "Doubtful. After all, this was a marriage of reciprocal convenience. There was no love match made when Emron was chosen to be Grace's mate. Leon and Decker would have wanted Grace for the same reasons."

"For her family connections," Sammy said. "It's sad werewolves rarely marry for love."

"They probably get fewer broken hearts doing it that way," Finn said.

"You sound cynical," Zandra said.

Finn shrugged. "All this relationship stuff gets messy. At least the werewolves know what they're getting themselves into. They have terms and conditions prepared before making an alliance with anyone. It takes away all the hearts and flowers chaos."

"You're definitely cynical." Maybe Finn took losing his chance with Zandra harder than I'd realized. He always wore a jokey exterior and acted like nothing bothered him, but Finn was an angel with layers. Not all of them pure.

"It's also the reason there are so few werewolf pups born," Sammy said. "Not much hanky-panky going on when you don't have an attraction to your mate."

"That's one side-effect," Finn said. "But that's what the werewolves have to do to ensure the packs don't blaze out in a fury fought furry war."

"Did you discover any problems in Grace and Emron's marriage when you dug into her history?" Zandra said.

"Grace's family excels in keeping bad news out of the media. The only things I could find were stories about her charity work, PR puff pieces where she was at social events, and various stories about the privileged position she holds."

"Grace sounds too good to be true." Zandra rolled down the window and let in a welcome blast of fresh air.

"She's an old-school werewolf, and that comes with baggage. She also comes with a heap of social expectations. It must have been drilled into her from an early age that she had to act a certain way, or she risked being ousted from the pack or sold to the highest bidder."

"What kind of family would do that to their daughter?" Sammy said.

"Pack status and standing is everything," Finn said. "If a werewolf steps out of line too many times, they're out. It doesn't matter if they're the daughter of the overlord alpha or the offspring of a bottom pack member. They know the rules. They break them, and they face the consequences."

"I'm glad I'm a familiar." Sammy leaned against me and rumbled out a purr. "Life is so much simpler."

I nuzzled him. If he knew my heritage and what was expected of me, it would blow his fuzzy mind.

Ten minutes later, we arrived at the edge of a private gravel driveway. A sign said: *trespassers will be eaten*.

"That's some greeting," Zandra said. "Should we be worried?"

"We have an invitation, so the risk of being eaten is minimal." Finn chuckled as he steered the vehicle along the gravel driveway.

As we rounded a bend, a huge, white painted log cabin came into view. It wasn't your typical log cabin and stretched over three thousand square feet. Surrounding it was a thick forest of dense fir trees. Perfect territory for werewolves to run free.

Interior lights lit up most of the lower level, and as Finn pulled his vehicle to a stop, the front door opened.

We piled out and walked over to meet an immaculately dressed female with short, dark, salt-and-pepper hair. Her pantsuit looked tailor-made and draped off her slim figure in pale cream waves.

Her intense, dark gaze took in each of us before she spoke. "I'm Grace Laker. Welcome to Pentacle Ridge."

Finn bowed at the waist. "I'm Finn." He stepped forward and held out his hand. "I appreciate you taking the time to see us."

She took his hand and gave it a single shake. "You left me little choice. Although I've already spoken to Angel Force and the Wolf Council. I'm not sure what else I can do for you."

"We have follow-up questions," Finn said. "This is Zandra Crypt and Juno. They work in animal control. And this is Sammy."

"My trusted companion," I said. "Greetings. You have a wonderful home."

"Thank you. Come in. I have refreshments ready." Grace stepped back and opened the door wider, revealing a high-ceilinged entrance hall with vast glass windows.

As we moved through the cabin, it felt like they'd brought the outside in. There were large ferns and potted plants dotted around. The color scheme was different shades of green and brown.

Grace led us into a large lounge with comfy couches arranged so you could look out over the forest. A pitcher of drink and glasses were set on the table.

Once everyone was seated and drinks had been served, Grace settled back in her seat, expectation on her face.

"Do you have someone here you'd like to join us? This must be a difficult time for you," Finn said.

Her gaze remained fixed on him. "Although I appreciate the offer, there's no one else here. I'm used to being alone."

Finn took out a notepad and rested it on one knee. "You were married to Emron for how many years?"

"I married him when I was eighteen. We were paired for forty-two years."

"It was a pairing of convenience, rather than a love match?"

"It was. It was a time of instability for my pack, and we needed to solidify our place in the community. As I'm sure you're aware, two of my brothers fought to get the position of alpha." Grace shook her head as sadness shifted across her face. "They were too young and headstrong to take on such responsibility, but nothing I said would convince them otherwise. The challenge was laid down, and they fought to the death. Isaiah died first, and Saul a few days afterward. His injuries were so bad he couldn't recover. It was a dark time for the pack. After that devastating event, it was decided to forge appropriate alliances to regain stability."

"And Emron was considered the most suitable match for you?" I said.

Grace's gaze flickered to me. "He was. There were various interested parties, but it was believed, with Emron's connections and prospects, he'd offer the most effective joining. We needed someone who could calm the chaos. Emron excelled at that."

"It must be hard to be with someone you're not in love with," Zandra said. "How did you handle it?"

She lifted her chin a fraction. "As I should. Marriage is rarely about love."

Zandra took a sip from her glass. "If you don't mind me asking, were you romantically involved with Emron, or was it purely business?"

Grace's delicate nostrils expanded. "There was a time when we attempted a romantic relationship, but it was because of what we wanted rather than any feelings of desire."

"A pup of your own?" I said.

She nodded. "I was unable to become pregnant. Emron believed I was barren, and therefore, the romance was extinguished. Neither of us were sad about that. It was an act we didn't enjoy performing with each other. Although, I was sad not to have a pup of my own."

I winced. That must have been a burden for Grace to bear. It was always expected females would continue the lineage by providing many pups. To be declared barren and written off by her mate would have been heartbreaking.

"Neither you nor Emron could create werewolves through a bite?" Finn said.

"Emron tried on numerous occasions, and I know I should, but it's such a responsibility. Even though there are always willing candidates, the risk of death is high. Over seventy percent of those bitten don't survive. I wouldn't wish to have those deaths on my conscience."

"That must be difficult for your family to accept," Zandra said.

"They recognized the sacrifice I made by joining with Emron. Thanks to that alliance, we've had no serious skirmishes to resolve. Emron's connections were excellent, and his negotiator powers meant no one wanted to tangle with us." Grace neatly crossed one leg over the other. "He's a loss to our pack."

I tilted my head then nudged Sammy. "Did you hear that?"

He closed his eyes and cocked one ear. "No, what was it?"

A faint thud reached my ears again. "That."

He nodded. "What do you think it is?"

"Something to explore." I stretched and hopped off the couch. "If you'll excuse us, we have business to attend to outside. Cat needs. I'm sure you understand."

Grace gestured to the door leading into the hallway. "Of course. The back door is unlocked."

Sammy followed me out of the room. I stood in the hallway and listened for more noises. There was another gentle thud then soft footsteps.

"Grace said she was on her own. Why did she lie to us?" I headed toward the footsteps.

"Maybe it's someone breaking in." Sammy scurried along, his belly low to the floor. "I was surprised there were no werewolves watching the cabin. You'd think Emron would want to protect his wife."

"The more I learn about Emron, the more of an egotistical scoundrel I realize he was. Numerous affairs, all that smooth talk and false platitudes. And what was the obsession with owning a sword? A werewolf shouldn't need a weapon to defend himself. He's a natural born predator."

"Just like us." Sammy stumbled over his paws.

I turned the corner, and my heart kicked up a gear as someone rounded the bend in front of us.

We broke into a run, chasing after the barefooted individual.

As we dashed around the corner, I slammed into what felt like a brick wall. But there was nothing there. Sammy had bounced off the invisible barrier so hard, he lay on his back, staring at the ceiling.

"What was that?" His words slurred out of him.

A spiral of gray magic swirled around me, and my stomach somersaulted as the air was sucked from my lungs. "It's danger. We need to get out of here." I hurried over and helped Sammy to his feet, my lungs burning.

"Let's go back the way we came."

We turned around but made it only a dozen paw steps before discovering an equally strong barrier in place. Each time I hit it, I bounced off.

Sammy dashed away and scrabbled at the other barrier. "I can't find a way through. We're trapped."

I slammed my front paws on the barrier and shot out a destruction spell. It flooded across the obstruction, but it remained intact. I tried again. Nothing.

I turned to Sammy. "We must combine our strength. It's the only way to blast through this wall of magic."

He staggered toward me, his power flickering around him. "What should we use?"

"A destruction spell. Simple but effective." It was a blunt instrument and damaged anything it touched, but we had no time for discretion. Black dots sparked in my vision. I had only seconds left before I passed out. "Ready?"

Sammy nodded. "I trust you, Juno."

I lowered my barriers, and my magic flooded out. Sammy's power mingled with mine. It smelled faintly of cinnamon and apples. Our magic spiraled together in a charming dance then flared out in an intense blaze of green and gold.

Sammy glanced at me. "You've gotten strong. Different from when we first met."

"Let's see how strong we are when we work together."

We smashed the destruction spell into the barrier. It flickered several times then vanished.

I sucked in much-needed breaths and rested with Sammy for a few seconds. Then we turned, and I was glad to discover the other barrier was also gone. We were free.

We raced along the hallway and came to a door at the end that was open an inch. We slid inside and discovered a vast room full of expensive artwork and treasures gleaming gold in the spotlights.

None of those treasures captured my eye, though. Not when the most interesting object in the room was the butt-naked guy with magic on his fingertips, his teeth bared, and his amber eyes blazing.

Chapter 15

The naked werewolf

The stranger was tall and muscular, with a carpet of dark chest hair and solid thigh muscles. He had a head of shaggy dark hair that came down to his shoulders.

"Werewolf?" Sammy whispered, his magic still flickering over him.

"Smells like one," I said.

The guy snarled, grabbed an engraved potion vial off a mahogany sideboard, and hurled it at us. It slammed into Sammy, and he groaned and slumped to the floor.

Rage hazed my vision red, and I hissed. No one hurt my Sammy and got away with it.

I slammed my paws onto the wooden floor, and a knockback spell rippled out and knocked the guy off his feet. Then I flew through the air and landed on his chest. My murder mittens went to work, slashing at his flesh. Each cut healed almost instantly, which proved he was a werewolf. And a strong one.

He howled as I blasted another knockback spell into him, making his bones rattle. Every time he tried to grab me, I slashed his hands until his arms were red with his own blood.

The guy pushed himself off the floor, but I clung to his chest with my claws buried in his curly hair and hissed in his face. "What have you done to Sammy? If he dies, so do you."

He bared his teeth again and growled.

I punched away one strong hand and hit him with another spell. "Answer me. What was in that potion vial?"

The sound of bones cracking and joints extending told me this werewolf meant business. He'd be harder to fight when he was on four paws and had a set of razor-sharp teeth to snap at me.

I threw out a strong restraining spell to slow him then bit his bicep. The bite wasn't meant to be painful, but it was full of slowdown magic. He'd still be able to shift, but it would be so intensely painful, he'd pass out from the shock.

The werewolf tipped back his head and howled again as his transformation took a terrifying turn. Every bone crack lasted for seconds, and the fur he'd been sprouting vanished.

"What are you?" he wheezed out.

"Your worst nightmare. You hurt my Sammy, so I hurt you."

His gaze flicked to Sammy, who hadn't moved since the potion hit him. "He won't die. It's a disabling potion. Some old antique magic. I didn't even think it would work."

"Liar! He's unconscious and barely breathing. You didn't have to hurt him."

"You were chasing me. What was I supposed to do?" His amber eyes flickered darker, and he heaved out a breath. "What manner of creature are you? I've never felt magic like this."

"That's not important."

His head tilted. "You're ancient. Why hide in such a tiny, fluffy body?"

I dragged my claws slowly down his arm to ensure he had my full attention. "I'm asking the questions."

The werewolf tipped back his head and roared. Idiot. He'd exposed his neck so I could go in for the kill. I bit down, intending to end his life as punishment for what he'd done to Sammy.

My magic was gone! The power that flowed through me was suddenly an icy drop I could barely feel.

He sensed something had changed, and his huge hands wrapped around me and yanked me away from his throat. His eyes gleamed as he realized victory was his.

I hissed and prepared for one final attack. Then I was flying, no longer in the werewolf's painful grip. He was falling back and slamming into a wall, while I twisted and landed nimbly on my paws.

"Juno! What are you doing?" Zandra rushed into the room, holding one hand out to keep the werewolf pinned, while her free hand settled me on her shoulder. "Are you hurt? Did he bite you?"

"Only my pride took a beating. I almost had him."

"It looked like you were trying to kill him. Why?" Her hand ran over me, her fingers probing for injuries.

"Look what he did to Sammy." Rage still flickered through me as I glared at the pinned werewolf.

"Is he alive?" Zandra stared at my fallen companion.

Finn was crouched over Sammy. "He's breathing. I think he'll be okay. What went down in here? Who's the naked guy?"

Grace stood in the doorway, her expression tight as she took in the scene.

Zandra glared at her. "You told us you were alone. Do you know him?"

"It's no concern of yours who I have as a houseguest."

"It is when that houseguest tries to kill us," I said. "His magic is toxic. He trapped me and Sammy in the hallway. We were unable to breathe."

"How did you get out?" Zandra said.

I licked her cheek. "You know me. I'm amazing. And combined with Sammy's power, we were unstoppable. We got free and chased him, but he threw an old potion at Sammy. That's when I attacked."

"Finn, we need to take this guy in. We can't have a dangerous, magic-using werewolf causing chaos," Zandra said.

"No!" Grace dashed into the room and stood in front of the naked werewolf. "He was defending me."

"Who is he to you?" I said. "What right does he have to defend you?"

"He's my brother-in-law. Rhett Laker."

That news jerked me from my rage. "Why is your brother-in-law naked and in a froth of killer intent?"

Sammy groaned, and his eyes flickered open.

I leaped off Zandra's shoulder and joined him on the floor. "Don't move. You've got a nasty potion running through you."

"What happened?" Sammy's gaze was unfocused as his head rocked from side to side.

"The naked werewolf got you."

"That sounds like a cooking show," Finn said.

Sammy's eyes rolled back in his head. "I don't feel good. What did he hit me with?"

"You'll be fine. Finn, stay with him. Keep him conscious. We need to figure out what the potion was."

"I'll be okay. Just so sleepy."

I tapped his cheek. "Don't sleep. That's an order."

Finn laid a hand on Sammy's side, and a gentle wave of his magic rolled over Sammy until his breathing was even and his eyes weren't rolling in his skull. "I'll keep him safe for you."

My appreciation for this half-angel, half-demon grew. Finn was an asset to this group.

I returned to Zandra, who'd been guarding Rhett and Grace while I looked after Sammy. "You were about to tell us why your naked brother-in-law was attacking your guests?"

"Rhett's helping me," Grace said.

"To do what?" Zandra said.

Grace's mouth twisted to the side. "We should return to the lounge. Rhett, join us once you're dressed. Then we can explain everything to our guests."

The rage in his eyes faded as he studied Grace. Then he nodded.

That was a stalling tactic. Grace needed time to figure out a plausible reason Rhett was here. I'd already figured one out but was waiting to hear if she'd be honest.

"I'm not sure it's safe to release Rhett from my spell," Zandra said. "What if he attacks Juno and Sammy again?"

"Or us," Finn said.

"Rhett must have been provoked," Grace said.

"We wouldn't have provoked him if he hadn't been hiding," I said. "He could have spoken to us rather than blasting us with toxic magic."

"I'm sorry about that." Grace clasped her hands together and drew in a slow breath. "There's no need to fight. And after everything that's happened with Emron, I'm done with violence."

Zandra jabbed a finger at Rhett. "Behave."

He growled at her, but an admonishing look from Grace silenced him. "Of course. My apologies."

Finn carried Sammy back into the lounge and settled him on his lap, still flooding him with healing magic.

I watched for a moment, content Sammy was on the mend, even though when I checked, his heartbeat was too fast.

I sat with Zandra, flickers of uneven magic pulsing through me. My reacquired power still had kinks, but working out those kinks when fighting to the death with an angry werewolf was the last thing I should do.

Grace paced the room, refusing to settle until Rhett appeared, thankfully, fully clothed.

After introductions had been made, Rhett's gaze went around the group before it settled on me. He gave me a half-bow. "My apologies again for attacking you and your companion. When you chase a werewolf, we fight back."

"We shouldn't have needed to chase you," I said. "We heard you walking around and came to investigate. We thought Grace had an intruder."

"This is my fault." Grace gestured for Rhett to sit, and then she joined him on the couch.

"No, it's mine. I'd stopped by to run over some business details with Grace when I got distracted. This is a difficult time for her. For both of us," Rhett said.

"You had to do that naked?" I said.

A muscle ticked in his jaw. "Much like you, I thought I heard a noise. I was planning to shift when you disturbed me."

I wrinkled my booping snooter, not convinced by the lie.

"You should ask questions before firing out dangerous magic or flinging potions at innocent supernaturals." Zandra rested a hand on my head.

"And my apologies to you, too. I didn't mean to injure your familiars. He will be well. It was an old vial, used for display. It contained nothing deadly."

Zandra didn't correct him as to Sammy's position in our lives.

"What was in the vial?" I said. "You mentioned a disabling spell."

"It was a sleep potion," Grace said. "My family has connections with a number of supernatural groups. That vial was gifted to my grandmother to help with her insomnia. She passed it on to me so I could keep it here when she visits. Not that she uses it anymore. Your companion won't have any long-term side effects."

Sammy was calmly slumbering on Finn's knee, easing my concern for his well-being.

"I hope not. Or I'll be back."

Rhett nodded. "I'd expect nothing less. You're a formidable fighter."

I accepted his praise with a tail flick. "Before the interruption, we were talking to Grace about Emron. Since you're here, too, you won't mind answering a few questions."

"I've nothing to hide. From what I've heard, the investigation is almost over. They've arrested an alpha wolf, and he's been charged, hasn't he?" Rhett said.

"Not yet. The investigation is proving tricky," I said. "There is evidence to implicate this werewolf, but I have doubts as to its reliability. We're interviewing all suspects again to get a fuller picture of Emron's life and death."

"Do you consider us suspects?" Rhett sat stiff in his seat.

"You must admit, the way Emron conducted himself with other women would give Grace cause to wish him dead," I said.

Rhett growled softly, but Grace placed a restraining hand on his arm. "You're mistaken. Emron was always respectful around me. I assumed he had romantic relationships with other females, but we never spoke about it, and I never looked into it. It would have done me no good. Why be jealous? We didn't love each other."

"You had no interest in who Emron fooled around with?" Zandra said. "Surely, your family would have needed to know, in case he was involved with anyone inappropriate, and she attempted to divide the pack by bonding with him."

"Emron was formally linked to no pack. The closest connection he had was through his marriage to me. That suited him. And my family kept an eye on things. It was of no interest to me." Grace glanced at Rhett. "As we matured, we grew apart. Emron's career blossomed, so he was barely around. It suited us. We were free to pursue other passions."

"And romantic relationships with people of your choosing?" My gaze was on Rhett.

"Don't be disrespectful," Rhett growled out. "This is my sister-in-law. I'll always be around to protect her, even when Emron isn't."

"Grace is a stunning female werewolf. You can't deny that."

Rhett's gaze softened as it settled on Grace. "I don't. But there are boundaries."

"You're seeing what isn't here," Grace said. "And Angel Force has the investigation under control. This will all be over soon."

"And we were aware of Emron and Decker Duke's history," Rhett said. "It's no surprise it ended this way."

"What history?" Zandra said.

Rhett shrugged. "They had an unpleasantly twisted relationship, full of deceit and fighting."

Grace lowered her head but said nothing.

"That's the first we've heard about that," Finn said. "Did you mention their fighting when we collected your statement?"

"I wasn't asked. But when I learned Decker was the prime suspect in the murder, it came as no surprise. I'd be happy to amend my statement if it would speed things up. The sooner this is over, the better."

I didn't believe Rhett. He was saying this to get him and Grace out of the spotlight. Pin Emron's murder on another werewolf and shift the blame from them.

"You must find it hard to cope with the loss of a beloved brother," Finn said, not a trace of sarcasm in his calm, impartial tone.

Rhett looked over Finn's head and out the window behind him. "Half-brother. Naturally, we had our rivalries, but to lose someone in your family is devastating."

The lack of sincerity in those words rang in my ears. "Was Emron your only brother?"

"I have various half-siblings. None of us are close."

"Including you and Emron?"

That same muscle ticked in Rhett's jaw. "We had our trials, but we'd worked together for years on various businesses. He had a way of convincing people to support him."

"Until Emron got what he wanted and abandoned you?" Finn said.

Rhett's gaze cut to the side before he focused on Finn. "My half-brother was always the family charmer. It got him exactly what he wanted. I can hardly begrudge him that."

He did. By the tense set of Rhett's shoulders and the way his hands involuntarily flexed, there was no love lost between Rhett and Emron. Sibling rivalry often ran deep and was as bitter as day-old coffee.

And from Grace's lack of tears, she also didn't miss Emron. It must be a relief to be free from a marriage that gave her so little. To be without love and affection for such a long time was hard to bear.

"When you last spoke to Angel Force, you said you'd taken a step back from Emron's businesses. You didn't mention why that was," Finn said to Rhett.

He shrugged. "Priorities change. I wanted to take things in a different direction. Emron didn't, so we parted ways."

I nodded slowly. Perhaps that hadn't been an involuntary parting. Emron could have forced Rhett out of the business. Or they'd fought and been unable to reconcile. The more I discovered about Emron, the more cutthroat he was.

The mobile snow globe in Finn's pocket buzzed. He checked the caller and stood. "Excuse me. I need to take this."

Finn left the room, Sammy tucked under his arm, leaving us with Rhett and Grace. Although they sat a respectable distance apart, their bodies leaned into each other. There was more to this relationship than they'd let on.

"Would you mind telling me your alibi for the night of Emron's murder?" Zandra said.

Rhett shook his head. "The angels already know."

"It's okay," Grace said. "I appreciate them being thorough. We want Emron's killer charged, after all."

"They've got Decker in custody. This is a waste of time."

Grace gently patted his knee before leaning back. "We were together. I don't have a head for business, so Rhett's been helping me puzzle through Emron's business affairs and the estate. There's so much to deal with. I don't want any mistakes."

"That's decent of him," I said.

"It's what anyone would do."

"You were together that late?" Zandra obviously thought the same thing as me.

"I'm a night owl. And most werewolves work best under the moonlight." Rhett sounded too relaxed.

Finn came back into the room, Sammy resting in his arms with his paws sticking in the air. "I think I've got everything here. Have either of you got more questions?"

"We're done." A glance at Finn revealed he was desperate to say something.

After we'd said our goodbyes and Grace had shown us out, we were back in the vehicle, safe from prying werewolf hearing.

Finn exhaled and dropped his head against the headrest. "We have a problem. Cythera is ready to charge Decker. She believes there's enough evidence to make a conviction stick."

"It's too soon," I said. "There are still suspects to discount. We've just spoken to two of them."

"And they conveniently alibi for each other," Zandra said. "Neither of them are sad Emron's dead, and they're clearly in a relationship."

Finn nodded. "I wondered about that, too."

"What gave it away? Rhett sneaking around naked in Grace's house?" I said.

"Or the way he could barely keep his hands off her?" Zandra chuckled.

Finn half-smiled. "That was a more obvious clue. The first time Grace was interviewed, Rhett was also around. And according to the statement, he acted protectively. More than he should with his sister-in-law. They were asked if they were together but denied it."

"They would. Because it gives them an excellent motive for wanting Emron dead." I placed my paws on Finn's knee and sniffed Sammy. He smelled like sour wine. "Cythera can't charge Decker."

"Once Cythera makes a decision, she rarely changes her mind." Finn gently petted Sammy. "She wants final reports by the end of tomorrow. Then she's charging Decker with Emron's murder and closing this investigation."

If I had anything to do with it, and I did, that wasn't happening.

Chapter 16

Someone's keeping secrets

Zandra and I had slept little last night. After speaking to Grace and Rhett, I was convinced there was more going on in this murder investigation.

On the surface, Emron had been a smooth talking charmer with luck on his side, but the more we dug, the more we discovered he'd left waves of dissatisfaction with the people he dealt with.

His own wife and brother thought little of him, and Hugh and Nico had seen behavior they didn't approve of. Behavior that went against Emron's persona of being a charming good guy who wanted the best for everyone.

"We need fuel." Zandra grabbed her keys, and we headed up the basement stairs and out the front door. "I won't be able to focus on anything today. Not while there's a chance Cythera will pull the trigger on Decker."

"Since Angel Force is focused on Decker, that's exactly what'll happen." I trotted beside Zandra toward town.

She looked down at me. "Are we letting them get away with it?"

"No innocent furball goes down for a crime they didn't commit. Not on our watch."

Zandra held her hand out, and we high-fived.

"We should go to Sorcha's café," I said. "You get the best brain fuel there. I recommend the salmon. It always works for me."

Zandra laughed. "What a shocker. Smoked salmon and poached eggs aren't a bad idea, though. But Sorcha's warm waffles with pecan cream are to die for. And as for her chocolate muffins..." She kissed her fingers and lifted her hand. "Perfection."

"We could combine the two. Suggest she make a salmon flavored muffin."

Zandra wrinkled her nose. "Have I ever told you that you have seriously disturbing ideas? Muffins should never be savory. Muffins are a dessert."

"It's been mentioned once or twice. Let's go eat."

We arrived at Bites and Delights, and while Zandra went to the counter to order, I found myself unable to settle. I tried each seat around the small table I'd selected, but none felt right. I lay on the floor. Still no good. I even opted for the window seat I often shared with Sammy so we could stare at passers-by.

Nothing did it for me this morning. There was only one thing that would relieve my tension and give Zandra a nice surprise.

I hurried outside and slid into the alleyway behind the café. I'd find what I needed here. That's not to say Sorcha didn't run a clean ship, but she left food waste outside to be collected. That waste attracted the finest rodent to devour. Although in this case, there'd be no devouring. I planned on finding a fine treat for Zandra to help take her mind off this difficult werewolf situation.

I crouched low, listening intently for signs of rodent life. At first, there was nothing. They must be able to smell me. And of course, my magnificent white fur made me stand out, but it was barely a disadvantage. I was the perfect hunter, thanks to my speed and a little magic when required.

I stayed crouched for ten minutes. If something didn't show up soon, Zandra would wonder where I was. But I was determined not to let her down. She would get a gift. If I couldn't grab a mouse, I'd find a juicy toad.

My whiskers twitched. There was something under the furthest waste container. I inched forward, slowly, slowly, slowly. These rodents startled easily, and I didn't want this one getting away.

I coiled, wriggled my butt, and leaped. It was over in seconds. There was no point in causing unnecessary harm or suffering during a hunt. I was, after all, the most benevolent of magical creatures when it suited me.

A quick crunch, a hard shake, and I had the perfect warm, soft gift in my mouth.

Zandra wasn't at the table when I returned, or at the counter chatting to Sorcha, which gave me the perfect opportunity to place the gift on her chair, so she'd see it when she pulled it out.

I hopped onto the seat next to hers and washed my face with my paws, feeling proud for locating such a splendid find in such a short amount of time.

Zandra appeared out of the washroom and strolled over. "Where did you go? Food's almost ready."

"I had a small mission to attend to." I lifted my chin and waited for her to pull back the chair. She was about to do so when Vorana walked in with Sage beside her.

"Hey, come join us." Zandra yanked out the chair and plopped into it. The second my warm gift oozed underneath her thigh, she froze. Her head turned slowly to me. "Juno. What did I just sit on?"

"Ah, you found your gift. You were supposed to see it, not sit on it!"

Zandra squeaked and leaped out of the seat, bashing her knee on the edge of the table. She yelped again, grabbed her knee, and hopped around, swiping at the back of her jeans with a napkin.

Vorana hurried over with Sage to see what the problem was just as Sorcha appeared with our platefuls of food.

"You okay?" Vorana said. "It looked like you got bit by something."

Zandra pointed at the chair where the sad little squashed mouse lay. She was still hopping around and rubbing her bashed knee.

Vorana and Sorcha peered at my gift, and their noses crinkled.

Sage had a look and nodded at me. "Excellent find. Lots of fat on that. Be nice pan-fried in bacon grease."

"I'm glad someone appreciates my hard work. It's difficult finding such wonderful gifts."

"That is not a gift." Zandra jabbed a finger at the squashed mouse. "I have dead rodent all over my jeans. I can't go to work in these."

"You've worked with red panda poop in your hair. And you spent a day covered in dragon ooze from those infected glands that spurted on you. What's wrong with a dab of mouse entrails?"

Sorcha set down the food. "I've got plenty of clothes you can borrow. I'll get you some pants. You can change in the washroom."

Zandra kept scowling at me. "Thanks. No rodents in here. Or anywhere. Rodents in a café are bad for business."

I hadn't considered that. I didn't want Sorcha to be forced to close. "My apologies, Sorcha, but Zandra has been under stress. This gift was supposed to make her smile."

"I'm not a cat! What did you expect me to do with it?"

I huffed under my breath. I sometimes got a little too involved with my cat side. It seemed the longer I stayed in cat form, the less of a demigoddess I felt. Well, that wasn't strictly true. Cats were once worshipped as gods. But every now and again, I lost touch with who I was, and that was terrifying.

When my feline side dominated, all I wanted to do was curl into a cardboard box, catch mice, and sleep for most of the day. It was a balancing act to get things right.

"I'll grab you those pants. Then you can enjoy breakfast." Sorcha hurried away.

"Thanks." Zandra shot me another glare.

I refused to apologize and instead inspected my murder mittens. I was only doing what came naturally to me. Well, the cat version of me.

Five minutes later, Zandra was dressed in a pair of floral harem pants, sitting on a different seat, and making her way through a plateful of muffins. I was enjoying my usual smoked salmon along with Sage, and Vorana was eating avocado on toast.

The mouse wasn't mentioned and had been taken out the back and given an appropriate funeral.

Sorcha hurried over and joined us with a mug of coffee. "I've got two minutes. How's the murder investigation going?"

"It's about to end and not well," Zandra said. "Cythera is ready to charge Decker Duke, the alpha of the White Ridge pack."

"We don't think he did it," I said.

"I've heard there's evidence to show he's guilty." Sorcha shrugged. "You know everyone gossips when they come in here. There's enough evidence to convince Angel Force of his guilt?"

"It seems that way. And he has no alibi," Zandra said.

"That's not true," I said. "He has an alibi, but for some reason, he's refusing to share it with us."

"Why do that if it proves he's innocent?" Vorana said.

"Beats me," Zandra said. "Decker says he's innocent. And he's got a convincing argument. After all, he's about to lose everything. His pack will merge with Leon's, and he'll be stripped of his alpha role."

"If he's lucky. The Wolf Council could demand an eye for an eye. Decker's life is on the line." I slurped down a strip of salmon before Sage could grab it. She was so greedy. "I was pinning my hopes on the bitter, power hungry, magic stealing girlfriend."

Sage swiped a hunk of salmon. "Why her?"

"Katrine is pregnant and claiming it's Decker's pup. She plans on trading the unfortunate pup to the highest bidder. And she has her eye on a trade with Leon."

Vorana whistled. "That's insane and dangerous. Not just for the werewolves, but for all of us. When werewolves fight, other supernaturals get involved. People pick sides."

"That's what Katrine gets off on. She likes guys fighting over her. What bigger compliment would there be than the werewolves starting a war over her pup?"

"What's her alibi like?" Sorcha sipped her coffee, her eyes bright with interest.

Zandra shook her head. "Airtight. She had a doctor's appointment. Angel Force confirmed she was there. There's no way she could have done it."

"That's a shame," Vorana said. "Katrine came into my bookstore. She was vile about everything. She kept complaining it was mainly second-hand books, and what was the point of those? I tried to explain the concept of recycling, but she said she felt cheated and stormed out."

"She loves to complain about everything," I said. "Some people are like that. What's that saying? Misery loves company? She wants to drag other people down because she only feels delight when ruining things for everyone else."

"Harsh but fair. We visited Emron's wife, Grace, last night," Zandra said. "There were no tears falling because of Emron's death."

"They probably didn't marry for love," Sorcha said. "Werewolves favor alliances over romance."

"That's what happened with this pairing," I said. "But most interesting of all, we discovered Rhett Laker, Grace's brother-in-law, running around naked."

"Typical werewolf." Sorcha cast her gaze to the ceiling. "Can't wait to show off their six-pack."

"We wondered the same thing, but he's got some serious magic and used it against us. Sammy is still recovering."

Sorcha nodded. "Poor little guy is still tucked up in his bed. He could barely string two sentences together when Finn brought him in."

"You reckon Grace and Rhett are having an affair?" Vorana said.

"I'm certain of it," I said.

"Which is a great motive for murder. Maybe Emron found out and planned on exposing them," Sorcha said.

"And they're each other's alibi." Zandra finished her second muffin. "Kind of convenient if you're trying to get away with murder."

"But the angels still want to charge Decker, even with these other suspects?" Sorcha said.

"They want to stop the werewolves from tearing each other apart while they're in Crimson Cove," I said. "They're under pressure to get it solved fast."

"I expect the Wolf Council is on their back." Vorana fed Sage a small piece of buttered toast. "They want justice for Emron."

"An innocent werewolf is about to be imprisoned because people won't take the time to investigate properly." I shook my head. "That can't happen."

"The Wolf Council is like any governing body," Sorcha said. "The idea is sound, but with all these institutions, when they get big, the wheels turn slowly."

"You're describing Angel Force," I said.

"Angel Force, the Wolf Council, they're all similar. Their heart is in the right place, but unfortunately, it's buried under a mountain of paperwork."

"What about Leon?" Vorana said. "You said he's getting Decker's pack. That's a great motive for wanting Decker out of the way. Could Leon have killed Emron and set Decker up?"

"It's a great motive, but he has an alibi," I said. "His entire pack is standing behind him."

"And to make matters trickier, Decker's pack is saying they killed Emron." Zandra tugged on her hair. "It's a mess. And Angel Force deals badly with mess."

We ate more breakfast in silence as we digested this information.

"Is it possible Decker did it?" Sorcha said. "I heard the negotiations were faltering. Sometimes, the simplest explanation is the right one. If there's evidence..."

"I've considered that," I said. "We watched the interview when the angels laid out the evidence to implicate Decker. He was genuinely shocked. To begin with, he was relaxed and seemed to have nothing to worry about. But the evidence rocked his world and not in a good way. He's keeping a secret about what he did that night. I just don't know what it is."

"It must be something huge if he's prepared to go to jail for murder," Vorana said.

Sorcha tapped her fingers against her mug. "You know, I saw Emron and Leon together not long before he died."

"Where was that?" Zandra said.

"In the woods. They asked me to do some catering for them, so I'd take over a couple of snack baskets every day. I got there early and saw them huddled together. Whatever they were talking about, it looked intense."

"Did you hear what they were saying?" I said.

"I wasn't close enough. But whatever it was, they came to an agreement. They shook hands before going their separate ways. I kept as quiet as possible until they were gone because I didn't want them to know I'd been eavesdropping."

"That's interesting." I washed the last of the salmon off my face with a paw. "We were told the alphas agreed to stay away from Emron to avoid accusations of favoritism."

"Well, whatever they were talking about, it looked pretty favorable to me. Neither of them seemed unhappy."

There was a massive bang, making us jump in our seats. Hugh had been thrown against the café's window. He slid down it, scrambled to his feet, and ran off. Half a dozen angry werewolves hotly pursued him.

"What the heck is going on?" Zandra shoved back her seat and dashed to the door.

We left the table and raced after her.

"Leon's pack is chasing Hugh. What's he done?" Sorcha said.

"Whatever it is, he stands no chance against them." Zandra was off and running, leaving me with no choice but to chase her to make sure she didn't get injured in the furry chaos.

Vorana, Sage, and Sorcha were also on her heels.

I glimpsed Tinkerbell, Sorcha's sort of familiar, sitting in the window and watching. I gestured for her to help, but she looked the other way. She was a terrible creature.

Hugh looked over his shoulder and yelped. He sped up, but he was tiring, and the blood down one side of his face showed the werewolves had gotten in a few good hits.

"Hey, stop that," Zandra yelled.

Unsurprisingly, the werewolves ignored her.

"Big, fury-fueled wolves need a more direct approach. Allow me." Vorana spun a spell around the werewolves' feet, tripping them.

They stumbled, but the magic barely slowed them.

"Nice try, but there's no messing around with werewolves." Sorcha flashed her fangs.

"Before you bite them, let's see what we can do." I leaped onto Zandra's shoulder and checked our bond had a strong spring to it.

"What you thinking?" Zandra pumped her arms, her breath shooting out of her.

"No silver to paw, but a suppress spell will quell their werewolf forms. It could even force some of them to shift."

"It'll hurt them."

"They've hurt Hugh."

A werewolf snapped at Hugh's ankles. He was out of time.

"Let's do it." Zandra raised her hands, and I spun out my power. Our energy combined and blasted over the werewolves.

They slowed. Two of them dropped and shook as they curled into a fetal position, while the others lost their sense of direction and ran into walls.

Once the werewolves were sufficiently subdued, I leaped off Zandra's shoulder, raced past them and over to Hugh. He was face down in the dirt and out cold. The spell had hit him, too.

I turned on the werewolves and hissed. "Why do this? Hugh is no threat to you. He's bottom of Decker's pack. He never seeks trouble."

A broad-shouldered werewolf lifted his head. He'd been turned from his shaggy form and lay naked on the ground. "We found that jerk planting evidence that Leon killed Emron."

I stared down at Hugh. That was a risky move. It was the move of a werewolf desperate to protect his alpha.

"Are you certain?" Zandra stood with Vorana, Sorcha, and Sage, guarding the rest of the werewolves.

"We know what we saw," the werewolf said. "That kind of treachery is punishable by immediate death. We intend to make that happen."

Chapter 17

A desperate move

I looked up at Zandra. "We need Angel Force to deal with this. Go get Finn. The others will watch the werewolves."

She nodded and dashed away to summon the angels. Within five minutes, she was back, and the street was alive with stressed out angels and fluttering feathers.

Finn bounded over to us. "The werewolves were battling in the street?"

"They were trying to kill Hugh," Zandra said. "One of them said he tried to frame Leon for Emron's murder. They found him planting evidence. I'm not sure where or what, though."

Finn's eyes widened. "If that's true, it looks even worse for Decker. His werewolves must be desperate to clear his name. Hugh is crazy to think he could get away with this. Where is he?"

"Still out cold in the dirt," I said. "I tried a few healing spells, but nothing roused him. He got a few knocks to the head, so it might take him a while to wake. We also hit him with our suppress spell."

Finn scrubbed the back of his neck. "Could this be Decker's doing? He knows he's about to be charged, so he sent an order that forced Hugh to plant evidence. He tried the group confession tactic, and when that didn't work, he moved on to his next plan?"

That idea sat uncomfortably with me, but I couldn't deny it was possible.

A group of angels had surrounded Leon's feisty, snarling pack, and were maintaining order, although there was plenty of jostling and feathers flying around. The werewolves were twitchy and loudly demanding justice for their alpha.

I marched over to the group with Finn and Zandra. Vorana, Sorcha, and Sage had moved back but were watching everything.

The werewolf who'd told us why they were chasing Hugh was on his feet, his hands fisted as he glared at the angels. "This gross act of sabotage deserves justice. I want that werewolf's head."

"Settle down," Finn said. "Werewolves have no jurisdiction in Crimson Cove. And Hugh is badly injured and needs treatment."

"Why bother?" the werewolf growled out. "He's a dead wolf walking. Healing his injuries is a waste of time."

The other werewolves growled their agreement, while the angels glowered and fluttered.

"Ember Cross pack, stand down." The alpha tone in Leon's voice shivered through me.

He stalked into the center of the group, staring at each of his werewolves until they dropped their gaze and hunched forward, accepting his dominance. Then he turned to Finn. "No more lives will be lost or blood spilled. There's been enough tragedy since we came here."

"We caught this werewolf trying to frame you for Emron's murder," one of the werewolf's said. "He must be punished."

Leon glared at Hugh, who was being protected by three angels. He let out a long breath. "Most likely because he received a command from his desperate alpha. All this proves is Decker is guilty of this crime. It doesn't make me happy to believe that, but with the evidence found, and now this, what other conclusion can be reached?"

"The case is still open," I said. "The investigation is ongoing, and there are other suspects. We haven't charged Decker with anything."

"True. But I've been informed he soon will be," Leon said. "The sooner the better. Then I can claim his pack, and we can move on. This unhelpful rivalry will be squashed, and the two packs will live in peace."

His werewolves grumbled their agreement.

Leon stepped forward and held his hand out to Finn. "I'll deal with this. I'm sorry my werewolves took matters into their own hands, but you must appreciate how tense this situation is."

Finn nodded and briefly shook his hand. "I appreciate that, while werewolves do things their own way, you can't administer justice around here. This isn't your territory, and you don't have control."

That comment provoked several unhappy grumbles.

Leon raised his hand, and there was immediate silence. "I only want the best for Angel Force and my werewolves. And I want the best for Decker's pack, too. It won't be easy for them to assimilate, but they'll see this is the best thing for them. Their alpha has fallen, and they need to be under the command of someone strong who follows the werewolves' true path. Charge Decker before someone else dies." Leon's gaze settled on Hugh.

I studied Leon as he handed out platitudes and reassurances. I wasn't convinced. His sudden charm was as fake as Emron's.

"If you could move your werewolves on and let us deal with Hugh, I'd appreciate it," Finn said.

Leon nodded. "Whatever you need. We're focusing on our future and have our new home to find and settle into."

It took less than a minute before the street was cleared of werewolves, and only the musky aroma of testosterone and hot fur lingered.

I walked over to the others, who had amassed around Hugh.

"How's he doing?" Zandra said.

"He's breathing, but we need to get him medical treatment," Finn said. "His injuries aren't healing."

"What did Leon mean by finding his new home?" I said.

"I'm guessing he meant Decker's territory," Zandra said. "What else would it be?"

I looked in the direction the werewolves had loped off. "He already knows where that is."

Everyone was focused on Hugh, who remained dead to the world.

"Finn, have you checked Leon's finances?"

He glanced up from his inspection of Hugh's injuries. "Sure. All suspects get run through the system to see if anything strange pops."

"Did anything unusual show on his accounts? Any lump sum payments going out?"

"Nothing. It showed he's a seriously wealthy guy, but that's it. What are you thinking?" He stood and pulled out his mobile snow globe.

"Sorcha just revealed she saw Emron and Leon talking in the woods not long before Emron died," I said. "What if Leon bribed Emron, so he'd win the negotiations?"

"He's hidden any money trail, if that's the case."

"Maybe it wasn't a money payment," Sorcha said. "What else could Emron have wanted?"

"When we met him at Finn's animal sanctuary, he mentioned wanting land," I said. "What if Leon didn't gift him money but purchased him land instead? Was there anything on Leon's account to show he'd recently done that?"

Finn shook his head. "There were no odd financial goings on with any of the suspects."

"It would be a great sweetener, though," Zandra said.

"Land purchases take time," Vorana said. "Maybe it was still going through when Emron was killed."

Finn looked up from his mobile snow globe. "True. I'll investigate and see if there are any transactions in the works that link Leon and Emron."

"You need to hurry," I said. "These werewolves mean business. Hugh is living on borrowed time."

"As soon as Hugh is safe, I'll get on it."

We stood back as Hugh was lifted by two angels and taken away to receive treatment.

"We can't stick around any longer," Zandra said. "We have to get to work."

"And I must get back to the café. My customers will want all the news!" Sorcha dashed away.

Vorana headed off with Sage, leaving us with the angels.

"I'll let you know if I hear anything useful about Leon's financials. But it's a long shot. Catch up with you later." Finn swooped off.

My gaze shifted along the street. Crimson Cove felt on the edge of a werewolf war. If the balance tipped the wrong way, it would be chaos. And that meant my witch would be vulnerable. Since I couldn't let that happen, I had to figure out exactly who killed Emron and why.

Chapter 18

Did he do it?

"You're sure Cythera won't catch us?" Zandra glanced around Angel Force's open-plan office.

"Nope. And what she doesn't know won't hurt her." Finn hurried as past a row of desks. "Besides, animal control is involved in this case. And I need your expertise."

"And naturally, our involvement stretches to interviewing the prime murder suspect." I inspected a half-eaten ham sandwich on a desk.

Finn tapped the side of his nose. "You said you wanted to talk to Decker, so I made it happen. It's just happening when Cythera isn't around."

We were on our lunch break from work, so we had little time. But after mulling over the options with Zandra during our morning shift, we'd agreed talking to Decker face-to-face could be worthwhile. Although he'd been open during his initial interview, there was something this werewolf was hiding. If I could figure out what it was, it could be the key to solving this mystery.

"How long have we got?" Zandra said, as we stopped by the interview room.

"No more than twenty minutes. Cythera goes out for a walk at lunchtime, but she could come back early since she's under pressure to get this case resolved."

"Then let's get in there and see what Decker has to say for himself," I said.

"I've laid the groundwork, so he knows you're coming to speak to him," Finn said. "I'll sit in, too. Just in case he gets mean."

I was happy to have Finn as backup. Werewolves were an unpredictable bunch, especially when looking death in the eyes.

We headed into the neutrally decorated interview room. Decker was already seated on one side of the table. He wore an air of resigned defeat as he nodded at us. It wasn't a good look on an alpha wolf. It must be hard for him to accept his fate, especially since he kept saying he was innocent. Why would an alpha werewolf give up everything? There had to be something bigger than his pack that made him hold his tongue.

"Decker, you know Zandra and Juno," Finn said.

"From the sanctuary. Sure. I have no new information for you, though. This is a waste of time."

"Let us decide that." Finn remained standing by the door, while Zandra took a seat, and I hopped onto the table.

He shrugged. "Do what you have to do. I know all the departments involved in this case need their paperwork in order. If you're sentencing a werewolf to death, you need to make sure everything is signed off. Don't want the Wolf Council getting in your business."

"We don't," Zandra said. "And I suspect, neither do you."

Decker raised an eyebrow. "Is that right? What makes you say that?"

"You're hiding something about the night Emron was murdered," I said.

"The evidence shows I was in his tent. We fought, and I killed him. What else do you need to know?"

"You're now saying you did it?" I flicked my tail.

"It doesn't matter what I say. No one believes me."

"You've given up?" I shook my head. "It's a sad day when an alpha werewolf loses his edge."

Decker growled softly at me. "Watch your step. I eat small things like you for a snack."

I extended my claws. "You could try. You wouldn't get far."

Zandra rested a hand on my back. "We're your allies. We're not here to cause trouble. But we're also not prepared to sit back and watch an innocent werewolf lose everything."

He shrugged and crossed his arms over his chest. "Sometimes, you have to let the dice roll and land where they will. It's out of my control."

"It doesn't have to be," I said. "Talk us through the night Emron was murdered."

"The angels know all this."

"Perhaps something was missed. You said in your initial interview you were alone in your tent when Emron died."

"That's what I'm still saying."

"Do you have werewolf guards outside your tent?" Zandra said. "Like Leon?"

A cold smirk crossed Decker's face. "I don't need bodyguards. I can look after myself. What Leon does is up to him."

"Were there any werewolves around your tent at that time of night?" Zandra said. "We just need one of them to come forward and tell the truth."

"I sent them away."

"Why?" I inched closer. "Were you doing something you shouldn't?"

"Like murdering Emron?" The smirk hardened.

This werewolf was still concealing something. "They all believe you're innocent."

"I know what they've done to protect me, coming forward and saying they murdered Emron." Decker tipped back on the chair. "I appreciate it's given me a few more days before the charges become formal, but you won't believe any of them if they change their statements and say they saw me. You'd all think I ordered them to say that."

I tilted my head. "Most werewolves on a murder charge would use every weapon they had. Why are you different?"

"If by different, you mean loyal and honest, I couldn't tell you. I won't misuse the pack bond." Decker's cool gaze settled on me. "You're this witch's familiar?"

"Correct."

"Then you understand our pack bond. Packs operate differently. Some are run on coercion and fear. Others forge alliances and have expectations they must meet. My pack is held together because we're honest, true, and loyal to each other. We think about pack needs before our own."

"That's a good way to live."

"The best. It isn't always the easiest of rides when pack desires go against your own wants, but it's effective. And it's a strategy I've used with my werewolves since I took over. During my time as alpha, there have been no internal challenges for my role, no unauthorized killings, and no battles lost. It's because we work for the benefit of all."

"It's a noble way to run a pack," I said. "And having been around your werewolves, I recognize they're a solid group. They'd die to protect you."

"I never asked them to do that. My pack means the world to me. Which is why I'd never insist any of them lie and give me a fake alibi. Unlike some werewolves."

"Leon, you mean?" Zandra said.

"That's not for me to say. As an alpha, you're always under observation. Perhaps his pack was watching him at the moment of Emron's murder. But it seems convenient."

"We thought that, too," I said. "And from what Finn told us, their individual accounts of that evening are identical."

"As if they'd been given a script," Zandra said, "or an alpha command."

"It's not important. The angels have made their decision about me. I'll be charged. At least the angels are being decent about it and keeping me informed about the investigation. And I'll get a final farewell with my pack before they're torn apart."

This stubborn-headed werewolf would never reveal his secret. It was time to stop pussyfooting around. "You were untruthful in your first interview with Angel Force."

Decker bared his teeth at me. "You're saying I'm a liar?"

"I'm saying you omitted information. Why do that?"

He pressed his lips together and looked away.

"Decker, the angels aren't messing around. The tension in Crimson Cove is growing hourly because of the packs clashing. If you're hiding something that shows you're innocent, reveal it. If you don't, you won't be released, and you won't be able to control your pack."

"They can control themselves. And I am innocent, but I've accepted my fate."

"You've accepted the grim fate of your pack, too?" I said. "If you do this, Leon will win. He'll ruin your pack."

Decker lowered his gaze and took several deep breaths, his shoulders heaving up and down. "It's always what he wanted. And I know there'll be suffering. But my pack is tough. They'll find a compromise."

"Do you know what Hugh did for you?" Zandra said.

Decker raised his head, his eyes narrowed. "If you mean that he led my werewolves when they came to confess to Emron's murder, I do."

"Not that. He's so desperate to get you out of here, he got caught by Leon's pack planting evidence to implicate Leon in Emron's murder."

Decker's eyes flared amber, and he gripped the edge of the table then gave a small shake of his head. "I underestimated that werewolf. When he came to me, dropped to his knees, and begged to be a part of my pack, I didn't expect him to make it six months. He was the runt of the litter and had been treated appallingly by previous packs. But when I learned he'd been trying to survive solo, I couldn't allow him to remain alone."

"Which shows you're a principled werewolf," I said. "You gave Hugh a chance when no one else would. You looked beyond his so-called physical imperfections."

"He's got a heart as big as a mountain. I couldn't let that go. All werewolf packs need someone with their emotions on display. You could say he's an empath. After I took him in, Leon would jibe at me about him and say I'd gone soft. I was letting in the misfits and damaged werewolves because I wasn't alpha enough to turn anyone or sire my own."

"Taking in those who don't fit in is an exceptional quality," I said. "Most people see difference and shun it or ridicule it. Only the best recognize difference makes this world so wonderfully unique and special."

"Hugh may be special, but now he's done this, he'll be put to death." Decker snarled. "This is a taste of how Leon will treat my pack. During the negotiations, he talked about how easy it would be to integrate them, but it was empty words."

"He actually said he wanted your pack?" Zandra said.

"Leon wants me to retire. He came ready with a dossier of my mistakes." Decker air quoted the last word. "He thinks compassion is weakness. Leon said it was the right thing to do so they could live as actual werewolves and not gelded freaks."

"I've watched him interact with his pack," I said. "He's callous to those that don't meet his standards."

"And we've seen how he treats his bottom of the pack," Zandra said.

"They're basically unpaid servants." Decker's top lip curled. "They're terrified of him. Always living on their nerves, waiting for the next strike or bark to tell them they've done something wrong and how worthless they are. Every werewolf has value."

"Why let this happen, if you know he's so bad for your pack?" I thumped my front paws on the table. "What are you hiding that's so important you're prepared to let your entire pack fall under such unkind rule?"

Decker's gaze roamed the room. "You wouldn't understand. I can't tell you."

"You mean you won't," I said. "If you have an alibi, reveal it. Once it's been checked, you can walk out of here, return to your pack, and the angels will find Emron's killer. If you take the blame for this, whoever did this will get away with it."

He sighed and looked away.

I glanced at Zandra, and she shrugged.

"I hope whatever you're hiding is worth it," I said. "Although you're more stubborn than a mule with the last enchanted carrot, you'll be a loss to the werewolf community."

"It's worth it. I can guarantee you that."

My whiskers twitched. I could test my power by beguiling this werewolf to tell the truth, but I'd bring his pack's wrath down on my head. And that was a harm I wasn't directing my way, not when Zandra would stand on the path with me.

"We've got the angels looking into the possibility Leon bribed Emron," Zandra said. "They were seen talking outside of the official negotiations."

"I'm not surprised to hear that. Leon was determined to get what he wanted. And Emron was greedy. Don't be shocked if you find no proof. Emron knew how to work the system."

"There's no proof yet, but we're not giving up," Zandra said. "And if we can find any truth behind this idea, it'll give you more time."

Decker lifted one shoulder. "Time for what? To sit around and await my fate?" His gaze shifted to me. "Why are you so intent on helping me? You barely know me. You owe me nothing."

"We're here for justice," I said. "If you're innocent, you can't be charged with this crime."

He shifted in his seat, and his eyes flickered amber. "It's a quality I teach my werewolves. Do the right thing, even though it's not always easy."

"Why aren't you following your own advice?" I said. "The right thing would be to give us your alibi and then help us find Emron's killer. You'd get your pack back, stop Leon from destroying them, and ensure the person responsible for this crime is caught."

Decker didn't speak, and his head went down again.

I walked over and placed a paw on his hand. "Decker, from one immensely powerful alpha to another, we always know the right path. You lead an incredible pack. Another werewolf shouldn't be allowed to corrupt them. You've worked hard to lift them up. Leon will undo that."

He lifted his head, and his gaze met mine. I couldn't be certain, but he sensed my power. Decker may not have a full grasp of how ancient I was, but he got a tickle of my life experience and the horrors I'd seen. Horrors caused by people not living up to their truth and shivering behind masks of indifference.

There was a knock on the door, and Bertoli strode in. "I've got news. Oh, Juno, here's a packet of your favorite fishy treats. I've been carrying them around, hoping we'd get time together." He set them on the table beside me.

I nodded my appreciation. He'd bought a deluxe-sized pack. "What have you got for us?"

"Finn asked me to look through any land or building purchases Leon made in the last year."

"I did. What did you find?" Finn said.

"Castle Dreadnought! It's Leon's ancestral home."

"What about it?" Zandra said.

"Leon arranged for a lawyer to sign the deeds over to Emron."

Decker growled, the noise rumbling in his chest. "He was bribing Emron to swing the negotiations in his favor."

"This gives Leon a strong motive for murder," Finn said.

"How big is Castle Dreadnought?" Zandra said.

Decker shifted forward in his seat. "Enormous. I've been there several times. It comes with over a hundred acres."

"So they made a deal. Leon started the deed transfer but then changed his mind?" Zandra said.

"Maybe. And if Emron learned he'd been lied to, he'd have confronted Leon and threatened to reveal his secret, so Leon silenced him," I said.

"What about his alibi?" Bertoli said. "Leon's pack confirmed they were all in the pizza parlor together."

Cythera appeared by the open door, her face etched with panic. "I need all angels outside immediately. The non-magicals are rioting."

Chapter 19

When is a party a riot?

After swiftly securing Decker in his cell, Finn and Bertoli dashed out of the office. We followed them.

"You should stay back," I cautioned Zandra. "You never know what to expect with non-magicals. I've seen them riot before. It gets ugly. They lose all control and destroy anything close at hand."

"Why are they rioting?" She slowed but kept following the hoard of angels as they poured out the main door.

As we grew closer, music filtered toward us.

"Music at a riot?" I said. "It's not that unusual, but when I've led skirmishes, we put on heavy metal or rock. It inspires a heightened level of bloodlust."

"Skirmishes? When have you ever led a skirmish? Unless you count those five mice you brought in one night. I still haven't forgiven you for that. It was like a miniature pet morgue had sprung up in the kitchen."

"Oh, you know, when out hunting with Sammy, Sage, and Elijah. Music inspires us."

Zandra didn't look convinced by my explanation, but she didn't need to know I'd once led an army of over fifty thousand magic users. It might concern her.

We stopped by the open doors and peered around the line of angels standing out the front.

"This isn't a riot," I said after a moment's inspection. "It's a street party."

There were groups of non-magicals dancing around. Someone had set up a barbecue in one corner, and there was a drinks' table covered in tins and several punch bowls. A couple of people were going around, offering colorful flower garlands, and another non-magical had a sound system set up that boomed away as he spun the tunes.

"Cythera, is this what you meant?" Zandra pointed at the exuberant crowd.

She gestured at the scene. "They're inciting trouble. It feels unsafe."

"It's called fun," I said. "You should join in. Shake your tail feathers. Well, wing feathers."

"Not here! We don't want them having fun on our streets. It's bad enough they're coming in as tourists and poking around. The next thing we'll have to deal with is them setting up home." She glared at a non-magical who came too close to us.

"No laws are being broken, so long as you discount those limp looking burgers being chargrilled," I said.

Her icy gaze zoomed around the chaotic merriment. "Are you sure this isn't a riot? Things feel out of control."

"It could turn into one if they drink too much." I hopped onto Zandra's shoulder and leaned against her head. "They're not doing any harm, though."

"Hey, pretty blonde lady. Dance with me." A skinny guy with a dark ponytail wearing a flowered shirt and shorts boogied over to Cythera and grabbed her hands. "And smile! The world is so much better when you smile."

Cythera didn't move as he danced in front of her.

"Act natural," Zandra whispered to her, "or he'll think there's something wrong with you."

"There is. Cythera doesn't know the definition of fun," I muttered.

"I'm not dancing in the street. I have a reputation to maintain." Cythera glowered at the non-magical. "Unhand me."

"I'm having fun. The burgers will be ready soon. Come join us. What's your name, Blue Eyes?"

She withdrew her hands and tucked them under her armpits. "I'm working. Go away."

My fur prickled, and a quick glance around showed it wasn't only the angels interested in this party. The werewolf packs lurked in the shadows. And although they weren't paying that much attention to the non-magicals, the partygoers were in the firing line if the packs clashed.

I huffed into Zandra's ear. "We have company. Check the alleyways. On the rooftops, too."

"Uh-oh. Do you think the noise attracted them?"

"Maybe. I expect Decker's pack is hanging around to see what'll happen to him, so Leon's pack is here to watch them. If the angels charge Decker, then we'll see a riot. And it'll tear this place apart, taking out all these non-magicals."

"And Leon will ensure things get extra bloody just to prove a point," Zandra said.

Cythera looked down at us, concern flickering across her glorious face. "I can't allow that. As much as I don't want non-magicals in Crimson Cove, I have a duty to protect them. If they get in the middle of a werewolf skirmish, questions will be asked. And if any die, we won't be able to cover it up. There'll be an investigation."

"So get your angels to move the non-magicals somewhere safer," Zandra said.

Her wings flickered out for a second before vanishing. "We're avoiding contact with them as much as possible. There have been one or two incidents."

"You mean your giant wings have been noticed when you get too flappy," I said.

"How do you know that?"

"I'm an excellent guesser. And the non-magicals have been blundering into areas that should be out of bounds. They messed up a load of Randal's tech by playing with his equipment. Equipment they shouldn't have been able to see."

Cythera shook her head as more non-magicals danced past. "This ends now."

"You're breaking up the party?" Zandra said.

"No, I'm charging Decker with Emron's murder. Once it's official, Leon will be entitled to take both packs under his rule. They'll leave Crimson Cove, and this will be over."

"That's the opposite of fixing things," I said. "If Decker's pack learns of this, they'll be the ones rioting through Crimson Cove."

"Not if Leon acts swiftly. I'll contact him before issuing the charges."

"You can't do that!" Zandra said. "Decker's innocent."

"That's impossible for you to know."

"It's not." She jammed her hands on her hips. "We've just been speaking to him."

"I did not give authority for that." Cythera loomed over us.

Zandra stood firm. "Decker has an alibi, but he's not willing to reveal who it is. He didn't murder Emron."

Finn joined us. "I think they're right. I've been looking into Leon's financial dealings with Bertoli. Leon planned to transfer his ancestral home to Emron."

Cythera's nostrils flared. "Why am I only hearing about this now?"

"We just found out," Finn said. "I arranged for Zandra and Juno to speak to Decker while we investigated. It's thanks to them we found the perfect motive for Leon wanting Emron dead. Charging Decker would be a mistake, now this evidence has come to light."

"Decker isn't telling you the truth about what he was doing the night Emron died," I said.

"But there's evidence to show his guilt," Cythera said.

"Evidence that was most likely planted."

"You can't know that for certain." She hesitated, her attention on the revelers. "I've made my decision. Decker killed Emron to end the negotiations. Maybe he hoped his tactics of ordering his werewolves to confess would hide his guilt or confuse us, but he made an error and left behind damaging evidence."

"Do I have to say it again? It would have been easy to plant that evidence." Why were angels so annoyingly stubborn when they got an idea into their heads?

"We need Decker's werewolves out of Crimson Cove. They won't move on until they have a new alpha. Everyone is vulnerable because they're here. Once Decker is charged, Leon takes over, and the werewolves go."

"And you send an innocent werewolf to jail and let a killer go free," I said.

Cythera opened and closed her mouth several times. "I... I... This is for the best. Crimson Cove feels unsafe. My job is to ensure the residents and visitors aren't at risk."

"Then you'll never succeed," I said. "Our community is full of immensely powerful individuals. A third of the residents could blow this place apart with a poorly timed sneeze. We live with danger every day because of who we are and what we can do. Don't be afraid of that."

"But the non-magicals." She gestured at the crowd again. "They must be protected. Two werewolf packs are about to go to war, and I have to find a resolution."

"Speak to Decker one more time." Zandra rested a hand on my side. She must sense my frustration. "For whatever reason, he thinks he's doing the noble thing by concealing his alibi."

"When all he's doing is ensuring his pack will suffer," I grumbled.

"That makes no sense. Alphas work for the good of their pack. Decker is guilty." Cythera turned to go back inside.

"We can't let her do this," I said to Zandra.

"No plans to." Zandra turned to continue the argument with Cythera.

Standing in front of the Angel Force building was a petite, hugely pregnant brunette. She had one hand on her stomach and the other on her hip, blocking our way inside. Even though she was tiny, power flooded out of her and dazzled me.

My eyes widened, and my fur stood on end. "You're the overlord alpha's wife."

She nodded, her dark eyes blazing with anger. "I'm Scarlet."

Cythera bowed in deference to the female werewolf who held an extraordinary position of power. "Welcome. This is an unexpected visit. You catch us at a difficult time."

Scarlet's dark hazel gaze flickered around as she took in the scene. "I'm aware of what's going on. I've had regular communications from a pack I have connections to in the area."

"Is your overlord alpha concerned about the situation?" Zandra said.

Her chin lifted, her gaze boring into my witch. "And you are?"

"She's not important. Please, come inside," Cythera said. "All this noise is unbearable."

Scarlet ignored Cythera. "My alpha mate is aware of the situation. It always concerns him when a respected pack leader is in the spotlight for a terrible crime." She chose each word carefully, as if weighing them up to determine the reaction they'd cause. Here was a werewolf who lived every day with threats looming over her.

"Let him know he has nothing to worry about. This case has been fairly and thoroughly investigated, and we're about to resolve matters," Cythera said. "Now, perhaps we should—"

"You've resolved them incorrectly," I said. "Greetings, Scarlet. I'm Juno, and this is my wonderful witch, Zandra Crypt. We've been working closely with Angel Force to ensure there are no miscarriages of justice undertaken during this investigation."

Her clever gaze assessed me, and she nodded at Zandra. "I appreciate that. Although, when I heard what was about to happen to Decker Duke, I had to step in."

"How do you know what's about to happen?" Cythera said.

"She's the overlord alpha's mate," I said. "He knows everything about his werewolves."

"He does. If there are any misdeeds occurring, he ensures a suitable punishment is handed out."

"Reassure him there are no problems." Cythera's hands were clasped. "No punishment is needed. The Wolf Council doesn't need to be involved."

The tension was so thick, I could cut it and eat it on a slice of toast with a pickled herring.

"They will be. If you charge Decker, one of our most respected alphas, the Wolf Council will have questions. So will my mate." Scarlet drew in a breath. "But I'm not here for those reasons. I can no longer hold my silence. Decker is innocent."

"How could you know that?" Cythera said after a short pause.

"Because he was with me when Emron was killed."

Chapter 20

Who's the daddy?

After a stunned silence, interspersed by the party goers booming out tunes and laughing, Cythera shook herself. "Let's take this inside. Angels, watch the party. Make sure no one steps out of line."

Scarlet's expression remained defiant, but she allowed Cythera to open the door and guide her in.

I followed with Zandra and Finn, and within a few minutes, Scarlet was seated in an interview room, her hands protectively clasping her bump.

Finn joined the interview, but we were relegated to the room next door so we could watch.

Cythera ran through the usual formalities, getting Scarlet's name and her role in the werewolf community.

"You have information regarding the murder of Emron Laker?"

Scarlet nodded. "I don't know who killed him, but you have my word, Decker Duke had nothing to do with it. I was with him that night."

Cythera's wings shivered. "Why are you only coming forward with this information now?"

"Because word reached me you were about to charge him with murder. That's a mistake."

"Perhaps you believe that—"

"I know it. He was with me." Scarlet smoothed her hands over her baby bump.

"They're asking the wrong questions," I said. "They must see what's going on."

"What is going on?" Zandra said. "It makes no sense for Decker to hide this. If it's true, it means he's innocent."

"Look at her situation. Scarlet is mated to the overlord alpha, a werewolf she most likely respects but doesn't love, and she's pregnant."

"That kind of happens when you're in a relationship. Especially if you're a female werewolf."

"Yeah, but who is she pregnant by?"

Zandra's mouth dropped open. "You think that's Decker's pup?"

"There's only one way to find out." I rapped my paws on the glass.

Cythera's gaze slid to the glass, but she made no comment. "Perhaps you've provided this alibi because of an incentive. Did Decker offer you something to lie for him?"

Scarlet growled softly. "I have a huge incentive for not wanting Decker to go to jail for a crime he didn't commit."

I thumped my paws on the glass again. "It's Decker's pup! Ask her who the father is." Of course, they couldn't hear me.

Cythera sighed. "Finn, could you see what our... associates wish to speak to us about?"

He nodded, pushed back his chair, and left the room. He opened the door and poked his head around the side. "What's up?"

"We need to be in on the interview. Cythera hasn't put the pieces together," I said.

Finn rubbed the back of his neck. "You know she's a stickler for protocol."

"We are involved in this case," Zandra said. "We're your animal control experts."

He raised his hands. "If she yells at you, you've been warned."

"Noted. I'm happy to be yelled at." I dashed past Finn and into the interview room.

Cythera's wings fluttered behind her the second she spotted me. "We're in the middle of a confidential interview."

"I'm aware of that. But I'd like to ask a question. With your permission, Cythera." A touch of deference to those who liked to appear important worked wonders.

"I don't mind who asks me questions," Scarlet said. "This needs to be resolved as fast as possible. I want Decker out of here."

Cythera sighed then gestured for me to continue.

I glanced around to see Finn and Zandra enter the room. Finn eased the door shut.

"Scarlet, this may be an uncomfortable question to answer, given your pairing to the overlord alpha, but you need to be honest."

Her expression grew weary. "Of course. I'm tired of hiding things."

"The pup you're carrying is Decker's, isn't it?"

Scarlet gave a single nod. "It is. I love Decker, and he loves me. And he'd do anything to protect me."

"Including going to jail for a murder he didn't commit to save your reputation and possibly your life?" I said.

Cythera drew in a deep breath, and her large nostrils flared. "Is this true?"

Scarlet's gaze flickered around the room. "Before I say anything else, I need to see Decker. I must make sure he's safe."

"We need answers first," Cythera said.

Scarlet's hands flexed around her belly. "You're all aware of who I am. If I desire, I could bring packs of werewolves here to ruin you. You will do as I say. I see Decker. Now."

I hopped on the table and calmly met her fierce gaze. "You won't do that. If you summon the werewolves to do your bidding, your secret will be revealed. The overlord alpha will ask questions about why you're protecting a single werewolf. And if he learns the truth about your affair, he'd imprison you and put you to death once your pup was born. Decker, too. Although his end would be more violent and unpleasant."

Her beautiful eyes flared amber, but then the heat died. "I want this over. I'm sick of sneaking around and hiding my feelings."

Finn took his seat again, while Zandra leaned against the wall.

"Start at the beginning," he said. "How long have you been with the overlord alpha?"

"Since I was sixteen. Many decades. My parents run the Black Creed pack."

"That's an ancient werewolf pack," Cythera said.

"It is. They value the importance of strong alliances. I always knew my destiny and that I wouldn't be paired with a werewolf I loved. I accepted my fate. And I was honored when the overlord alpha decided I was to be his. Not all overlords pick a single mate, but he was focused on building his reputation, so he needed a steadying influence by his side. I'm not a wild werewolf. I respect our ways of doing things. So, I accepted the joining. It was my duty."

"That makes you happy?" I said.

"Not all of those years have been easy but, equally, not all difficult. Ruling over the werewolf packs has its challenges. The overlord alpha is often physically challenged by those foolish enough to think they can best him. It's never been done, and he's yet to reach his prime." Sadness filled Scarlet's eyes but was swiftly replaced by a stoic expression. "It's good he has me as a mate. Single male werewolves in positions of power are dangerous."

"You don't like your mate?" Finn said.

"He's not a bad male, but I don't love him. I'm with him because of an expectation set by others."

"And you were content to do that until you met Decker?" I said.

"I was. I had brief moments when I wondered what life would be like if I found love. A complete bond with another werewolf. You hear these incredible love stories, where the werewolves meet as strangers, but a single gaze and that's it. The bond is locked, and there's nothing you can do about it.

I used to read those stories when I was a child. I never thought it would happen to me. It's so rare."

"Then Decker came into your life," Zandra said.

Scarlet nodded. "We met at a wilding event eighteen months ago. His pack has been occupied with other work, so that was the first time we met. It felt like getting hit with a lightning bolt. When he looked at me, everything vanished. I couldn't stop staring. A hot, urgent feeling buried into my heart, and he was all I could think about. Day and night, I became obsessed with him."

Cythera pitched forward in her seat, a rapt expression on her face. "Decker felt the same way about you?"

"He did. I did everything to resist him, and he was doing the same, but it was as if fate dragged us together. We kept bumping into each other. And then my mate asked me to show Decker around one of our estates. I spent the day with him, and it was the best day of my life. But also the worst. Since then, I've been disloyal. It's not something I'm proud of." Scarlet stroked her belly. "But then I got this. My biggest joy. Also, my biggest fear. My pup is so vulnerable."

"You're in an impossible situation," Cythera said on a sigh. "You have an allegiance to the overlord alpha, yet your primitive bond has linked you to another."

Scarlet growled again. "Nothing I feel about Decker is primitive. It's perfect. It's as it should be. If only I'd met him before I'd been joined to the overlord."

"Dwelling on what could have been gets you nowhere," I said. "I suppose there's no option for you to leave the overlord alpha and be with Decker?"

"There's one way. For Decker to be with me, he'd have to take the role of overlord alpha. He'd have to claim me, and there'd be a fight to the death."

"Which would ripple out across the werewolf community," Zandra said. "Packs would pick sides, and war would begin."

Scarlet's gaze dropped for a second. "I cannot allow that. As I said, although I don't love my mate, he has my respect. I wish I'd been stronger and fought my feelings, but you cannot deny a true mate bond. Now, I find myself here, and everything is tumbling down around me. Everything I've tried to prevent is coming true."

"How did you know what was going on with Decker?" Finn said.

"One of his werewolves, Hugh, keeps me informed. But I hadn't heard from him recently and became concerned," Scarlet said. "I reached out to another member of Decker's pack and learned Hugh had been attacked. Then I heard the charges were about to be finalized, so I had to come forward."

"That was risky, meeting Decker during the pack negotiations," I said.

"It was a calculated risk. My mate was curious how the negotiations were progressing. I have friends who live out this way, so I suggested a short trip to visit them and, while I was there, stopping at the negotiations and getting an update."

I flicked my tail. "And giving you the chance to have one-on-one time with your bonded mate."

Scarlet lifted her chin. "Of course. That's where I was when Emron was killed. I was wrapped in Decker's arms. When word circulated something bad had happened, Decker begged me to stay silent so I'd be safe. I did for a time, but I won't see him lose everything. Not for me. It would destroy me."

"You'll both lose everything if this gets out," I said. "The overlord alpha won't let you live."

Scarlet pressed her lips together. "The punishment will be severe. Werewolves with such power can become corrupt and dangerous. And not just those with power. I'm finding, more and more, female werewolves need a haven from the primal violence they encounter."

"Why do they need a haven? Female werewolves are as strong as their mates," Cythera said.

Scarlet arched an eyebrow. "Being as physically strong doesn't mean they have the mental strength to survive a difficult situation. If you're with your bonded mate, they can command you to do anything. Sometimes, those commands leave a bad taste in the mouth."

I nodded along as she spoke. Werewolves' love of violence was often bleak.

"Then there are werewolves who never achieve a bond, so they don't settle. These lone wolves are the most dangerous to females. They try to take what they desire. It's why I set up RFW."

"The Refuge for Female Werewolves?" I said.

"You've heard of it?"

"Of course. You do great work."

"Thank you. I had to plead with my mate it was a worthy cause and wouldn't interfere with my duties, but he agreed I could set it up. We operate on donations, often from anonymous sources, and run safe houses and emergency hostels for female werewolves in fear of their lives." Scarlet's smile was tinged with sadness. "We're always busy, but I'm working toward the day when my services are no longer needed. I suspect I'll be working on that for the rest of my life."

"I'm aware of RFW," Cythera said. "It's saved many female werewolves. I had no idea you established the organization."

"You wouldn't. That was a condition from my mate. He didn't want my name associated with it. Of course, those who dig eventually find out I'm involved. But I must be discreet. It's a difficult balance."

"You may need to use your own services if the overlord alpha finds out about your relationship with Decker." I pushed sympathy into my words.

"The irony has not escaped me. But I won't lose Decker. He's an example of how an alpha should be. Strong without using extreme violence. Others can learn from him but not if he's charged with killing Emron."

"When news reached you there'd been a murder," Cythera said, "what did you do?"

"Decker insisted I leave. He said no one could know I'd been there. Of course, some of his werewolves know we're involved, but they've been forbidden to speak of it. I wanted to stay with him and argued my alpha expected me to visit Decker.

But he was right. It was late, and there would have been no easy way to explain why I was in his tent and we were alone."

"I'm assuming the overlord alpha doesn't know Decker is the father of your pup?" I said.

"He's never questioned that he isn't the father," Scarlet said. "And I've had no reason to tell him the truth. I perform my bonded duties, so why couldn't it be his?"

"It's definitely Decker's?"

"I'm certain of it. And I'm thrilled to be with pup," Scarlet said. "I'll protect her with my life."

"The pup is a girl?" I said.

"She'll be strong, proud, and will stand up for the rights of female werewolves."

There was a knock on the door, and Bertoli entered. He looked miserable, and one of his wings seemed bent out of shape. "Sorry to interrupt. Katrine Nominski is here. She's demanding to see Decker."

"Why?" Scarlet stiffened in her seat.

"She's his mate, isn't she?" Bertoli smoothed his wing. "She's not friendly. I could do with some help."

Scarlet's gaze flickered over him, her breath coming out in tiny huffs. "His mate? The last I heard, she was still involved with Emron. She's already moved on?"

"Yes?" The word came out as a question. His gaze went to Scarlet's belly. "Maybe you can help her. Katrine's having cramps. I don't know much about pregnant ladies. She wants a hot water bottle and ginger tea. Is that okay?"

Her top lip peeled back to reveal sharp teeth, and she drew in several deep breaths.

"Thank you, Bertoli. We'll be out in a moment." He needed to stop talking before this werewolf turned savage.

He remained in the doorway. "What should I do with her? She keeps saying Decker needs to know. She pulled my wing and told me she'd break it if I didn't do what she said."

"Go see to Katrine." Cythera's sharp tone showed she meant business and had Bertoli hurrying out.

I winced. He'd just stamped his big old angel boot into a tricky situation. I touched Scarlet's hand. "You didn't know about Katrine?"

Scarlet closed her eyes for a second. "I told Decker to find someone else because I wasn't free to love. I didn't mean it, though. Decker is mine."

"If it's any consolation, it was only one night. Decker got drunk, and Katrine pressed herself on him." I doubted it would be much consolation.

Scarlet nodded slowly. "I cannot condemn him for his actions. I've been intimate with my mate. And sometimes we didn't see each other for weeks. He's a prime werewolf, and he has needs."

"And Decker resisted them. I'm not saying you should accept this or be happy, but Katrine has been raised to use her charms to maximum effect." I briefly touched her hand again. "She may even benefit from your services at the refuge to help her see there's another way to live."

The anger faded in Scarlet's eyes. "It's not the first time I've heard such a story. Some females are raised to believe they have only one thing to offer males. They get told it so many times, they believe it, and it becomes a habit. They see how much power they have when they offer themselves to a male werewolf. But the power is an illusion."

"Katrine holds a lot of bitterness inside her," I said. "Even though she doesn't realize it, she'll need support when her pup arrives."

"She'll get it," Scarlet said. "But right now, I'm focused on making sure Decker is released."

"We'll need a formal statement from you," Cythera said. "Is there anyone else who can confirm you were with Decker at the time of the murder?"

"Several of his pack saw me. Decker swore them to secrecy, but when he releases that order, they'll confirm his alibi."

"Good enough," Cythera said.

I sat back as the angels ran through a few more details. Although I was glad to get to the bottom of Decker's secret, that still left an enormous problem. Who killed Emron and why?

Chapter 21

Back to the start

By the time the interview concluded, it was getting late.

Scarlet had been taken to visit Decker while her statement was written up, and I was relaxing with Zandra and contemplating whether to investigate Bertoli's desk drawer for treats, when he bounded over, a big smile on his face.

"How about I treat everyone to dinner? Today's been an adventure. We should celebrate how clever you are for solving this mystery, Juno."

"Um... we were just heading home," Zandra said. "It's been a long day."

"I'll come with you," Bertoli said.

"Haven't you got somewhere else to be?" Zandra shot me a panicked look.

"I can't think of anywhere else I'd rather be. Juno, perhaps we could spend the weekend together at the beach? I know you like to fish. I could hire a boat, and we could see what we can catch together."

"I do. I usually take Sammy there when we go on a date." I tried to act casual, despite Zandra's incredulous expression.

"I could join you the next time. Unless you think I'd be a third wheel. I wouldn't get in the way. I'd make myself useful."

Bertoli's puppy dog expression had me wavering. "I'll think about it."

Cythera called him into her office, and after flashing me a smile, he dashed away.

Zandra scooped me into her arms. "What have you done to that angel? It's freaking me out."

"What makes you think I've done anything?"

She raised her eyebrows. "He's being nice to Finn, wants to be your best friend, and keeps buying you things. He'll ask to adopt you next. Should I be worried?"

I huffed out a breath. "Don't be angry, but I used a tiny amount of beguiling magic on him."

"Juno! Why do that?"

"Because he was so mean to Finn. Finn works hard at fitting in and doing a good job, and Bertoli is always unkind to him. I snapped. Perhaps I pushed a little too much magic into the spell, so he's enchanted by me, too." I accepted a tickle under my chin. "Of course, he could have come to his senses and realized what a magnificent creature I am, but..."

"You need to be careful. He's getting obsessed with you. Remove the magic. He wouldn't normally behave like this. It could harm him."

"If I do that, we get the snappy, sarcastic Bertoli back. I've been having fun getting all the treats. I particularly enjoyed the kippers."

"They stank, and they gave you indigestion. I had to endure your fishy burps on my face for most of the night. No more gifts, especially no kippers." Zandra glanced over her shoulder. "We'll have to get used to grumpy Bertoli again. He's too weird like this. It's unnatural. He's not behaving like himself, and that won't do him good in the long term."

"Being positive, encouraging, and generous with his friends are bad traits?"

"They're amazing traits, but they aren't Bertoli's traits. Deal with it. Do we have an understanding?"

"Unfortunately, yes." I flipped my front paws over her shoulder and looked at Bertoli through the glass window into Cythera's office. He noticed me and gave me a finger wave.

I raised a paw in acknowledgement. Perhaps he was becoming clingy. And Finn seemed uncomfortable when Bertoli was nice to him. I'd leave the magic for a few more days, so I could maximize my gift-receiving opportunities, then I'd remove it.

Finn walked over and joined us. "Scarlet's thrilled to be reunited with Decker. It was kind of sweet. He kissed her belly."

"It was foolish of him but noble to hide her involvement," I said.

"At least she came forward before it was too late," Zandra said. "And I get why she hesitated. She's in for a world of hurt when this news gets back to the overlord alpha."

"And unfortunately, it will," Finn said. "He has connections everywhere. Even inside Angel Force."

"You mean you have a traitor in your midst?" I hissed softly.

"Don't look at me, but information has a habit of leaking out."

"And there I was, thinking angels were incorruptible."

"I blame the change in policy. They let anyone in these days." A tiny flicker of Finn's demon energy danced across his wings before vanishing.

"Angels are like the rest of us," Zandra said. "They do their best, but sometimes, they get distracted."

"Much like Scarlet. She didn't request to be born into a world with expectations about alliances and marriage for political gain. Scarlet accepted her situation and made the best of it. It wasn't until she discovered what she could have from a relationship that things changed. It often takes a shocking revelation to shift the status quo," I said.

"And a lot of pain. The overlord alpha will kill her," Finn said. "He'll imprison her until the pup is born, take it away, and use Decker to set an example to other werewolves. It'll be a public and violent death for both of them."

"You can't allow that," Zandra said. "All Scarlet's done is fall in love."

"While being mated to the overlord alpha," I said. "It's an awful situation, but that is their heritage. It's how they've always done things. I'm not saying it's right, though. Just because something has a history doesn't mean it's the correct way to do things. But

Decker and Scarlet have a battle on their hands if they're to survive this."

"We'll help them, right?" Zandra looked from me to Finn.

My heart swelled at the determined look in my witch's eyes. She never stepped back from helping the underdog. Or in this case, the under werewolf.

"Let's get Decker cleared of murder first and find out what happened to Emron," Finn said. "Then we'll figure out how and if we can help Scarlet and Decker without bringing even more werewolves to Crimson Cove."

"This mission calls for strong coffee," Zandra said.

"I'll get it," Bertoli called out as he left Cythera's office. "And whatever else you need. Snacks? Sparkling water? Whatever you want, just ask."

"Just a coffee, thanks, buddy." Finn looked at me. "Juno, I could do with your help with the Bertoli situation."

"I've spoken to her about it," Zandra said. "Things will get back to normal soon."

"They will. You'll soon have your grumpy, unpleasant companion back to snipe at you, belittle you, and question everything you do," I said.

Finn grinned. "I prefer him that way."

We settled in seats around a desk as Bertoli hurried back and forth with coffee and packs of cookies he'd discovered in the kitchen, looking proud of himself for making our lives more comfortable. Or more uncomfortable, in Finn's case.

"Angels have gone to speak to Decker's pack," Finn said. "Decker has lifted the restriction on them talking about his relationship with Scarlet, so we can confirm they were together."

"And since they were together at the time of the murder," I said, "it means someone planted the evidence to show Decker killed Emron."

"If we find out who did that, we find the killer," Zandra said.

Finn dunked a cookie into his coffee and sucked on it. "It wasn't Katrine. I checked her alibi myself. The doctor confirmed she was at her appointment. So did his receptionist."

"Katrine could still have planted the evidence, though," I said. "She found Emron's body."

"Leon is a possibility," Zandra said. "His pack could have lied and said he was at the pizza parlor when he was killing Emron. Maybe he formed an alliance with Katrine. Did a deal with her so she'd plant the evidence."

"What would she get in return?" Finn said.

"Revenge because Decker rejected her," I said.

Finn grabbed another cookie. "It's a possibility. How do we prove it?"

"Can I get you anything else?" Bertoli said. "Soft drinks, peanuts, whatever you like, it's not too much trouble. I can order in. Or make a booking at a restaurant. My treat."

"We're good," Finn said. "How about you wait by the reception desk for the other angels to come back and confirm the information from Decker's pack?"

He shot Finn a salute. "It's a pleasure to serve my best friend."

We waited until Bertoli left the office before continuing.

"How about Grace and Rhett?" I said. "They claimed they were together when they got news about Emron's murder, but could they be covering for each other?"

"Again, it's possible, but how do we get them to reveal their deception?" Finn said.

No one spoke for several minutes as coffee was sipped, snacks munched on, and twisty problems mulled over.

There had to be a way to figure this out. At the start, this investigation had seemed straightforward. There'd been evidence of Decker's guilt. He had no alibi, and we'd discovered a reasonable motive. But murder was rarely simple, and it felt like we were back at the start with no idea how to progress. We needed to dig deeper to sort this out.

I swallowed the fishy treat provided by Bertoli. "Is the crime scene still intact?" I said to Finn.

"Sure. It was warded. No one's been allowed in since Emron's body was removed. Why?"

"We need to go back to the beginning and see where it happened."

"You think we missed something when we investigated?"

I twitched my nose. "No offence, Finn, but it wouldn't be the first time Angel Force missed something critical at a murder scene."

"Definitely taken. I'll have you know, I have excellent crime scene analysis skills. I almost aced my class."

"And you're a wonderful exception to the rule. But we're missing something. Perhaps seeing where it happened will bring things into focus."

"It's not a bad idea." Zandra didn't sound enthusiastic.

Finn brushed cookie crumbs off his fingers. "I need to get the okay from Cythera, but if she has no objections, we can go there now. See if anything clicks."

"Then make it so," I said.

Zandra grimaced as Finn walked away. "I can think of better things to do this evening. I don't feel like I've had a break in weeks. What with Adrienne, a busy work schedule, and you being shady, I need a time out."

"When am I ever shady?"

She arched an eyebrow. "When are you not?"

"We can relax later. Once we've found the killer."

Zandra grabbed another cookie and closed her eyes. "Let me know when the fun begins."

❦

After an hour of us kicking our heels, Finn got approval from Cythera for us to go to the site of Emron's murder.

"I have to fly in," Finn said as we headed outside. "Emron set up exactly halfway between the two werewolf camps. Here are the coordinates."

Zandra checked them and nodded. "I don't mind translocating us all. You're welcome to hop on board the spell."

Finn flexed his wings. "It's tempting, but Cythera gave me a talking to about being more angel. She's watching me like a hawk after my recent rule break. Even though we're not supposed to fly in case a non-magical spots us, she wants me to show I don't disobey her. And that means I take to the wing. Discreetly."

I patted his arm with one paw from my position on Zandra's shoulder. "With those beautiful wings, that won't be possible. Happy flying. We'll see you there."

Finn shot into the air, and Zandra cast a translocation spell, taking us deep into the warm, green embrace of Crimson Cove woods.

"Holy bubbling cauldrons! That's not a tent." Zandra set me on the ground as she stared at the enormous woodland home Emron had established for himself.

I sniffed around the green and gold fabric. "Emron liked everything to be top of the range and expensive." The first time I'd met him, I'd noticed his designer jeans and fresh out of the box shoes.

"This is something else, though. You could live in this all year round." It took Zandra several minutes to circle the tent. "It's too much."

"Some people need to show off their wealth. It's got something to do with ego. Or the size of a certain male appendage."

"No kidding," she muttered. "Emron's must have been tiny."

The front of the tent had a shimmering magic ward across it, which prevented anyone from going inside and nosing around.

We waited for Finn, who descended through the trees a few moments later.

He nodded at us then swiped his wings across the wards to make them vanish. "It's quite some place, isn't it?"

"We were considering which deficiency Emron was making up for by investing in something so elaborate," I said.

Finn chuckled. "I'm not going there. Shall we?"

I stepped in first and got a whiff of old blood. Zandra followed me, and Finn came in last. The inside of the tent was as elaborate as the exterior, with gauzy drapes, full-sized furniture, and even pictures on the walls. All of them were of Emron posing with various celebrities.

"There's an actual king-sized bed in here." Zandra was shaking her head. "This werewolf had gone soft."

"He's worse than Leon for spending money," Finn said. "But their accounts were similarly impressive in terms of savings."

I slowly walked around the tent, noting various bloodstains on the fabric floor covering.

Zandra stood with her hands on her hips. "What are you thinking, Juno? Anything standing out for you?"

I walked to the smaller of the bloodstains. "This was where Emron was axed in the shoulder?"

Finn nodded. "We believe so. He was struck with the axe first. The injury weakened him enough that his killer got him on his knees and then removed his head with the blade over there. You see the second bloodstain by the sword holder and then the spatter on the floor and walls?"

"Unfortunately, yes." Zandra grimaced. "His head landed by the door?" She pointed at a much larger stain that was so deep red it looked almost black.

"Right again. I'm not sure if that's what his killer intended, but the blow was so powerful it took the head off in a single strike. It must've flipped in the air and landed by the door." Finn made a spiraling motion with his hands.

"Could the killer have kicked it?" Zandra said. "Or deliberately moved it? Maybe they were going for full shock factor for whoever found Emron. Making a statement?"

"There was a small mark found on the side of Emron's head, but it was most likely from where it landed rather than from being kicked. There were no other injuries to suggest it had been manipulated."

I walked around the bloodstains again. "Emron's head was taken off from front to back. You believe he was brought to his knees after receiving the axe wound, and the killer took the sword from its holder and then hit him with it?"

"It's the only thing that could have happened," Finn said. "After they used the sword, they placed it back in the holder and left."

"Emron was slumped on the floor in front of the sword holder?"

"Yes. He was on his knees, sort of slumped on his left side," Finn said. "From what we can tell, his killer didn't touch him after he took off his head. He must have realized he had little time.

Alpha werewolves are rarely left on their own for more than a few minutes. There's always someone watching them."

I paced the scene several more times. The small stain from the axe blow then the beheading. It made little sense. "A werewolf wouldn't have been slowed by such an insignificant axe wound."

"Maybe his killer surprised him," Zandra said. "Or there was silver on the axe?" She looked at Finn for confirmation.

"No silver on Emron or the axe. He wasn't poisoned. We ran a blood work panel, and nothing odd showed up."

I looked from one stain to the other. "I know what happened. And our killer has already confessed."

"They have?" Finn said. "It was one of Decker's werewolves?"

I nodded. "Finn, we need a new werewolf negotiator and the suspects to be brought together. It's time to solve this mystery."

Chapter 22

Who killed Mr. Wolf?

It had taken Finn all of the previous night to secure an experienced werewolf negotiator to help us tidy the loose ends of this investigation.

In that time, I'd grabbed food, sleep, and revealed to Zandra what I believed happened in Emron's tent.

"You're sure we need this negotiator?" Zandra strode beside me as we headed to the small medical facility on the edge of Crimson Cove.

"Better to be safe. I expect tempers will flare when the truth comes out. We need to make sure no one else is harmed." I trotted along, my tail up. It felt good to be at the end of this mystery. If only I'd paid more attention in the beginning, we wouldn't have needed to wade through an army of angry suspects and motives, and I could have been relaxing in Sorcha's café with Sammy, while Zandra explored her relationship with Randal.

Still, that fun would come. Every mystery was a learning experience. And for that, I was grateful.

As we drew near, Finn stood outside the medical facility. Standing beside him was a broad-shouldered, burly male werewolf with mutton-chop whiskers and an impressive head of messy dark curls.

Finn raised a hand, his clothing crumpled and his eyes tired. "This is Marmaduke Lupin. He's the best the werewolves could offer at such short notice."

Marmaduke slid a glare toward Finn. "Watch your tone, angel. You're fortunate I'm here at all. I barely received enough information to consider it worth my while. If I didn't know Decker, I wouldn't be here."

"Sorry. No offence meant. It's been a long night."

"Greetings. I'm Juno, and this is Zandra Crypt. We appreciate your visit. I'm hopeful your services won't be needed, but this is a delicate situation."

Marmaduke huffed out a breath. "Sure. I know the basics. I knew there was something dodgy about this investigation when I learned Decker had been locked up for murder. If I can help, I'm glad to be here."

"Decker won't be the problem. But there will be egos to handle. Is everyone here?" I said to Finn.

"Decker and Scarlet are inside. So is Leon. He brought Nico with him. Katrine arrived five minutes ago, complaining bitterly about what a waste of time this was."

"What about Grace and Rhett?" Zandra said.

"They were invited, but they've yet to make an appearance."

"It's not crucial they're here," I said, "but I'd have thought Grace would want to know who actually killed her husband."

"And shake their hand?" Zandra smirked.

"I wouldn't put it past her."

"I'm still uncertain why we have to do this around Hugh's hospital bed." Finn pulled open the door, and everyone walked in in front of him.

"Hugh muddied the waters early on by confessing. Which prompted all of Decker's werewolves to do the same."

"You're talking about Decker's bottom werewolf?" Marmaduke said as we walked into a quiet, cool corridor.

"That's right. And Leon's pack discovered him planting evidence to implicate Leon in the murder. It's how he came to be in here."

Marmaduke winced. "I'm amazed he's still in one piece for pulling a stunt like that. How's he doing?"

"It's a weird one," Finn said. "Hugh was badly beaten, but he should have healed from his injuries. He was knocked out but has yet to regain consciousness. And his physical injuries are slow to heal, too. The doctors are worried. They think something else is going on."

"Perhaps when he learns we know Decker is innocent, it'll encourage his healing," I said. "Which room?"

Finn led us to a large private room at the back of the facility. Everyone was crammed in there. Decker and Scarlet sat close to Hugh's bed, and Scarlet had hold of one of Hugh's hands and talked quietly to him.

Leon and Nico stood on the opposite side of the room. Leon smiled, although there was no kindness in that expression. His gaze was on Decker and Scarlet. Nico was in his usual cowed position.

Katrine sat in a chair, her arms and legs crossed as she swung one heeled foot. She glanced at us and rolled her eyes. "At last. Why have we been dragged here? The angels said something about new evidence. What is it?"

Finn stepped forward, and I joined him. "We've had a break in the investigation. And since you're all involved, we thought you'd like an update."

"Get on with it," Katrine said.

"It's been an illuminating morning so far." Leon's gaze was still on Decker and Scarlet. "I'm getting all sorts of useful information by being here."

Decker glowered at him.

"This is Marmaduke Lupin. The Wolf Council has asked him to ensure everyone cooperates in the final stages of this investigation," Finn said.

Marmaduke nodded at everyone.

"You won't have any problems from me," Leon said. "Although I would like a chat with the Wolf Council and our overlord alpha once we're done. How long will this take?"

"Not long. Juno, you're up," Finn said.

I arched my back and smoothed a patch of fur that was sticking up. "At first, this case seemed simple. An alpha werewolf lost control and killed the negotiator who was attempting to establish peace between two warring werewolf packs."

"That's what happened," Leon said. "The evidence is clear."

"And Decker seemed guilty," I said. "But the evidence of him being at the murder scene was planted. He has a solid alibi."

Leon pulled himself upright. "What alibi?" His gaze flickered to Scarlet. "You mean her?"

Scarlet stood, assisted by Decker. "Show respect, wolf. You know who I am."

The power in Scarlet's words reverberated down my spine.

Leon must have felt it too, because he swayed and lowered his head. "My apologies, my queen. But it's a shock to see you being intimate with Decker. And I've yet to congratulate you on your pregnancy. You and the overlord alpha must be over the moon. Or... maybe not?" His gaze went to Decker's hand, which was tucked against Scarlet's spine.

Scarlet didn't flinch under Leon's acerbic tone. "I'm Decker's alibi. We were together that night. And I'm prepared to testify if required."

Leon rubbed his hands together, despite keeping his head lowered. "Our overlord alpha will tear you apart because of your treachery."

"That's never going to happen," Decker growled out.

"Keep it calm, gentlemen," Marmaduke said.

"I'm calm. But you won't be able to stop it. You've broken the rules, so you have to pay," Leon said to Decker. "And your friends on the Wolf Council won't be able to save either of you."

Marmaduke moved forward, his hands held out. "Let's focus on finding out who killed Emron."

"Happy to, but that doesn't mean I can't gather information to assist our overlord alpha," Leon said.

"Decker, step aside now and hand me your pack and territory. A dead alpha can't rule."

Decker's hands flexed, and claws poked through the skin.

Marmaduke stepped between the alphas. "I don't want to restrain either of you, but I will if this gets tenser. Both of you, back down."

Leon shrugged and looked away.

Marmaduke glanced at me. "Probably a good idea to hurry this up."

Scarlet gripped Decker's arm. "I need a moment."

"You want me to come with you?"

"No, stay. I want some water. I'll be back in a minute." She kissed his cheek and then walked out of the room.

Leon and Decker engaged in some non-blinking posturing, but the tension remained below boiling point.

The door opened, and Valerie walked in. She stopped and stared at everyone. Behind her were Grace and Rhett.

"What's going on?" Valerie hurried to the side of Hugh's bed.

"Greetings, Valerie," I said. "I'm glad you could be here, since this affects you, too."

"What affects me?" She caught hold of Hugh's hand. "You shouldn't all be in here. Hugh needs his rest."

"I left you a message to let you know we'd be here," Finn said.

Valerie didn't look up. "I didn't get it. I've been too busy making sure my brother doesn't die to check my messages."

"He won't die." I hopped onto Hugh's bed, walked up his chest, and sniffed his face. His breathing was deep and even, and to the unpracticed eye, anyone would think he was unconscious. But his eyelids flickered a little too quickly.

"Sorry we're late." Grace remained by the door with Rhett. "There were several vehicles blocking the road into town. They'd broken down. You have a non-magical problem here."

"Don't we know it," Finn said. "We're glad you could make it."

"We almost didn't come," Rhett said. "There's no point in us being here."

I settled on Hugh's stomach and resisted the urge to make biscuits on the white sheets with my paws. "Surely, you want to know who killed your brother."

Rhett's gaze cut to Decker. "I thought the killer had been found."

"He has been. And he's in this room," I said.

"I insist you all leave." Valerie finally looked up, although her gaze settled on no one. "Hugh isn't getting better. This stress won't help his recovery."

"He needs to hear this," I said. "If we'd listened to him and not ignored the truth, this mystery would have been solved days ago."

"What truth? What does Hugh know that can help solve this?"

"Hugh, why don't you tell everyone what's been going on?" I said.

"He's unconscious, thanks to Leon's vicious pack. He hasn't said a word since he was brought in." Valerie stroked Hugh's hair off his forehead.

Scarlet re-entered the room, carrying a cup of water. Her eyes widened when they settled on Valerie. "Hey!"

Valerie jumped away from the bed. "What are you doing here?"

Scarlet opened her arms, and they embraced. "It's a complicated story. How are you? I've been trying to get in touch."

"You two know each other?" Finn said.

I regarded the two women. "Of course they do. This makes even more sense now."

"This is ridiculous," Leon said. "Charge Decker with murder, and let's get on with things. My pack isn't happy being stuck here. Neither am I."

"Not so fast," I said. "Decker is innocent, but there are other reasons Emron could have been murdered. Not least of which involved his bitter, cheated-on mate and his frustrated brother. Did you turn to each other to seek comfort after Emron mistreated you?"

Rhett put an arm around Grace's shoulders. "You don't know what you're talking about."

"You're together. It's clear for everyone to see. And no one would blame you. Emron was unkind to both of you," I said. "Grace, you're a magnificent werewolf with a noble heritage, but once Emron claimed you and manipulated your associations, he basically ignored you. That must have hurt."

She looked away. "I understood our arrangement would never be about love. I would have been happier if he'd respected me, though."

I nodded. "The same goes for you, Rhett. You worked with Emron, but when you had a disagreement, he cut you out, didn't he? Emron tossed you aside like trash because you no longer served a purpose. You refused to do his bidding, so you were of no value to him. It didn't matter you were related by blood."

Rhett's fingers tightened on Grace's shoulder. "Maybe so. But that doesn't mean either of us had anything to do with Emron's death."

I hesitated to see if they'd say more, but they remained steadfastly silent. "It's true. Neither of you killed Emron, even though you're both happy it happened."

Rhett shrugged while Grace stared at the wall.

"There are other people who wanted him dead." I curled my tail around my paws. "Leon has had designs on Decker's pack for years. And although Decker was diplomatic when he spoke about their interactions, it was clear there were few lines Leon wouldn't cross to get what he wanted. His actions speak volumes about his true nature."

"Hey, kitty cat. Watch it. Just because there's a Wolf Council negotiator in the room doesn't mean I won't tear you apart." Leon's hands were flexed, his eyes gleaming amber.

Nico stood behind him, looking tense and ready to move if ordered, even though his eyes were full of an apology as they briefly met mine.

"I have nothing to fear from you," I said. "Despite you being a thoroughly unpleasant individual who uses any underhanded means to get what you want, you also didn't kill Emron."

"And it wasn't me, before you go pointing a fluffy paw in my direction," Katrine said.

"No, you also didn't kill him. Although you had an excellent reason to do so. Emron misused you for years. He used your enviable physical assets and desire to make him happy and turned you into a man-eating weapon."

Her gaze rolled to the ceiling. "Oh, please. I knew what I was doing." Her foot swinging grew faster.

"You were happy to go from bed to bed, forming no proper connections, and manipulating the men you gave pleasure to? Does it give you satisfaction to drag out people's secrets and use them against them? Is that what you want from life?" I wasn't judging. If it truly made Katrine happy to gouge misery into people, I wouldn't force her to change, but I'd actively avoid her.

"It's what I'm expected to do." Her nails tapped the arm of the chair.

"It doesn't have to be that way." Scarlet held one of Valerie's hands. "I've heard that story hundreds of times from women who come to my refuge. I set up RFW."

Katrine stilled in her seat. "You work with battered werewolves who are too weak to stand up to their mates."

"The females stand up to their mates many times, but they often don't know when to ask for help and when to get out of a situation that's ruining their lives."

Katrine's tongue ran across her teeth. "Whatever."

"The females who come to the refuge assume they must act a certain way to gain acceptance from a pack or a particular male. They're brainwashed into following every order," Scarlet said softly.

"I'm not brainwashed." Katrine's words faltered. "Emron told me to make the most of my assets before they faded. I had to get everything I needed fast because it wouldn't be long before I was invisible."

"You're a beautiful, intelligent, strong werewolf." Decker's tone was sincere. "You don't have to offer yourself to every male to get him to do things for you."

Katrine's expression changed from angry to confused then to sad. She focused on her nails. "I'm free to do what I like. And I like being with lots of men. There's no crime in that. I've broken no laws."

"No, you haven't," I said. "But someone has. And that someone planted evidence to frame Decker. They goaded him, challenged him, and demanded he take over his pack and territory. Isn't that right, Leon?"

Leon's eyes narrowed. "You've got nothing on me."

"You're not denying you had opportunities to get fur and blood from Decker," I said.

"I could if I'd wanted. It was easy to land a few blows on Decker. And he was half-hearted when we fought. It was another sign he'd given up being interested in the alpha role."

"I was attempting to settle our negotiation in a civilized way. It's a concept overlooked by most werewolves. Did you plant that evidence?" Decker said.

"Not me," Leon said.

My gaze settled on Nico, the timid, beaten down werewolf who'd barely made eye contact with anyone since we'd all entered the room. Now was his chance to shine. "Nico, is there something you want to tell us?"

Chapter 23

The underdog wins

Nico inhaled and exhaled deeply three times. He kept his gaze on the floor.

"It's okay. No one here will hurt you," I said.

"What's he got to do with this?" Leon didn't spare Nico a glance. "He knows nothing. And even if he did, he's loyal to me."

"Because he's werewolf-bound to be loyal," I said. "If Nico had a choice, he'd have left you a long time ago. That's what he wants."

Nico was inching away from Leon, his body shaking.

"Is that right? You've been flapping your lips to this smug little cat?" Leon whipped around and grabbed Nico by the throat.

Marmaduke lunged and pinned Leon to the wall. "That's not how we do things. Release your werewolf."

"If he's hiding things from me, he must be punished," Leon said. "I own him."

"Don't make me force you," Marmaduke snarled out. "It won't be pretty."

Leon resisted for a full minute before dropping his hold on Nico. "You're wasting your time by asking him anything. He's never involved in important werewolf business."

I hopped off the bed, walked over to Nico, and placed my two front paws on his calf. "Stand up to your bullies. It's the right thing to do."

Nico trembled, but he nodded. "It's hard. I've been with Leon's pack for years. I don't handle change well."

"You don't want to be in his pack, do you?" I said. "And if Katrine hands her pup to Leon, it'll be ruined. The creature won't stand a chance. Leon will bend its innocence to his will, just like he's done to you."

"I hate it," Nico whispered. "They all bully me. Leon encourages the pack to be cruel."

"Every werewolf needs to know his place," Leon said. "We all have a bottom werewolf. They know the situation when they join any pack. If they desire it, they can rise up the ranks. I don't stop anyone from achieving their ambition if they have talent and power."

I glared at him. "You also work hard to ensure Nico believes he's worthless and will amount to nothing. You keep him at the bottom because it's convenient to have a whipping werewolf. A werewolf who'll tremble every time you walk into a room. Does that make you feel powerful?"

Leon sneered at me. "You know nothing about werewolf politics. We all have ranks and positions. That's how it's always been. Decker has a bottom werewolf, too. I don't hear you complaining about unfair treatment."

"Hugh is treated with respect," Decker said. "Sure, he gets the less glamorous jobs, but he's always praised when he does well. He's a true member of the pack and is treated kindly by the others. I tolerate zero bullying. Anyone who can't stick to that rule is out."

"Which goes to show, your way of running the pack is wrong. It's no wonder they're soft. They'll welcome a change of leader," Leon said.

"Never going to happen," Decker said slowly and menacingly.

Marmaduke lifted his hands, and they crackled with magic.

Both alphas got the hint and stepped back before they got a taste of negotiator power.

I nudged Nico with my head until he stood in the center of the room. "Keep telling your story. You've put up with so much abuse that it became your normal, everyday, didn't it?"

"I did. It was normal to expect a beating and to go hungry. I'd accepted my fate." Nico's tongue darted out across his lips. "When I heard about Leon's plans for Katrine's pup, it broke my heart. I was sick to my stomach thinking about what he'd do. He wanted to show Decker he was the stronger werewolf and would always defeat him."

Decker was shaking his head. "You're disgusting, Leon. Even though that werewolf pup isn't mine, I won't let you get your hands on it."

"It's not yours?" I said.

Decker nodded, one hand on Scarlet's shoulder. "I'd never betray my soulmate. Katrine may claim we were together, but I don't find her attractive, not in that way. There's only one werewolf for me, and she's by my side. We're bonded. Scarlet is all I think about. All I desire."

Katrine hissed at him. "We were together. This pup is yours!"

Sympathy flickered in his eyes. "I'm happy to wait for the pup to be born so you can run a DNA test."

"Is this true?" Leon snapped at Katrine. "You lied to me about the father?"

Katrine flipped her hair over one shoulder.

"Is it any surprise she lied?" I said. "Katrine knew what you'd do if she failed to get pregnant by Decker. You must have bullied her until she agreed to work for you."

Katrine's granite exterior crumpled, and her eyes hazed with tears. "I know how much you wanted the pup. I tried everything to convince Decker to be with me, but he refused."

"You're a filthy liar!" Leon advanced on Katrine, his hands in fists.

"Easy now." Marmaduke rested a broad hand on Leon's shoulder. "Our pregnant females deserve careful treatment."

"She deceived me. She said that pup was Decker's." Leon jabbed a finger at Katrine. "What else has she lied about?"

There were tears on Katrine's cheeks. "You want to humiliate Decker and spoil everything he cares about."

"Why do you hate me so much?" Decker was shaking his head. "I've done nothing to you."

"You exist! That's enough," Leon spat out. "And you act like you have the perfect pack, the perfect werewolves, and the perfect life. No one is that good or that decent. I wanted to expose you for the weakling you are."

Decker growled. "Bitterness is a bad trait in an alpha."

"So is softness, and you have that in bucketfuls."

"It's not soft to help others. Nor is it soft to protect those who aren't as strong as you. Holding out a hand and pulling others up is the biggest strength an alpha can have."

Leon snorted. "Look where it's gotten you."

"You don't deserve to be an alpha," Decker said. "If you treat the rest of your werewolves like you do Nico, it's no surprise they're so tense and run on testosterone. Werewolves don't always have to be ready to fight. There are other ways."

"Only if you're a coward with no backbone," Leon said.

Finn cleared his throat. "Juno, maybe you could let me know who I should arrest for Emron's murder."

"This is all relevant to the investigation. Our killer needs to hear this, so they know this is a safe place. And although murder is never right, they won't be severely judged," I said. "So, how about you open your eyes, Hugh, and tell us why you murdered Emron?"

Everyone looked at Hugh.

Hugh drew in a deep breath, and his eyes flickered open.

Valerie gasped. "You're awake! How do you feel?"

He clasped his sister's hand. "Bad for lying. Terrible for worrying you. I just couldn't think what else to do."

"It'll be okay. Ignore everyone. I'll make them go. And I'll get the doctor to examine you."

He shook his head. "No. Juno's right about me. I told everybody I killed Emron, but no one believed me."

"You really did it?" Decker moved to stand beside Hugh's bed. "Why? You know I want peace between the packs."

"He did it for me." Nico shuffled forward, still trembling.

"You two are good friends, aren't you," I said.

"Hugh's friendship is the only thing that keeps me going," Nico said. "I'm overlooked by everyone. I don't stand a chance with any females, and my pack taunts me or ignores me. But when I met Hugh at a wilding event, he understood what I was going through."

Hugh nodded, a small smile on his face. "I found a true friend the day we met. More than a friend, a brother."

Nico returned his smile. "Hugh found me when I was in a dark place. Leon had threatened to remove me from the pack. He said I was an embarrassment. I tried my hardest, but it was never enough."

"What happened to you?" I said.

Nico's chin sank to his chest. "I'd lost hope. I went to the edge of a cliff and stood with my toes over the edge. I was waiting for a powerful gust of wind to decide for me. Even when attempting to take my own life, I was too weak to act."

Hugh shook his head. "You should never have been pushed so far. Your alpha should have supported you. He should have known you were struggling and helped."

"Watch what you say, pup," Leon growled out. "I'm within my rights to beat you for speaking to an alpha in such a way."

"You won't go near Hugh," Decker said. "And you won't hurt or belittle Nico again." He pulled a small blade from his back pocket, sliced it across his palm, and then held it out to Nico. "Join my pack. You'd be welcome. We have hierarchies, but everyone is treated fairly."

Tears flooded Nico's eyes as he grabbed the knife. "You're serious?"

"I never joke around with pack matters. We want you."

"You can't have him! He's mine." Leon lunged at Nico, but Decker and Marmaduke blocked his path.

"No more bullying," Decker said. "That's not how a healthy pack operates. Nico, if you wish to join us, share your blood with me. Then your tie with Leon and his pack will be dissolved. You won't have to live in fear anymore."

"Do it," Hugh said. "You won't find a better pack."

"Don't you dare," Leon snarled. "I forbid—"

Decker punched Leon in the stomach, preventing him from issuing a binding order. He glanced at Nico. "Hurry if you want this to happen."

Nico didn't hesitate. He sliced open his hand and then gripped Decker's outstretched one. There was a swirl of heat as Nico's old bond dissolved and a new one formed with Decker. The magic smelled of damp trees and earth.

"You're with us now." Decker rested a hand on Nico's shoulder. "We'll find a role to fit your talents."

"Share the bottom with me." Hugh's smile faded. "Or, of course, I won't be around, so the position is yours full-time."

"You're going nowhere," Decker said. "The pack will protect you."

"Hugh needs to answer for what he's done," Finn said.

"I'm still uncertain why Hugh killed Emron," Grace said.

"Go on, Nico," I said. "You knew a secret about Emron, didn't you? Something that meant the negotiations would never be successful for Decker's pack."

Nico glanced at Leon then nodded. "Bottom pack werewolves are invisible. We overhear plenty we shouldn't as a result. I was in the woods one evening and overheard two guys talking. It was Emron and Leon."

"You're not the only one who's seen them sneaking around together," I said.

"All that means is people are lying about me." Leon's gaze flickered with rage. "I demand to know who."

"Never going to happen. You'll only punish them." Although I was certain Sorcha could stand up for herself if confronted by an angry werewolf.

"To ensure things were fair, we weren't to speak to Emron outside the negotiation process," Decker said. "You knew that."

Leon smirked. "Some rules need to be bent."

"You broke them. You forfeited the negotiations by doing that."

"Leon hated how things were going." Nico was still hunched, but his head was lifted. "So, he arranged to gift Emron Castle Dreadnought."

Grace sucked in a breath. "Emron said nothing to me about this."

"Why would he? He raked in the assets and kept them for himself," Rhett said. "That's how he did business. It was always about what he could get for himself."

"There's one problem here. I don't own Castle Dreadnought," Leon said. "You can't prove Emron planned to gift me anything. This is a pathetic lie from Nico to make himself seem important."

"We can prove it," Finn said. "And if Nico will testify, that'll help. We also have testimony from a legal team about the deeds of Castle Dreadnought being prepared for transfer. It hadn't been completed, but the process was underway."

Leon huffed out a breath but said nothing.

"I was shocked when I overheard their conversation. I didn't know what to do," Nico said.

"So you turned to your closest friend for advice," I said.

Nico nodded. "Hugh got angry. He knew how important these negotiations were to Decker and how desperately he wanted peace."

"You're a disgrace," Leon muttered.

"I got so mad when Nico told me what was going on," Hugh said. "I already knew how badly Leon treated him and told him to break the bond and request entry into our pack. But Nico kept saying he couldn't be disloyal."

"You've lost yourself a fine werewolf." Decker placed a hand on Nico's shoulder.

Leon sneered at him. "Not by my reckoning."

"Go on, Hugh," I said.

"I hated to see my best friend beaten down and broken. But what pushed me over the edge was Leon and Emron's deceit. Emron was a lousy werewolf, all charm and promises but only when it got him what he wanted. I had to act. I grabbed an axe and went to Emron's tent to confront him about his plans."

"You intended to kill him?" Finn said.

"I suggest you don't answer that," Marmaduke said.

"I'm done living in a world full of deceit." Hugh looked Finn in the eyes. "Yes, I wanted Emron dead. I was tired of the fighting and tension. Emron was supposed to help us, but he made things worse. I thought if I spoke to him, reasoned with him, he'd realize his mistake. But he laughed at me."

"That's when you threw the axe at him?" I said.

"I knew I had no hope of defeating a prime werewolf in a fist fight, which was why I took the weapon. I threw the axe, but it missed his heart and hit his shoulder. I figured I was dead when Emron lunged at me."

"Then you grab the sword to defend yourself?" Finn said.

"No. The crime scene revealed Hugh went nowhere near that sword," I said.

"It's true. I didn't. I dodged out of Emron's way at the last second, and more out of luck than judgment, he didn't get me." Hugh looked around the room at his sister's anxious face, Leon's sneer, and Decker's supportive nod. "Emron stumbled and fell on his own blade."

Leon snorted. "You expect us to believe that?"

"When I entered the tent, Emron was sharpening his sword. It's the one he always has on display. The one with the gold on the handle."

"You're lying. Emron wouldn't waste time sharpening his own blade. He'd get one of his werewolves to do it for him," Leon said.

"No. Emron never let anyone touch his swords," Grace said. "They were too precious to him. He was possessive of those wretched things. Even I couldn't go near them. Not that I'd want to."

"He had the blade on a display stand with the sharp side up," Hugh said. "It all happened so quickly. One second, he was lunging, and the next, his head rolled across the tent, and he was on his knees. I promise, I never touched his blade. I only hit him with the axe."

No one spoke for a moment as the revelation settled around us.

"You should have come to me," Decker said. "I would have helped you."

"Covered up the crime, you mean," Leon said.

"Your reputation is hardly angel white in this situation," I said to Leon. "You made a deal with the negotiator who was supposed to end the feud between your packs. And you planted evidence in Emron's tent to make Decker appear guilty."

Leon jerked back his shoulders. "You can't prove that."

"I... I saw what you did that night," Nico said.

"Keep your damn mouth shut! If you say another word, you won't live to see the next full moon."

"He'll live to see many full moons, thanks to being in my pack and under the protection of all my werewolves," Decker said. "Back down, unless you want a werewolf war."

"Gentlemen, keep this under control. No blood needs to be spilled," Marmaduke said.

The tension simmered at boiling point, but no punches were thrown.

"What did you see on the night of Emron's murder, Nico?" I said.

"Leon running through the woods. He was excited about something. So, I followed him. He found Decker outside his tent and jumped him. Leon punched him in the back of the head and knocked him to the ground. They shifted. There was a brief fight, and then Leon ran off. It was so quick. Like he'd changed his mind about attacking Decker."

"Or because he'd gotten the evidence to frame Decker for murder," I said.

Nico nodded. "I watched Decker for a couple of minutes. He changed back and stared after Leon, looking bewildered. Leon had bloodied Decker's face."

"He gave me a split lip," Decker said. "I had no idea why he came at me. And Nico's right. The fight was over before it began."

"Leon had discovered Emron's body," I said. "Had you arranged to meet him again, and when he didn't show, you went to his tent? You found him dead and realized it was an opportunity too good to miss. You fought Decker to get evidence to plant."

Leon's nose wrinkled, but he remained silent.

"I watched you do it," Nico said. "I've not been able to say anything because you caught me, and after you'd beaten me, you ordered me to remain silent. I'm no longer in your pack, so I can speak the truth. It feels amazing not to keep this a secret."

"You scheming, deceitful, traitor," Decker growled out, his fury aimed at Leon. "You never wanted these negotiations to work."

"Only wimps and those past their prime negotiate for power. The rest of us take it."

"I have a question." Katrine had been dabbing her face and attempting to repair her make-up. "Hugh, you confessed to Emron's murder at the start of this but then went quiet. Why? You should have kept confessing. Eventually, someone would have believed you."

"I can answer that," Scarlet said. "Valerie, with your permission?"

Valerie swallowed then nodded. "Sure."

Scarlet clasped one of Decker's hands. "I met Valerie eight weeks ago. She came to one of my refuges. She was shaking, in tears, and terrified because she was being forced into an unsuitable alliance. Her parents had picked a violent male werewolf as her mate. Valerie begged them to change their mind, but he comes from a strong pack, and he's wealthy."

"Much like me, our parents never amounted to much," Hugh said. "We've always struggled for money. And Dad was injured when he was a pup, so he has trouble working."

"Like father like son," Leon said.

"My parents thought if I married this werewolf, their problems would be solved," Valerie said.

"But they'd only be beginning for Valerie," Scarlet said. "I told her to find an ally, someone who'd support her on this journey. Her family and most packs would ostracize her for turning down this offer."

"So, she turned to you, Hugh," I said. "That meant you could no longer confess to the murder because you needed to help your sister."

Hugh nodded. "After Emron fell on his sword, I panicked. I hoped Angel Force wouldn't figure out what happened, and the case would remain unsolved. So, I kept quiet. Then I was stunned when they took Decker in for questioning and revealed the evidence at the crime scene."

"So you acted to protect Decker. You confessed, but then the rest of the pack stepped up, too," I said. "They thought they were being helpful."

"Werewolf loyalty is something else," Zandra said.

"I was willing to accept my punishment for the good of the pack. Decker is an amazing alpha, and we can't afford to lose him," Hugh said. "But then Valerie got in touch and told me what was going on, and I couldn't turn her away."

"You took a different route," I said, "and attempted to frame Leon."

"It was a dumb move, but I was desperate. I was loyal to Decker but also Valerie. We've always looked out for each other. I couldn't let Decker go to jail, but I needed to be free to help my sister. I had to make sure they were both safe."

Decker clapped him on the shoulder. "I commend your courage and your honesty. You shouldn't have attacked Emron, but I understand when rage takes hold. We'll work together to ensure you find a positive way to release your anger."

"That won't happen. That idiot is going to jail." Leon turned his glower on Nico. "And I'll make sure the Wolf Council hears about your deceit."

"And I'll ensure they hear about yours," Decker said. "You'll be lucky to be bottom of any pack after they're done with you."

Leon's bluster evaporated. The Wolf Council didn't mess around when handing out punishment. Best case scenario for Leon was that he'd be stripped of his alpha rank. Worst case, he'd be cast out, and no werewolf would acknowledge him. That was a death warrant against his name.

"I know what I did was wrong, but I can't leave Valerie." Hugh grabbed his sister's hands. "Not now. She can't be mated to that monster. She won't survive."

"Don't worry about your sister," Decker said. "Scarlet and I will ensure she's safe."

"Of course." Scarlet's tone brimmed with compassion. "Whatever it takes, I'll make sure she's protected."

"Hugh, you need to answer for your crime," Finn said. "You attacked Emron. Even though you didn't kill him, you sought him out to hurt him."

He sighed and closed his eyes. "I know. I'll take my punishment. So long as Valerie is looked after, I won't fight this. You'll have my confession."

"In partnership with the Wolf Council," Decker said. "This is an unusual situation, so both angels and wolves must be involved."

"Agreed. I'm sure we can find a solution between us." Finn turned to Leon. "You're coming with me. You'll be charged with tampering with a crime scene."

"You can't do anything to me," Leon said.

"I'll contact the Wolf Council as soon as I can," Decker said. "I'll let them know how you treat your pack members. You have crimes to answer with them, too."

Leon snarled, and it was only Marmaduke blocking his way that prevented him from lunging at Decker.

I looked at Zandra, and we nodded at each other. This mystery was solved.

⁂

Three days had passed since the werewolf trials and tribulations had ended. And I was glad of it. All the werewolf angst made me twitchy.

I lounged on a bookshelf in Vorana's store. Zandra sat in one corner in a high-backed plaid chair, flicking through a spell book. Vorana sat opposite

287

her, immersed in a thick tomb titled *How to Find Your Perfect Warlock*. Sage reclined on the floor beside her, while customers browsed around us.

Vorana glanced up from her book. "You see. Books are relaxing. Everyone loves this place."

"It would be better with coffee and cake." Zandra didn't look up from her spell book.

As if by magic, and there was definitely some in the air, Finn pushed open the main door with his butt. When he turned, he carried a tray of takeout mugs and a white box. The delicious smell drifting from it told me there were foodie treats inside.

Zandra snapped her book shut and grinned. "Perfect timing. Vorana was about to launch into a speech about how amazing books were, and I was about to make my excuses and leave."

Vorana swatted Zandra's knee. "You're a disgrace to the bookish community."

Finn laughed as he handed around the drinks and placed the box on the table. "I've just been dealing with the last coachload of non-magical tourists. I needed a reward for not bashing any of them with my wings."

I glanced out the window. Gus, the tour operator, was herding a few gray-haired old ladies into a coach. "May they never return."

"Now the werewolves are heading out, the risk of non-magicals being eaten has been minimized," Zandra said.

Finn dropped into a seat and grabbed a blueberry muffin from the box. "I had a debrief with Cythera first thing. Angel Force and the Wolf Council have negotiated a deal for Hugh."

I rolled over. "What's the verdict?"

"He'll serve a year inside for assault and wounding. Knowing him, he'll be out in six months because of good behavior. The Wolf Council argued he defended his pack from Emron's attempt at misdirection. And Emron would have healed from the axe wound without medical treatment, so it wasn't a fatal blow."

"Cythera was okay with that?" Zandra snagged a cherry tart from the box and took a bite.

"She knows it's better not to get tangled in a confrontation with the werewolves. And she's more worried about the non-magicals that keep descending on Crimson Cove than angsty werewolves."

"What about Valerie?" I said. "She'll be safe? She's not being forced into the unwanted mating?"

"Valerie is safe," Finn said. "Decker and Scarlet are supporting her. And there's change for them, too, since it's likely Leon will want payback. Decker came to an agreement with the Wolf Council. Valerie will join his pack, and he's relocating them to a secret location in Alaska. Scarlet is going with him. She's severed her link with the overlord alpha and is in a safe house until the details are figured out."

"That's some move," Sage said. "Does Decker realize how cold it gets there?"

"Werewolves have shaggy, dense fur. I'll doubt they'll notice the difference," I said. "And at least they'll be safe."

Sage shivered. "I like a little sun on my fur. It warms my old bones."

"Leon could still track them if he's determined," Zandra said. "He strikes me as a guy who doesn't give up easily."

"Which is why Valerie, Decker, and Scarlet are getting new identities. It's kind of like witness protection. The pack is getting new identities, too. They're also coming up with a new pack name that suits the expanded group."

"It's an exciting time for them." I watched the coach full of non-magicals as it chugged along the street.

"And Leon? Is he getting away with messing with the negotiations and planting evidence?" Zandra said.

"We're working out the details for Leon, but the Wolf Council appreciates he didn't work in the best interests of his pack or werewolves as a whole. They're willing to accept the punishment we give him." Finn blew on his coffee and took a sip.

"What about Katrine?" I said. "What will happen to her pup?"

"She approached Scarlet yesterday, just before she went into the safe house," Finn said. "She's been doing some thinking and wanted to talk things through with her."

"Scarlet got Katrine to see there could be other options," I said. "Perhaps no one ever told her there was a different way of doing things. Katrine could have a better life."

"I like to think she'll change. She spoke to Scarlet for hours," Finn said. "She's even considering keeping the pup and raising it herself."

"And Grace and Rhett get to live happily ever after, I suppose," Zandra said. "She'll inherit Emron's wealth."

"I see no problem with that," I said. "Not after she put up with him for all those years."

"That's it in a nutshell. There are provisions for family members in Emron's will, but Grace gets most of it."

"It's a happy ending of sorts," I said. "Let's hope Grace has better luck with Emron's half-brother."

"If she doesn't, she'll be ridiculously wealthy and free to do as she pleases," Vorana said. "Lucky lady. I wish someone would leave me a fortune."

"You do okay with the bookstore," Zandra said.

"Sure, I get by. But a sack full of gold left by the front door would be put to good use."

We were settled in our seats or on our shelves, happy to munch our way through the box of treats Finn had brought, when movement outside the store caught my eye.

"You have got to be kidding me." I hopped off the shelf and joined Sage at the window.

Another coach of non-magicals had arrived, and right behind it were two huge camper vans, the engines groaning and complaining as they fought our magic.

"How are they here? The wards have just been checked. We've got to get a handle on this non-magical invasion." Finn peered out the window.

"We get rid of the werewolves and then get the marauding non-magicals back," I said. "It's like Crimson Cove is cursed."

"Maybe we'll have to get used to them," Zandra said. "Perhaps this is our new normal."

"I like the old normal," Sage said. "This version stinks."

I agreed as I grumbled along with Sage while we watched the coach belch out tourists. Still, the werewolf murder mystery was solved, there were no angry wolves stalking around Crimson Cove putting my wonderful witch at risk, and I'd just enjoyed a delicious savory muffin. Sorcha had agreed to test a salmon muffin. It was divine.

If a few non-magicals were the only things I had to worry about, then life with Zandra and all our friends was as close to perfect as it could be.

"To non-magicals, muffins, and mutts going home," I said.

Sage gave me the cat-like version of a smile. "Don't get too comfy. Whenever you're around, there'll always be a mystery to solve."

I hopped onto Zandra's lap and made biscuits on her stomach, while she chatted with her friends. Sage wasn't wrong, but life was dull if there wasn't a dash of mystery to solve.

But the next one could wait a while.

About Author

K.E. O'Connor (Karen) is a mystery author living in the beautiful British countryside. She loves all things mystery, animals, and cake.

If you want to practice spells, solve a few murders, and spend time with amazing witches and their talking familiars, join her weekly newsletter.

Sign up today.

Newsletter: https://BookHip.com/GXDVFRA
Website: www.keoconnor.com/writing
Facebook:
www.facebook.com/keoconnorauthor

Also By

Witch Haven: Welcome to Witch Haven, where nothing is what it seems. Meet four fabulous witches as they struggle with their destinies, deal with misfiring magic, murder, and the irksome Magic Council.

Crypt Witches: Meet Tempest Crypt, a witch who swallows demons, and Wiggles, her talking hellhound, while you enjoy magical murder and intrigue.

Lorna Shadow: A cozy mystery series set in the fun world of a personal assistant who sees ghosts. Meet Lorna, her ditzy sidekick, Helen, and Flipper, the dog who senses ghosts, as they solve crimes and save the day.

Holly Holmes: An adorable cozy culinary mystery series set in the beautiful English village of Audley St. Mary. Each book is full of treats, murder, and twists. Join Holly and Meatball, her clue-hunting dog, as they solve murders and eat cake.